To the power that lies within us all

THE DARK CHRONICLES®
VOLUME I
THE BEGINNING
A Flash Blasters Series/November 1993

Fiction by Cynthia Soroka:
The Dark Chronicles®
Volume I

EVIL AT HAND

As Thaddius walked through the North Woods, his whistle echoed in and out of the trees. But small sounds that came from the woods began to make the hair on his back stand on end. He began to hurry. The feeling of being followed permeated his entire being.

He felt his feet betraying him. He could not move fast enough; all the while he was tripping over branches and stones. And then, a swift vision of darkness struck him, and he fell into nothingness.

THE DARK CHRONICLES®

Volume I
The Beginning
by Cynthia Soroka
Poetry by Cynthia Soroka

The World of Ancra

Ranker
Red lake
Spearhead
The Enveloped forest
Twanka
Arisna river
Hope Plains
Calib Mts
Devon
Hillard river
Anchor head
Sompin
Pin lake
dessa river
Valhaia river
Shang desert
Trident
Wanna river
The Crolix Mts
Lionow river
Mau lake
Barct Plains
Boix
Thea
Edsel
The Hills
The North forest/
Guam
CandleSpar
Keneley lake
Cran
Winter Channel
Ewer
Donyer
Hawker
Homer Islands

To the power that lies within us all

THE DARK CHRONICLES®
VOLUME I
The Beginning
A Flash Blasters Series
Third Edition Printing October 1995

For information address: Flash Blasters, Inc. 1-800-Flash-09

ISBN 1-881374-70-X

Prelude - The Birth Of The Dark One

It began on an autumn day like any other. All the leaves were turning colors as the sun streamed through to warm the ground below. It was towards the end of September, Sunday September 20th to be exact. Most families were out taking in the last days of warmth before it got cold outside. But not too far away, in a small house surrounded by woods, things were different. A woman with long chestnut hair lay upon a wooden slab. Her swelling belly had been covered by a dark blanket, and a man in a black cloak stood beside her. Soon her screams echoed throughout the small house, but oddly enough, outside, the birds were still chirping, and anyone passing the unfamiliar house could not hear a thing.

Shades of Darkness rose above the house as the cloaked figure picked up a pair of dark leather gloves, donned them, and lifted the baby. The baby, beginning to cry, was thrust back upon the wooden slab. The figure then backed away. A deep male voice began to chant words of magic from the cloak. As the words flowed through the air, the baby began to rise from the slab and was transported into a black cradle. The man in the black cloak walked over to the woman and vehemently said, 'It is a boy!' The walls then began to shake and the wails of dismembered bodies from hell echoed in the house. Then the figure and the cradle vanished to distant sounds of a woman crying.

The baby began to grow in his small cradle, seeing only four dark walls surrounding him. Once in a while a creak at the door would signify a visit from the man in the cloak. Ominous shadows filled the room as the man would enter, look down, snarl, feed the baby, and leave. The baby was dressed each day all in black. His blankets were black, the sheets were black, and most of the time he was left in darkness. No matter how much he cried or struggled to leave his crib, no one came to him.

As he began to grow, the man in the black cloak showed him few things. Most of the time he was left alone. Soon, when he began to walk, he explored the strange place called home. He realized that the stone walls that sailed up over forty feet were much bigger than he was, but he continued on. Halls led to more halls, which led to doors and more doors. Finally, after much exploration, he came to a door that was a little different from the others. He reached up his small hand, but he could not reach the door knob. He began knocking and knocking. The door suddenly opened, and he almost fell face down. When he gained ground, little blue eyes peered in the door. What he saw made him want to run, but he stood and looked up and up into the big dark person's eyes. The sight of this man horrified him. The man smiled, picked him up, and carried him into the room.

"Yes, my son — I am here," the dark man said as he strapped him to a stone slab in the middle of the vacant room. The child began to cry, and as the tears fell from his new eyes the man removed a big sharp blade and a thick black rope from the far corner. All through the big empty castle, screams of horror followed and a woman with chestnut hair cried herself to sleep.

Things went on like this for quite some time, until the child was ten years old. By this time the child's face had the facade of a twenty-year-old, almost etched in stone. He rarely cried, and now he knew his place.

When he turned ten, his father walked up to him, opened his hand, put ten gold pieces in it, and told him he had to leave for good. The next thing he knew, he was thrown on the floor and tied head to foot. Then he was gagged, blindfolded, and taken away.

As the darkness subsided, he saw a door to a small wooden house which was engulfed by the woods that surrounded it. He was told he could never return home. The two men carrying him set him on the doorstep and left. He spent the next two days unravelling his bindings, and when he was free he walked into the house and collapsed.

The next morning he awoke. Nobody was around, and he found a note sitting on the table in the small kitchen. He opened the note as he rubbed the sleep from his eyes.

Cynthia Soroka

Dearest Son,

   This is your home now, to exist
in and to do as you please. I hope
you disintegrate in hell!
Love,
Dad

His eyes widened, but he did not cry — he just tucked the note in his black pants pocket and went into town and ordered breakfast. He sat in the darkest corner and ate slowly as he watched the people. After he was done, he walked out of the inn and down the street. He stopped when he saw children playing games. He began to talk to them, but it was obvious the way he talked belittled them. The same children asked him his name, and when he said it, they began to laugh. Their harsh laughter echoed through his young ears, and their words began to eat away at his very soul. He grew angry at their ridicule. He looked at all of them, and his cold glare sent shivers through their spines. He turned and returned to his seclusion.

As he spent more and more time alone, he began to resent people, and his parents, whoever they were, became his enemies. He always rationalized his anger and never allowed it to get out of control, but his plotting began, and so did the strange feelings.

THE BEGINNING

Part I

Chapter 1

GUAM(the center of it all)
Guam is my roots
Guam is my strife
Guam is where I long to be
Guam the meaning of my dark and endless life.

"There's a legend that goes — an old man jumped across Guam, and the odd part is, it's probably true!"

A big hearty laugh is heard rippling about the room. It began with Bill, the owner of Big Bill's. Why big? Well you see, Big Bill dwarfs most others, if not by height then by bulk. He is the picture of a hearty barkeep who is getting a bit older, wiser, and rounder.

What is Big Bill's? It's an inn and a tavern, with a bar downstairs and upstairs a bunch of single or double bedrooms. And a mere two silver will get you a night's stay.

And now the tale begins....

The big wooden door to Bill's opened for the hundredth time that morning. Squeaks emanated from the wooden floor as another satisfied customer entered Big Bill's. The end barstool creaked again as the wood withstood another customer's weight. Big Bill then turned to his customer, with his eyes bulging out of his head.

"Gowen! How are you?"

The whole tavern looked to the bar to see a handsome young man who appeared to be in his mid-twenties, with a somewhat crooked nose and brown wavy hair cascading down to the base of his neck. He wore an oversized white shirt with brown pants and boots to match.

"Bill, I'm o.k. How are you?"

"Oh, just fine, Gowen. It's pretty much the same all around — get up, make food, tell jokes, kick somebody out — you know, that's Guam for you." The people in the bar began to smile as Bill's hearty laugh resounded round the room.

"What about you, Gowen?"

"Well things are pretty much the same with me, except for the fact that Minker and I will be leaving again."

"Minker? He will probably be the downfall of you, that lush! A happy one, but what a lush!" Bill's eyes crinkled up as he laughed again.

"Tell me, what's the special for today?"

"Oh the Special Cooked grill."

As the interior of Big Bill's filled with hearty laughter, outside things were a bit different.

The dark woods were void of sound. Everywhere the two looked the trees swayed to and fro, and the owls peered around, craning their necks, watching.

"It's unusual, I don't see one soul in this town," Casiopiea said, as the two women made their way down the winding road into the small town.

"Let's knock on one of the doors and find out where we can get a night's stay," Yasmin said.

As they made their way further into town, the silence grew and then suddenly ceased. In front of them was a tavern that was different from the rest of the town — there were loud noises coming from it!

"Cooked Grill!"

"Yes, Gowen, cooked grill — you know, grits from the good ol' grill!"

Bill laughed again while the door swung open and the two women walked in. One was rather short, with pointed ears and short white blond hair, wearing a skimpy outfit anyone's mother would shun. The other was a sight no one could behold, until she removed her hood. Then they saw her long thin blond hair flowing down her back, enhancing her womanly curves as she moved. And the sight of her almond green eyes could stop anyone dead in his or her tracks. Her robe was a deep grey.

As they walked to a table, Gowen turned to watch.

"Hey, Gowen, your kind of women!"

"Shush, Bill!"

The two women sat down and ordered some food. Anyone looking at them could tell they were strangers to the town — they did not wear what a farmer's wife would wear. Around Casiopiea's waist, pouches hung with archaic symbols that no one could comprehend. And around Yasmin's exposed neck a holy symbol lay. No, they were quite distinctive.

And as everyone in the bar looked at the two women with curiosity, a figure in a concealed corner watched them from the shadows.

Chapter 2

The darkness which enshrouded him shielded him, yet no one seemed to notice he was there. He watched from afar, seeing Casiopiea's long blond hair and then her fluid hand movements. Then he glanced at Yasmin, her pointed ears peeking out just above her short hair. What was different about them?

As Yasmin turned, the symbol she wore about her neck glistened to him across the room like a beacon of light. He could employ her.

And just as he was watching, he saw a man approach Casiopiea and Yasmin, and his blood began to seethe. His gaze went across to the bar to lock eyes on Gowen.

Their eyes met for a split second. Then, as if he knew what was going on, Gowen got up and approached the intruder at the ladies' table.

"Excuse me, but I do believe that neither one of them would dance with the likes of you."

Casiopiea began, her anger rising, "And I do conclude we do not require any of your —"

"What!" The man with the bulbous nose cried, as he turned to see Gowen across from him, nostrils flaring.

Gowen looked at Casiopiea, and then back to the man. "You heard me, the girls are with me — you see, that's my wife." Gowen pointed to Yasmin. "And that's my overgrown sister." Casiopiea raised her right eyebrow, but she allowed Gowen to continue. "And you wouldn't want to touch her. She has..." Gowen's eyes widened as he looked significantly at her robe and back to the man. "You know."

"Oh my God, no!" the man said in confusion. "But she has such a lovely face — no one would ever...!" He turned his head back to Gowen. "Thank you, my friend, for telling me," he said. He patted Gowen on the back and left hurriedly.

Casiopiea and Yasmin then looked at Gowen.

"Hi!" He introduced himself. "I'm sorry if you feel I got your pride, but I didn't think new folks in town would want that kind of a welcome." He looked at Casiopiea and extended his hand, but she would not take it. He frowned as Yasmin butted in.

"Nice to meet you, Gowen." She gave him her name as she studied Gowen's handsome face, not forgetting to blink her big long lashes at him.

"My name is Casiopiea," said the other in a monotone.

"Well, I'm glad to meet the two of you."

"Gowen, is it?" He nodded. "Tell me, what is it that I have?" she asked, glaring at him.

"Oh, I told the man you were more or less a leper."

"He must be moronic!" Casiopiea said curtly.

"He's our local one."

As their conversation progressed, the figure in the shadows began to shift.

"I just noticed . . . Oh, excuse me, I'll be right back," Gowen said as he walked back into the shadows.

Casiopiea watched intently, noticing the slouch in his gait. As she watched Yasmin began to talk, making her lose her concentration. "Don't you think he's cute, Casiopiea?"

"I didn't ask to be disturbed. Now leave me be."

"I don't think I'm the only one who is disturbing you," Yasmin said as a man with a green and red cap approached.

"Excuse me, little lassie," he said in a thick brogue. "Are you part of the race of elves or is it just you be being a little on the odd side?"

"Excuse me, but I think you are the one who is strange."

"Oh, but a wee sorry, I just thought . . . "

Fists began flying as Gowen, who had now returned, began pummeling the overgrown man.

While the confrontation was in full speed, Casiopiea took the time to steal away into the darkness that had previously encircled Gowen. As she approached the back of the tavern, she saw a figure and moved towards it, slowly, taking one step at a time. Suddenly she heard a sound behind her. Quickly turning, she glanced back to see bottles flying as the fight intensified. Ignoring it in disgust, she turned to see the figure — vanish.

The cloaked figure walked slowly down the street, breathing a little more heavily than usual as he disappeared into the folds of the night.

A shack appeared in the middle of town, and numerous figures dressed in black robes were leaving it. Uneasy at seeing these figures, the townspeople barred their windows and doors, fearing the worst. Then two robed figures emerged from the shack with gold embroidered appliques running down the length of their robes. They began chanting archaic words of sorcery as the road through the town began to shift.

As their words began to flow about, the people in the bar suddenly stopped dead in their tracks. Bill began quickly to secure the doors and windows shut.

"What's going on?"

"Shush!" Bill looked at Yasmin, his eyes wide with fear.

Casiopiea turned to see an astounding sight. The entire bar was frozen, listening and waiting as the wind outside began to whirl and the ground began to quake. Then, as she began hearing words, slow and quiet, she could see no one else could hear these silent forbidden words.

"Calib, Alcarus — Moor"

Then screams echoed as another innocent victim was taken by the night.

Chapter 3

Morning came as the two women awoke. Casiopiea and Yasmin looked around the room, feeling disoriented. In an attempt to get her bearings, Yasmin began to speak.

"What happened last night — I know I didn't drink anything."

"Yasmin, something very peculiar is happening in this town, and I'm going to uncover what it is." Casiopiea arose to find it difficult to walk. Slowly making her way downstairs, she could see she was still in Big Bill's tavern. She recognized faces from the night before, eating breakfast as if nothing had happened. She approached the bar and saw the man named Bill rubbing his eyes of the previous night's sleep.

"Excuse me."

"Yes?"

"Could you tell me what happened here last night?" Bill looked around quickly and then back at Casiopiea. He then handed her a note sealed with the emblem of a black claw.

She slowly sat down at a table and ran her finger across the seal:

Yasmin and Casiopiea — meet me at the Crystalbird Inn for an explanation and breakfast.

Gowen Aries

She crumpled up the note and proceeded upstairs to gather her things and to tell Yasmin about the note.

Yasmin smiled and giggled. "I'd like to see Gowen again."

"Let's go," Casiopiea said harshly, and they walked to the Crystalbird Inn. Casiopiea winced, barely tolerating Yasmin, yet knowing that getting rid of her would get rid of something she needed now.

The Crystalbird was a sight — all one could see was crystal. All the lights illuminating the inside of the place were made of crystal. The elegant red rugs leading to the left extended into a magnificent dining room, and to the right stairs climbed up to estate rooms. At the front of the inn stood a bar, and right in front of them was the roomkeeper.

Casiopiea and Yasmin approached. He was a thin man. From the lines in his face, he appeared ancient. His only saving grace was his outfit, which was made from the finest silks. He looked up from the book he was buried in and acknowledged the two women.

"May I help you?"

"Yes. How much is it here for a room?"

"Four gold a night."

"I would like to stay for a night. My name is Casiopiea."

"Casiopiea, I don't have that kind of money," Yasmin said.

"Well, you can stay with me," said a voice behind them.

The two turned to see Gowen.

"Oh, hi, Gowen. I couldn't do that to you — I'll stay at Bill's."

"Well, o.k., but I'm sure you both are starved."

"I know I am. I could eat a horse!" Yasmin exclaimed.

"I am also quite hungry," Casiopiea said.

"Well, let's eat."

Gowen escorted them to a table in the dining room and helped them sit down.

"Tell me, Gowen, what happened last night?"

Gowen began to explain. As he did, a figure in an all black cloak walked past. Casiopiea looked up and felt that something about it was familiar. When the figure had disappeared into the other room, she turned her attention back to Gowen.

"You see, something has taken over this town. A few of us have seen it going on, and as our loved ones and friends disappear, things begin to happen."

"Like what?"

"This used to be just one happy town with just one straight road which led straight to it — now you see our road has become twisted, and each time someone disappears, the road twists more. As soon as you two walked into Big Bill's, I knew you could help — will you help us rid the town of this plague?"

They said they would, and then suddenly the chandeliers began to shake and the ground below to rumble, as everyone began running for cover.

Just when the pictures on the walls and the glasses began to fall, a figure in a black robe emerged and began to speak. As he spoke everything ceased. "You will all give yourselves over to us willingly or unwillingly! If you do not heed us, you will all suffer!" The robed man left the inn, followed by the man in a black cloak. Casiopiea looked up as he passed. Things were starting to get very interesting.

After the cloaked figure was out of sight, Casiopiea wondered who this person was and why he hid himself. She was so curious about his presence that she wanted to follow him, but then through sheer force of will she stopped herself. She would know who he was in time.

This was not Yasmin's case; her curiosity got the best of her, and she got up, although Gowen tried to stop her, and left the inn, ready to follow the two figures, but they had already gone and in their place she noticed the deep uncertainty that lay before her in the street.

A small shack seemed to have appeared in front of her out of nowhere. Was it magical? As she approached it, she noticed the silence surrounding her, not a noise. Just then a black robed figure emerged from the shack, followed by another, and another, until a group of robes stood around the doorway.

As she watched, intently studying every detail, the shack and the figures vanished — or at least it seemed that way. Quickly she returned to the inn, and told Casiopiea and Gowen what she had seen.

Casiopiea listened to Yasmin's description, leaning in closer to get every detail.

"We should find out what's going on here — can you tell us anything, Gowen?"

"Not now."

"When then — in the next century?"

"Be patient, Casiopiea."

"Yasmin, show us where you saw this shack."

"O.k."

She took them outside and showed them where the shack had been. As Casiopiea watched and listened, the hair on her neck began to stand on end. She felt they were being watched.

After a couple of minutes, Casiopiea suggested going back inside. She had noticed it was awfully quiet, so much so that the leaves on the trees moved without a sound.

Chapter 4

"Gowen, when will we find out more?"

"You will first meet the person who will lead this expedition. He will be able to describe more."

"When is that?" Casiopiea asked. As she watched, something in Gowen's eyes receded — he was afraid. How perfect, she thought.

"Soon, you will meet him soon."

He cautiously entered the small house centered in the woods and sat down in his rocking chair. Waves of pain began shooting through him as he placed his head in his hands. He had lost their trail again. He needed to know more before they could vanquish this nuisance. Just when he knew he could not find anything yet, voices came inside his head. 'They want to meet you.'

'I know — tell them tomorrow.'

Gowen then turned to Casiopiea and Yasmin.

"You will meet him tomorrow — one at a time."

"When?"

"After breakfast. Meet me at my house — I will give you directions." Casiopiea's body filled with anticipation. She knew she could find out more before the next day.

They agreed to split up and meet them.

After Yasmin and Gowen left, Casiopiea began to investigate. She went to the area where the shack had been, and watched. Just then, a robed man appeared. Had to be magic, Casiopiea thought. He looked to the sky and held up his hands. All of a sudden his left eye began to glow red and the palms of his hands began to show crystal — one crystal in each palm, glowing.

After he had finished, he disappeared, and left in his place were one ruby and two crystals.

She picked them up and went back to her new inn room.

Yasmin made her way to another bar, which was not too crowded at the time. She approached a curved bar surrounded by wooden stools.

"Hello and good afternoon." She turned to see a broad shouldered man with shoulder-length blond hair and green eyes, who bowed to her and smiled. "My name is Englemare, and this is the Lionheart." He waved his hand around the bar. "Care to sit and drink a spell?"

"O.K., sure." Yasmin smiled quickly, looked at him, and batted her eyelashes.

As they drank, he began to talk. "So, Yasmin, tell me what it is you do?"

"Oh, I am a healer — or a cleric — if you get a serious wound, I can help it heal." She smiled as she rubbed his bare arm up and down. "So what is it you do?"

"I could show you."

"Oh!" she said as he picked her up and brought her upstairs where the bedrooms lay....

Meanwhile Casiopiea sat in her inn room studying the ruby and the two crystals. "There must be some link between these and whoever is controlling this town." She lifted the ruby and placed it in her left eye, and then took the two crystals and placed one in each palm. She stood and looked about the room and felt a tingle go from her head down to her toes. She began breathing heavily. "I revel in your power!" Casiopiea said as the ground began to shake and the windows began to rattle — and then suddenly it stopped. She let go of the crystals and removed the ruby, and then sank onto the chair. She sighed, not understanding what had just happened. She then opened a large black pouch and retrieved a book that appeared solid black, with little symbols covering it. She opened it and began to read. As she did, a hypnotic state came over her, and someone watched her every move.

"So this is what you do, Englemare?"

"Yes, I used to be a healer — such as you — but I decided to give it up for this."

"But you stopped worshipping?"

"Yes. I felt lost, and thought making somebody feel good was better than killing, I guess."

Yasmin moaned, "You know, you are proficient at this." She smiled at him.

"I know."

Chapter 5

Gowen's words, "You will meet him tomorrow," echoed in Casiopiea's head as she approached the door of the small house.

The door opened and there he stood, all dressed in black.

"Come in," he said in a harmonic voice.

She approached him and asked him his name. He replied as he removed his hood, and she saw . . . nothing. She awoke with a start and immediately looked around the room. She had to find out who he was, and why he was such a mystery.

She heard a knock on the door. She got up and opened it — no one was in sight. Annoyed, she looked around and down the hall, before she saw a note with the emblem of a black claw. Not again, she thought, picking it up. She quickly opened it and read it.

"It is time. Meet me at the Bat's Eye."

Another note from Gowen —- how tedious, she thought. She donned her deep gray robe and went out to find the place.

She entered the dark, secluded bar and sat down.

No sign of Gowen or Yasmin. She ordered a glass of red wine. It was placed in front of her, and she sipped it. Surprised by its taste, she asked a passing waitress what the name of the wine was. "Black wine, miss," she conveyed, on her way to another table.

"Black wine. How splendid," Casiopiea said, and, examining the glass, noticed the wine had indeed a black sheen to it.

She knew she had not ordered it, and this made her curious. She turned around and saw him. The darkness of the poorly lit bar swallowed him as he approached her. When he stood towering over her frail body, her heart began to beat with both excitement and terror.

With his hooded face positioned towards her, he motioned for her to follow him.

Yasmin strolled down the street to a small house off the corner of town. She got to the front door and knocked.

"Come in," Gowen hollered from his kitchen.

She opened the door to smell the wonderful aroma of breakfast wafting about the house. As she entered, she saw Gowen and a short, squat man-boy who had a flask to his lips.

"Hi, Yasmin, sit down — how was your night?"

"All right. Who's he? Are you a halfling?" Yasmin said looking at the three foot man-boy that distinguished the male element of the halfling race.

"Oh, hello. I'm Minker, and it's a pleasure to meet you. And yes, I am a halfling," said the fellow, pausing only long enough to hold the flask away from his mouth to speak, then bring it back again.

"What is that?"

"Oh — this — you want to try it? It's Bill's special brew!"

"Will put a hole in your stomach!" Gowen said, and smiled at Minker.

"I'll try it," said Yasmin showing off her bravery.

"O.K., here it is. Don't mind the color — it's . . . ."

"Blue!"

"Yes, it's blue. Try it." He pushed the flask into her hand.

"O.K." She brought the flask to her lips. The fumes that came forth could have stifled a horse. She sipped it slowly. As soon as the blue liquid touched her tongue, fumes came out of her mouth and her face turned beet red. She rapidly looked for as much water as she could down.

"Too much, Yasmin?" Gowen smiled as laughter bellowed from Minker's belly.

Gasping for breath, she glared at them and drank more water. As she calmed down, Gowen led her to a chair. She sat down in a huff.

"You call this stuff what?" She croaked.

"Bill's special brew."

"You mean Big Bill?"

"Yes — Bill and I made it," Minker said with satisfaction.

"Wow, that's powerful stuff!"

"Yes, it is!"

Casiopiea followed the figure down the small road, then beyond the town along a still smaller road. Soon there were only trees lining the beaten path.

Casiopiea looked up into the trees encircling them. Then she searched for the figure ahead, but he had vanished into the woods. She tried to follow his path, but she had lost him. She came upon a small wooden house, and, glancing around, hesitantly reached the door and knocked.

The door slowly opened — no one stood in the darkness before her, which filled the inside of the house. She walked around the house, seeing nothing but darkness: even though it was sunny outside, no light came through.

Then she heard a voice — a mesmerizing voice.

"Hello, Casiopiea."

"Who are you?"

"Not now."

"Show yourself!"

"Not now."

"When?"

"Now is not the time, Casiopiea. Listen."

"Yes," was all she could say, under the voice's spell.

"The items you found — give them to me . . . ."

"Yes — I will," she said, and began to search for them.

"Give them to me, Casiopiea," the voice said, and a hand reached out towards her. At that moment, the spell was broken.

She backed away. With venom spitting from her mouth, she screamed, "<u>No!</u>" as the hand clutched at her neck. Writhing for breath, she collapsed.

"So, Yasmin, are you excited about going out —
maiming, killing, and making a lot of money?"

"Don't scare her, Minker!"

"Oh, it's okay, Gowen. Yes, Minker, I am excited.
I have another person who would go with us as well."

"Oh? Tell us about this person."

"His name is Englemare, and he works at the
Lionheart."

"We know him . . . how could he help?"

"Well, he used to be a healer, and he could still be
one if I asked him to go."

"Really? I don't think I'd give up the job he has!"
Minker's eyes twinkled.

"Just watch." Yasmin twirled about and patted him
on the head as she sauntered out of the house.

"Hey, where are you going?"

"Don't worry, Gowen, I will be back, and I will have
Englemare in tow." She swayed her hips as Gowen watched
her.

"Hey, Gowen, that one is fascinating — yes?"

"Yes."

Chapter 6

He bent down slowly to her, brushing the locks of hair away from her polished face. Ever so gently, he lifted her and carried her down the small darkened hallway.

"Englemare, Englemare!" Yasmin yelled, above the hustle and bustle of the breakfast crowd at the Lionheart.

"Er, Englemare — he's upstairs with a customer."

"Thanks!" Yasmin said, as she bounded upstairs and began knocking on every door, yelling, "Englemare!"

As the inn doors began opening, and grumpy faces appeared, a man screamed, "Oh, Englemare — he's down there, Room B."

"Hey, lady, if you ever do this again I will personally cut the gizzard from your lizard."

Looking puzzled, Yasmin smiled and said, "Sure," as she strode down to Room B and banged on the door.

"Oh, Honeybunches, let me in."

There was no answer.

"<u>Englemare!</u> Let me <u>in!</u>" Yasmin screamed, banging on the door as it swung open, causing her to fall on her face.

"Let me help you up," he said sarcastically.

"Thank you, Englemare. I am so happy — let me talk to you. And you —" she pointed to the woman sprawled on the bed "get out. And if you don't, I'll call up the guy from Room Z!"

The woman quickly threw on her clothes and scrambled out of the room.

"Now, what was so important that you had to run a perfectly good client out?"

"I have a proposition for you."

"Oh yes? And what is it?" said Englemare leaning against the wall, folding his arms, and staring impatiently.

"I want you to go with me to help — well — I'll just get on with it. I want you to become a healer again."

"What?"

He laid her unconscious form upon the bed. Removing his cloak, he placed it over her as she opened her eyes to see him.

She looked up to see his perfectly chiselled nose, his penetrating deep blue eyes, the well-defined lips, all surrounded by thick, shoulder-length black hair. Her heart caught in her throat as his eyes gazed into hers. She lay still as he stood over her, watching her peering green eyes, and the thirst for fire that burned within them. Perfectly still, they gazed at each other — for what seemed aeons, but was only an eternity to them. He turned and left.

Chapter 7

"Yes, Englemare, I want you to go with us —- we need you," Yasmin pleaded.

"Well, who is going?" Englemare asked, considering.

"Gowen, Minker, Casiopiea — a woman you haven't met yet — and of course me." Yasmin smiled. "Oh, and a leader I haven't met yet."

"Well, let me think about it." Narrowing his brown eyes at her, Englemare sneered.

"Maybe," Yasmin beamed, as she crept up to his face and pressed her lips to his.

The figure sat rocking in the chair as the darkness broke. Casiopiea entered the room.

"What is happening here?"

He arose. "Keep your voice quiet. I merely saved your life."

"What do you mean, you saved — " her voice rising.

He turned to her, his eyes boring into her, as shivers went up her spine. "You would have been murdered. Now you may leave."

"What do you mean? Who are you?"

"That doesn't matter now. You should leave — your life is still in jeopardy."

"What is going on?" She looked up at him. "Please tell me."

He looked at her and said, "I give you one last chance — leave, before . . . ."

"Before what? Before you kill me?"

Silence fell upon them, as she looked up at him and felt warmth consume her. She admired him, but why? She sensed he was more than meets the eye, that he was mysterious and that she would be the one to uncover his secrets.

"So, Minker, Gowen — you don't believe that Englemare is going to give up his job to go with us? Well, tonight, you will find yourselves in the wrong." Yasmin smiled with glee.

"You mean to tell me that you have convinced Englemare to come?" Minker said.

"Yes, I have." She folded her arms in front of her as she smiled smugly at the two of them.

"I am impressed," Gowen said.

"So when do we meet the leader?"

"Tonight."

"I can't wait!"

"I can," said Gowen under his breath.

"I am not leaving," Casiopiea stated, as she turned to the figure immersed in darkness.

"You are a fool." He turned and began to walk away from her.

"Wait!"

"Yes?"

"Who are you?"

"Come quickly." He held his hand out towards her.

As he did, she quickly studied it, strong, masculine, and detailed to perfection. She felt she could trust him, and as her hand melted into his, she knew that this person was different — powerful — and someone she wanted to have for her very own.

They moved through the house and out into the woods, where darkness again engulfed them.

As their pace quickened, Casiopiea looked up to the figure in front of her to see him cloaked to the world again. Who was he?

They moved through the brush, and as they did she felt a sense of urgency. Up ahead, she saw a small house which stood apart from the forest greens.

They ran towards it, and as they ran, his grip loosened.

"Go, Casiopiea —- I will see you soon, trust me." He pointed to the house and, looking back at her, felt his blood rush.

"Go now."

"All right," She said, a little confused, as he disappeared again. She quickly approached the house and rapped on the door.

"Come in," exclaimed a familiar voice from inside.

She opened the door and, disappointed, saw Gowen, Yasmin and . . . who?

"Oh, hi, Casiopiea. We were wondering if you were going to come," Yasmin grinned.

"Gowen, what is going on? Tell me now!" She glared at him, feeling the weakness that permeated his being and that disgusted her.

"Are you ready?"

"Ready for what?" Casiopiea said.

"Ready to leave."

"What?"

"We leave in the morning," Gowen conveyed, turning to them all. "We are all in grave danger."

"What do you mean?

"If we don't stop what's happening here in Guam, we may all die."

"Why?"

"Not until tonight."

"What's tonight?"

"We meet the leader."

He moved through the woods to the meeting place.

"CALIB, ALCARUS, MOOR."

The skies darkened, and the man in the black robe began to scream.

"No, you will tell me what is going on!" he shouted at the robed figure.

"C - A - L - I - B."

His flesh began to tear, as his blood seeped out onto the dirt floor. But he continued.

He began to shake the robed figure . . . violently. But nothing.

He seized his dagger and shoved it below the robed figure's ribs, killing the man.

"Show that to your master."

He knelt next to the man, as his own wound began to spread. He began to search for the map that led to his possible demise.

Throwing off pieces of the man's clothing, he found a single pocket, and upon opening it, he found a small piece of paper, folded many times. He opened it cautiously. As he looked up into the sun, a glint held his blue eyes and he clenched the paper in his hand — a map.

"I have found you - finally."

He got up and, holding his bloody side, made his way back to the little house engulfed by woods.

'Gowen,' he heard in his head.

'Yes?'

'Bring them now.'

'Yes.'

"Gowen, is something wrong?"

"No. Yasmin, go get Englemare. And Minker, go get Symra. Bring them here. Soon we meet the leader."

Upon their return Yasmin, Englemare, Casiopiea, Minker, and his fiancee Symra stood near Gowen.

"Let's go."

They made their way through the thickening trees and came upon a path. The wind began to blow, and the skies shifted. Lightning struck and, as the day turned to night and heat to cold, they approached the single house in the woods. Casiopiea smiled. She knew she had been there before.

Chapter 8

He stumbled into the house just before the party of people arrived.

Gasping, he sat down in his rocking chair, holding his side where the blood flowed.

Slowly he closed his eyes and began to concentrate. As his breathing slowed, a strange phenomenon began to occur.

The darkness that had encircled him slowly disappeared, as a green glow began to spread around him. As the aura increased in strength, his bleeding began to stop.

And just as the power erupted within the house, the six visitors rounded the corner and came up to the door. The aura subsided, but not before Casiopiea had time to notice it and wonder.

Gowen slowly approached the door to the small house and knocked.

"Enter," came the voice from within.

They saw a silhouette in the corner.

"Don't move — I want to hear your names; then you may be seated."

Feeling compelled to begin, Gowen spoke first.

"Gowen Aries."

"Yasmin DeLovine."

"Minker."

"Englemare."

"Symra," she uttered, in the voice of a weasel.

"Casiopiea."

They all took seats on the floor; there was no other vantage point from which they could see.

"Thank you," the voice said. A small light burst, from the fireplace, revealing a figure in a black cloak seated in a rocking chair..

"Yasmin," he beckoned.

"Yes."

"I need you to use your powers to assist me."

His voice was steady — and oh so tempting to her. She got up without thinking and approached him.

As she did, Gowen began breathing heavily. Casiopiea watched Gowen and saw the concern etched upon his face.

"What is wrong?" asked Yasmin.

"I have been injured," the cloaked figure said, "and it is essential that you heal me."

"Certainly," she smiled, mesmerized by this man.

"Please help me — immediately," he said.

"Oh, sorry." She began to chant words of the Ancients. And as she did, his wound healed completely.

"Thank you, Yasmin — I'm indebted to you. You can sit with the others now."

"O.K.," she replied, following his order and returning to her seat.

"I want you all to know that we can all have faith in each other."

"How do we know?" Casiopiea inquired. "You haven't even divulged your name, and you don't show us your face."

"I understand, all our lives are in danger. You will find out who I am soon, but the information I am providing you now is more important. First you must all know — whatever we say together here must remain solely among us. And anyone who breaks this trust will destroy us all." He sighed. "Is this understood?"

"Yes" was all anyone could say, as Gowen's breathing continued to deteriorate.

"Now, all of us here know that this town is a little unusual. This town is infested, and we are the only people who can prevent it, and others, from being destroyed. But first, you should all know we are being watched. Right now we are safe, but that could change in an instant."

"Why?" Yasmin asked, perplexed.

"Because you have entered this place, — and for no other reason." The figure began moving closer. "We have all, in this town, wondered how to stop what is occurring. This is how." He pulled out a long scroll from his cloak and unrolled it. "I have found where we can stop this menace. Right here —", he pointed to an X on a map — "Castle Bilac. Or, as most of us have heard the word passed in the night, Calib. We will vanquish this. We have no choice but to leave tomorrow, ready or not — for in a fortnight this problem will strike again, and it may destroy what is left here. I will not allow my home to be destroyed. I am sorry for those of you who didn't realize what was going on here. It is unfortunate," he sighed looking down at Symra, a three foot halfling woman. "Now you may ask your questions, but only afterward will I disclose who I am."

As Casiopiea and Yasmin asked about the surrounding area, Gowen began to move away from the rest of them. He turned around, colors spinning, his eyes — and then the pain began to slice through his very soul . . . .

"Gowen, Gowen!" Yasmin shrieked, as the last of the color seeped away from his face.

She ran to him just before he fell to the ground, holding him, and the rest of the party turned to help.

"Wait — let me through," the cloaked figure declared, rushing to Yasmin and Gowen.

"Is he — " Yasmin trembled.

"No, he will be fine," the figure said, as he laid Gowen down on the floor, and placed his hands over him.

As he did, his hands began to glow green; Gowen's color came back, and he started to breathe normally.

Casiopiea then turned to the cloaked figure in amazement and said, "Who are you?"

"My name is Darkmere."

Chapter 9

Calib, Alcarus, Moor — those three words echoed throughout the small town as the sky turned blood red and the clouds began to part. Lightning struck as, oddly enough, only one area remained calm and still — a small wooden house deep in the tall woods, hidden to the rest of the world, for now . . . .

"Darkmere — what an interesting name," Symra replied in a shrill voice, bouncing around Minker, who was now drinking.

"Yes," was all Casiopiea said, as she watched Darkmere's subtle movements.

"Gowen, are you o.k.?" asked Englemare, as Gowen awakened to see Yasmin bending over him.

"Oh, yeah, I'm fine" Gowen smiled at Yasmin, and then got up to stand next to her.

"Before we all leave — I will show myself to Casiopiea — alone — and then to Yasmin, since I know the rest of you already," Darkmere said. They agreed, except for Symra who insisted to Minker she had never laid eyes on Darkmere before.

Darkmere brought Casiopiea into the bedroom that she recognized all too well.

"I need" she said, "to know a few things."

"Go ahead and ask."

"I want to know what happened before —"

"All you need to know is that everything is taken care of," Darkmere said.

"And you know also, Darkmere, that I am unlike the rest."

"Yes," he said. He removed his cloak once again for Casiopiea — and just stood, in all his majesty, as she gaped. "Casiopiea."

"Yes?"

"Do you still have those objects you found?"

"Yes."

"We will require the use of them to destroy the problem which infests this town."

"Very well. Tell me about yourself, Darkmere." she said, yearning for more information about him.

"In time, Casiopiea, in time," he replied, as he felt his own magnetism taking control of Casiopiea. He reveled in satisfaction.

"Gowen, are you sure you're alright?" Yasmin asked.

"Yes — I'm fine, Yasmin."

"He looks just fine to me," Minker smiled.

"Everything looks fine to you, Minker — you're drinking that blue stuff again", Symra said, and she kissed him on the forehead. "Now, tell me again where I met Darkmere, Minker?"

"You met him at a party in town." Minker curled his lip up.

"If you say so, Minker." Symra sighed and put her head on Minker's shoulder.

"I don't know about you, but if they don't come out soon I'm going to have to get back to work," Englemare said.

"Oh no you don't," Yasmin declared.

"Oh yes I do," said Englemare, as both Darkmere and Casiopiea emerged, allowing Yasmin to look up and see Darkmere for the first time . . . .

Shoulder length black hair, ocean blue eyes, perfect features, smooth lips, pale skin, *a body that wouldn't quit,* black clothes — oh, my!

"Yasmin . . . Yasmin," Englemare said, then turned to Darkmere. "You know, I can't believe you — you did it again. All the women can't take you. Put that hood back on so we can all —"

"No, don't. You are so <u>beautiful</u>," Symra said, and blushed.

"What about me?" Minker murmured into Symra's blonde hair as he stood behind her.

"Oh, sorry, honey — I didn't mean to —"

Suddenly the walls began to shake and the ground rumbled. Darkmere yelled, "Follow me!"

They all made their way to the basement, Englemare carrying the dumbfounded Yasmin.

"What's going on, Darkmere?" Casiopiea asked.

"Just be quiet and still — <u>everyone</u>."

They waited as they heard the door being smashed in, and footsteps above.

"I want him found — and don't let me down this time!" a voice of authority bellowed. Above them they heard things being smashed, then silence.

Darkmere glanced at everyone, warning them with his eyes to stay silent, and they heard the words from above:

"Calib Alcarus Moor." The wind began to turn and a chill crept over them all, then suddenly, all grew calm.

"It's all right now," Darkmere said, as he began to climb the stairs from the basement, followed by the others.

"What happened?" Yasmin asked, looking up at Englemare, who held her in his arms.

"Nothing," Englemare said.

As they entered the upstairs, they saw the path of destruction: glass lay scattered over the floor, the windows were gone.

"Are we safe here?" Casiopiea asked.

"No, but nowhere is as safe as here, for now. We must all part, and meet back here tomorrow, ready to leave. We meet at sunrise — understood?"

"Yes."

They had begun to leave when Yasmin glanced at Darkmere again and she fainted; again Englemare came to her rescue and carried her out of the house. Gowen gave Darkmere a look of disgust, and left.

"Tomorrow," Casiopiea said.

"Tomorrow," Darkmere responded.

Chapter 10

When morning came they met again at Darkmere's house, all complaining about leaving so early in the morning.

They emerged from the town not knowing exactly what to expect as Darkmere led the way to the future.

Not far away, a group of five met in a shack, planning to demolish the group who had just left the outskirts of Guam.

Waves of smoke filled the room as a single figure stepped into the circle of fire. As they stood still, an orb of red levitated before the figure in the center of the circle. The figure took the orb, raised it, and then began to speak.

"My son — he will die, and no one will stop it." He placed the orb in front of him, peered into it, and saw a face — Darkmere.

"Are you bored?" Yasmin asked Symra.

"Oh no, I have my fiàncee here, and I'm never bored when he's around." She grabbed Minker's puny hand as he drank some more from his flask.

"We stop here for the night," Darkmere said glancing around to make sure they were protected. They made camp as a group, for the first time.

"This is the watch order. First watch will be Yasmin and Gowen, second watch will be Minker and Englemare, and the third will be Casiopiea and me. Symra, you get to sleep the whole night through. I will switch the order tomorrow.

Let's get some sleep, and anyone who sees anything out of the ordinary, inform me," Darkmere said. They all went to sleep, leaving Gowen and Yasmin at watch.

As the moon rose above, Gowen moved closer to Yasmin. "So, tell me more about yourself."

"There's not much to tell — I'm a healer, so I heal people's wounds. I come from a small family. My brother — what a pain — all he cares about is himself. Well, anyway, I came here looking for money, adventure, and a good time — and so far, I've found two out of three."

"What do you mean?" Gowen watched Yasmin's small physic shift around.

"Well, I've found adventure and a good time," Yasmin grinned, with a glance towards Englemare's sleeping body. Gowen followed her glance with a glare. "How about you?"

"I am a fighter," he said, "but I rarely believe in fighting — I just decided to do it because I'm good at it. Let's see, I've been living in Guam almost all my life . . . ."

While Gowen and Yasmin talked, a pair of red eyes watched and listened.

"I guess it's time to wake Englemare and Minker," Gowen said, smiling at Yasmin.

"Oh yeah," Yasmin said, as she got up and approached Englemare. "Nice talking with you," she said to Gowen just before she turned and kissed Englemare awake.

"Good morning, sleepyhead."

"Good morning, Yasmin," Englemare yawned. He stretched and got up, noticing that Gowen watched them while he woke Minker.

The second watch went as smooth as butter — Minker drank, and Englemare watched the moon. Then came the third and final watch, when Englemare and Minker were relieved by Casiopiea and Darkmere.

Casiopiea examined Darkmere. In the darkness she could only see his silhouette, dancing with the light of the golden fire.

"Casiopiea, tell me how you and Yasmin met."

"Oh, that's dull. Don't you want to discuss something else?"

"Humor me."

"Well, we met as we were travelling towards Guam. We both were looking for adventure and wealth, and we felt that it might be easier for two of us to find it. That's it. She is not the best company, but I also felt that, if I had gotten into trouble, a healer would be a good thing to have."

"Thank you for telling me."

"Now explain to me what happened at the house."

"All right. I will explain what occurred in a different way. Don't be alarmed — just listen."

"O.K."

Darkmere then turned to face Casiopiea and met her eyes once again. He looked at her, and then she heard him, but not the usual way — she heard his voice inside her head.

'Now, I will tell you — are you ready? Just think "yes" or "no," and I will understand.'

'Yes.   This   is   a   very   interesting   way   of communicating!'

'When you followed the figure in the black cloak from the Bat's Eye to my house, you were not following me. I arrived just in time to see the you in agony, so I ran after the man, but I lost him. I came back and placed you upon the bed, and it was later when you awoke.'

'Do you know who the person was who tried to strangle me?'

'I'm not positive . . . yet.'

'Tell me more — about these items I found.'

'I know that the objects appear to be their central power, and the person who created the items is rather omnipotent.'

'Are we going to destroy it?'

'Yes.'

She looked into Darkmere's eyes and began to feel the strength in him; as with her, there was a fire beneath, but more. Then she got up, smiled, and thought about undressing him — button by button — inch by inch. Then she felt him — his burning desire overflowing, as he intently watched her. As she approached him, she looked into his eyes and placed her hands upon his strong shoulders. She knelt in front of him, and then smirked.

"So you read minds, too."

"Yes," he said as he rose and looked around.

"What's wrong, Darkmere?"

"Wake everyone — we're being watched."

Green eyes quickly fled as the party was awakened and made ready to move ahead.

Chapter 11

Cautiously, they proceeded through the forest; Minker broke open another flask of Bill's Special Brew.

"So, Minker — are you going to share that with anyone?" Englemare asked.

"No — but for you, anything." He handed the flask of blue stuff to Englemare, who sipped the brew and almost choked.

"Wow, I don't know how you take this stuff — it's like poison!"

"Anyone else want some? Yasmin?"

"No, thanks. That stuff could burn a hole through anything!"

"Hey, Darkmere, you want any?"

"No, thank you — and aside from you, I don't want anyone drinking. We have to be vigilant."

"Oh, Minker, you are the only one who could be manly enough to drink the most powerful drink that you and Bill could supply. I love you," Symra said. She smiled, her wide eyes growing wider, as she gazed up at him. She snuggled under his arm, and they walked on together.

"You know, they're really cute together," Englemare said.

"Just like you," Yasmin said.

'You know, Darkmere, shouldn't they be a little more quiet, and a little less repulsive?' Casiopiea asked in Darkmere's head.

'I'm not concerned with that now, Casiopiea,' Darkmere replied without speaking.

They marched through the second day of their journey, then made camp.

"We are coming closer."

"How can you tell, Darkmere?"

"Watch those ravens above. The more of them you see, the more you will know we are on the right track. The map indicates it, right here," Darkmere added, pointing to the sentence on the bottom of the map.

"What's the watch order for tonight?"

"Symra and Gowen, Minker and Yasmin, and Englemare and I. Casiopiea gets to sleep tonight. And remember, if you feel you are being watched, wake me."

They all went to sleep, and Symra and Gowen began their watch.

Red eyes peered from beyond the camp, watching Gowen's and Symra's movements.

As the two talked quietly, beyond them words began to be chanted . . . .

"CALIB, MOOR, CALIB, MOOR"

At first the chanting was no more than a whisper in the wind, but it began to grow. No one heard.

"CALIB, MOOR, CALIB, MOOR, CALIB, MOOR, CALIB, MOOR, CALIB, MOOR, GOWEN!"

Then came a large clap, startling them all.

"Did you hear anything?" Darkmere asked Gowen and Symra.

"Not until that horrid noise that everyone else heard," Symra replied, nervously.

"We must break camp again — and this time keep as quiet as possible."

They moved slowly and quietly until they found an area that felt a little more secluded. They set up camp, this time without the comfort of a fire, and began their watches again.

Two sets of red eyes now peered through the night, as Yasmin and Minker began their watch.

The trees swayed in the breeze. The third watch finished without a hitch.

They all awoke the next day refreshed and ready to go — except for Gowen.

"Gowen, get up," Yasmin said, prodding him.

"I really need more sleep."

"No, you don't. Darkmere, Gowen won't get up!"

"Gowen, are you all right?" Darkmere looked into his eyes.

"Yes."

"Then get up."

They began their third day's journey.

chapter 12

The sun shone on an overgrown path before them. Black birds flew overhead and the sounds of branches underfoot emanated about them. As they progressed, the path became unobstructed. Evidently, someone had been there recently.

"Proceed with caution," Darkmere said, holding onto his sword as they moved further down it.

The sun warmed the woods, and Gowen began to complain. "Darkmere, it's getting hot — can we rest here?"

"Not yet." He turned and stopped. Gowen's face was unusually flushed. "Are you sure you're O.K.?" Darkmere asked.

"Yes, I'm just hot — can we rest?" Gowen snapped. Beads of sweat stood out upon his brow.

"Not yet."

"Soon?" Gowen almost pleaded, his eyes anxiously scanning the rest of the group.

"Soon," Darkmere replied quietly.

They continued until they came to a fork in the road. One side went east, the other west. Darkmere took out the map and studied it before leading them on the westward path.

The path began to grow wider, and they decided to stop for awhile. As they rested, four pairs of red eyes watched and waited.

Suddenly, Gowen again spoke. "Darkmere, can you wait a little while, while I put on some of my armor? I have a feeling I'm going to need it." He still looked flushed and uneasy.

"Sure," Darkmere answered. He watched Gowen leave the camp to change, unusually stiff in the way he walked.

After they had waited several minutes, Symra remarked, "You know, he's been gone an awfully long time — must have had to relieve himself, too!" She giggled nervously.

"You know men — once they find a tree, they want to find ten others, for next time," Yasmin smiled. Englemare glared at her.

"I don't like this one bit," Darkmere said scanning Gowen's thoughts, not finding any. "We will wait only a few moments more."

He had barely finished speaking, when they heard Gowen yell, "We're being attacked!"

They looked above to see swarms of red-eyed birds descending upon them.

chapter 13

Casiopiea immediately ran out of range to ready a spell. Darkmere drew his sword and began swinging it with all the power and precision of a true swordsman. He killed numerous birds, but even as they were destroyed, more emerged.

And then the worst happened.

Englemare, Yasmin, Casiopiea, Minker, Symra and Darkmere were all attacked at once, and as the long beaks pierced their flesh, Darkmere cried out, "They drain blood! Stay away!"

. . . CALIB, ALCARUS, MOOR . . .

The robed man looked around, and his followers knelt about him.

He turned and peered into the orb. . .

The birds poured from the sky, attaching themselves to the individuals below. Blood flowed, as their beaks sliced their way through flesh . . . deeper and deeper. Then Darkmere, warding off the birds, looked up.

The once blue sky was now covered by the black wings of the birds; below the army of birds stood Gowen, not moving, concentrating on something, but what?

"Gowen! <u>Gowen!</u>" Darkmere yelled.

'Gowen! Gowen!' He bellowed in his head; nothing.

And as the swarm thickened and people began to feel the loss of their blood, Darkmere heard Symra scream, dropping below wings that covered her . . . then Englemare fell, and then Casiopiea. Darkmere's rage began to build, as blood poured everywhere.   He screamed into Casiopiea's head, 'Stay awake!'

Then he looked around to see only Gowen standing, birds encircling him.

Then Darkmere understood. Gowen was controlling the birds. A flash of lightning illuminated the sky. Darkmere ran as fast as he could and jumped upon Gowen. The vicious birds clung to his flesh as he pummeled the man to the ground.

While the birds took chunks of flesh out of his burning back, he turned Gowen's head to face his own, and peered into the blank void of his eyes. Then Darkmere began to speak slowly, unhindered....knowing this was not Gowen.

"Gowen, listen to my voice — you are not yourself. CALIB ALCARUS MOOR!"

The ground began to shake and the trees swayed. The wind picked up, and he repeated again, "CALIB ALCARUS MOOR".

The wind began to swirl, the black sky filled with birds began to disperse.

Lightning struck again, and a bright light encircled Gowen and Darkmere — and then suddenly, a tornado hit. The tremendous wind swept the birds away, like a giant swarm of flies, and the light around Gowen subsided as he dropped to the ground. Darkmere cried out, "Calib Alcarus Moor!"

The light intensified again and . . .

The man, who watched the now blank orb with disappointment, looked up, as lightning began to strike the ground in the shack. Then the words came, in a voice that could only be his son his son — striking him deep within:

"<u>Alcar.</u>"

The man in the black robe felt the light — it sliced through his very soul, and he collapsed, as did Darkmere.

Chapter 14

Gowen awoke and dragged himself to his feet. He was dazed: He could not remember what had happened.

He tried to focus his bleary eyes. Unable to, he took a step and tripped over — what was it?

He slowly bent over and touched the shapeless mass that lay before him. It was a person! He felt something on his hands and smelled it — blood. He backed away, wondering who it was and why his vision was becoming worse. He knelt down over the body, widening his eyes to see who it could be. Black hair — Darkmere.

"Darkmere! <u>Darkmere!</u>" he screamed. No answer. Then he screamed out everyone's names — still no answers. Were they all dead, except for him? It couldn't be. He knelt down beside Darkmere to see if he was breathing. Through the haze in his eyes, he saw the man a little more clearly, lying motionless on his back. Gowen tried to roll him over. He put his ear next to Darkmere's nose; he could hear some faint breathing. Gowen sighed with relief — but how could he help, if he could not see?

He began to concentrate. 'Darkmere. Hear me, Darkmere,' Gowen said in Darkmere's head.

'DARKMERE HEAR ME, OR ELSE I WILL PUT YOU IN WHITE ROBES!' There was no response.

He looked around and sighed. He could hardly see anything. He quickly kicked Darkmere in the side, trying to revive him . . . . Nothing happened. He was no healer. Then an idea came to him.

He knelt down and drew a small wooden box from an inner pocket.

"Darkmere, we need you now, more than I."

He opened the box, stepped back, and waited.

A green, glowing vapor began to flow out from the box. As the glow surrounded Darkmere, Gowen began to turn pale. His face lost all its color and he dropped to the ground, while Darkmere began to stir, then awaken.

Darkmere rose slowly, understanding what Gowen had done. He closed the box and placed it between Gowen's hands. Then he went to see how everyone else was.

He knelt beside Yasmin and closed his eyes, putting his hands over her head. As his hands began to glow, her eyes fluttered open. Yasmin looked at Darkmere and sighed.

"You are beautiful."

Darkmere looked her directly in the face, "There is no time for this, Yasmin. I need you to help heal everyone — first Englemare, and then the two of you can help the rest of us."

She went to Englemare, while Darkmere knelt at Casiopiea's side.

"Where is Symra?" asked Minker after he was awakened.

"Stay here and I will see. Don't anyone move. Minker, take care of Gowen."

Darkmere searched amid the dead birds for Symra, the stench nearly overwhelming him. As he turned to leave, he saw her blond hair and disfigured body, drenched in blood — and he cursed beneath his breath.

"You will die when I find you!" He swore. He looked skyward as his words flew through the shack where the robed figure now sat, laughing.

Darkmere returned to the party.

"Where's Symra, Darkmere?" Minker asked, everyone turning towards him.

"She's gone."

"You mean she got away?"

"No, Minker. She is dead."

Minker jumped up. "No! She's not — you're just making this up!"

"Minker! Minker! <u>Listen</u> to me," Darkmere declared, grabbing Minker by the shoulders and sitting him down. "She's gone."

"Minker, we're here for you," Yasmin said, kneeling next to him.

As Minker began to sob, Gowen opened his eyes to look around, alarmed, come to think of it he had never seen Minker cry.

Casiopiea came to Darkmere, and he slipped his arm around her waist. Yasmin snarled in disgust. Darkmere, noticing it, quickly took Casiopiea to see where Symra lay.

"We have to bury her."

"Why, she deserved this. And maybe her death will help put some sense into Minker. She was a twit."

"Don't you see," Darkmere asked, "her life taken jeopardizes our lives now?"

"We will do fine, I'm sure," Casiopiea said.

"I wonder, Casiopiea . . . we have to keep an eye on Gowen."

"Why?"

"Someone's put a spell over him — he wasn't attacked."

"What?"

"Yes. He just stood there, watching." Darkmere glanced around and then focused on Casiopiea. "It has to do with the loud noise we heard while Symra and Gowen stood watch."

Casiopiea stirred and smiled. "Maybe this is a way to help us."

"How so?"

"We could use Gowen to do things we don't want to do — things that could harm the rest of us."

"No. You must understand — we are working here to eliminate a common foe, not fight each other. There will be other times for that."

Darkmere turned and saw what a mess the people around him had become; Minker was sitting there crying, with the rest gathered round him. Then he noticed Gowen. Darkmere watched him intently, as did Casiopiea. Something about him seemed strange to her, though she was not sure what it was.

Gowen turned to Darkmere — his one eye glowing red with an intent to kill. And in that instant, Gowen began to bolt towards Darkmere, screaming, "I hate you, and you will die for it — brother!"

Casiopiea gasped as Gowen, sword drawn, ran head on at Darkmere.

Darkmere just stood his ground and watched Gowen bearing down on him. Then he commanded, extending his hand, "STOP NOW! Gowen! Listen and hear me!"

His words flowed through the stilled air. Gowen lowered his sword inches from Darkmere. His eyes widened, as if someone or something had hit him full in the stomach, and he collapsed.

Everyone gathered around the fallen Gowen and looked at Darkmere.

Astonished at the confession, they all asked in unison, "Brother?"

chapter 15

Darkmere looked around him. "Yes, he is my <u>half</u>-brother, but there is no time to talk now. Yasmin, Englemare, and Minker, watch Gowen while Casiopiea and I bury Symra." He left, Casiopiea following. They could hear Yasmin as she comforted Minker, on the verge of tears.

Casiopiea turned to Darkmere, "Tell me more. How are you and Gowen brothers?"

"Let's bury Symra first."

They pulled Symra's disfigured body from beneath the wings of the dead birds tangled around her. They placed her in a shallow grave and adorned it with flowers from a nearby grove. When they were done, it looked like a rose garden in spring; blooming, as once had Symra herself. Darkmere found a rock that could pass for a headstone, carved Symra's name on it, and how she had died defending Minker and the whole town of Guam.

"It's done."

"We're doing an awful lot for a dead person, and risking our own lives in the process."

"We would be risking our lives if Minker could not function properly. Casiopiea look at me!" Darkmere raised his voice and grabbed her wondering face in his strong hands, turning her gaze to his. "We are all risking our lives, I want you to stop and help me. Do you understand, or is it too hard for you?"

"Yes, Your Highness," she mocked. "I understand. You want me to shut up and follow you no matter what. Now will you let me go, or will I have to scream bloody murder?"

"I don't want trouble."

"Well, that's par for the course, isn't it, Darkmere?"

He felt his blood boil, as he returned to Minker leaving her to curse his every move.

He helped Minker and the others to where Symra's grave site was. They began a short funeral, with Darkmere keeping watch over Gowen and Casiopiea.

When Minker was finished mourning, they moved on. Darkmere carried Gowen over his shoulder.

Further into the recesses of the woods, Darkmere told them to stop.

"Darkmere?"

"Yes, Yasmin?"

"Can you tell us what is going on?"

"Yes." He explained that Gowen had become bewitched, that he was being controlled by the same thing that they were on the trail to find, the thing that had killed Symra, and it was in the process of trying to destroy Guam.

He stirred in the night air, waiting in the alcoves of his mind: 'He will die! Triumph!'

"Darkmere, look!" Englemare called. Gowen had begun to twitch.

"Everyone move away from him!"

They did watching Gowen, possessed, being jolted this way and that. Then, with a start, he awoke.

"Gowen," Darkmere called.

Gowen turned towards him and smiled.

"So, Darkmere, it comes to this: you and me, brother against brother, flesh against flesh.   Haven't you had enough?"

"Gowen, you are being controlled by another force, inside you. Listen! Look at me!"

Gowen did so intently, listening . . . listening. Suddenly something shifted inside him. He blinked his eyes; once, twice, . . . then a total change came over him. Like night and day, Gowen returned to himself. "Darkmere, what happened?" he asked, shaking his head.

"Just tell me what did you feel?"

"I don't know — like a wrenching inside. More like a knotting of my stomach. What happened to Symra?"

"We sent her back home, Gowen. Now let's move on. Is everybody ready?" added Darkmere, nodding towards the party, encouraging them to prod Gowen out of his near trance.

'Darkmere, you and he are half-brothers?' Casiopiea asked incredulously.

'Yes, unfortunately.'

"Gowen — come on, let's go!" Englemare snapped, bending down to help Gowen up from the ground.

'Will he be able to help us?'

'Not very well; at any moment he could switch back.'

'Then why not leave him here?'

'We need him.'

"Let's go," Darkmere called out, and they moved deeper into the folds of the dark and menacing woods.

Chapter 16

Only the beginning, Darkmere thought to himself, as they made their way through the treacherous woods in the slow, swirling wind — not willing to turn back, knowing a fierce fight was imminent.

"Tell us, Darkmere — how do we know we can survive this ordeal?" Yasmin queried, holding Minker's hand as he tagged along next to her, his face drawn and empty.

"The only way we can make it is if we all stay together," he replied bleakly, making Yasmin shiver. "Things might get a little difficult from here on but remember this — when we survive, we will know that, if we had stopped here, we would wind up in a hell worse than death, as would every living being."

"Don't worry, I'll be beside you," Englemare said, looking back into Yasmin's eyes and giving her a smile.

The sun rose above the trees to give a little light to the travelers' journey.

Time passed and they continued on. Gowen still walked as though in a trance.

"Not too much further," Darkmere thought aloud, trying to ease the party's progress.

The sun streamed through the trees, creating dancing shadows. Seeing this, Darkmere wondered, were they being followed . . . and if so, by what? Symra's dead body? The fight that lay ahead, or perhaps some fate worse than death?

All this thinking was hurting Darkmere's head. 'Forge on — keep going and don't look back,' he told himself.

Day turned into night, and the night watches began. Darkmere stayed awake all night, keeping Gowen in his sights.

"Darkmere," Casiopiea said, sitting down next to him.

"Yes?"

"What's next?"

"I have a feeling that we're in for a bit more than some of us bargained for."

"As long as I benefit in the end, I'll be around."

"I know."

She smiled, moving closer, her heart racing alongside his slow, even breath.

"Casiopiea."

"Yes?"

"Not now."

"What do you mean?" she said, panting slightly.

"You know." He moved away.

"I will hold you to another time, Darkmere."

They awoke the next day, ready to move on.

"Darkmere, I feel much better," said Minker, taking his first drink in a few days. Darkmere sighed with relief.

"I thought we had a problem with you, lad," Englemare said, grinning and patting Minker on his back.

"Don't worry, I'm back on track. Symra is better off. She would have had an awful time with me here."

"What do you mean?" Englemare asked.

"Well, I have a feeling it would have been a lot harder the other way round — and she's probably happy now."

"Happy for being dead? Oops!" Yasmin said, covering her mouth, as confusion came into Gowen's face, then glancing at Darkmere.

"What do you mean, dead?" Gowen asked.

"Well, we didn't want you to be upset," Minker told him.

"Upset? Minker, she was your wife-to-be — and you didn't want to upset me?"

"Yes. Things have been a little strange with you," Yasmin began, "and we didn't want to —"

"Look, Gowen," Darkmere cut in, "you were having a difficult time, and I felt you should be told later. I was looking out for all of us."

"Oh, so you thought you would take it upon yourself to judge how I would handle things — right?"

"No. Now let's move on, before we get into trouble here."

"O.K.," sighed Gowen. "Minker, I'm sorry."

"So am I," Minker took another sip of the blue stuff.

Towards evening, after a full day's travelling, they had arrived at a clearing when a feeling of doom suddenly overcame them all.

Would it be their worst nightmare?

"We'll go back a bit and rest for the night," Darkmere said, hoping they would be prepared for whatever lay ahead.

Chapter 17

The next morning, they ate quickly and looked out into the clearing.

From afar, the castle resembled a deserted isle — there were no animals to see or hear, no human beings, nothing. It stood before them like a silent mountain or a volcano waiting to erupt.

Stark grey walls loomed over them, seeming to peer down at them, as they approached. It was unnerving, yet in some way peaceful, as if they could look out over the entire world.

They all began studying the castle walls, — but could not believe what they saw. Places should have been smooth were now old and crumbling, and in some parts there were even gaping holes. No one could live there, it seemed. The place appeared completely abandoned. Could it be true?

Darkmere unfolded the map which had led them there. Was it wrong? Was this a trap?

He studied the map, then the castle. There were no ravens, as the map had shown. He looked skyward to see the sun directly overhead. How had it become noon so quickly? He looked to the left, towards the cool woods they had come from, and then to the right, over rolling fields of green. He looked at the map again.

"Is this the right place?" Casiopiea asked, noticing the wild ivy, which grew nearly to the top of the castle walls.

"Yes, it is," Darkmere confirmed, and motioned the others to follow him up to two double doors that were almost hanging off their hinges. He had a definite feeling about this place. "Wait," he said, holding up his hand. "Casiopiea, find out if these doors are magical."

She spoke arcane words and gazed at the door.

"Well?" Englemare asked, almost in a whisper.

"No, they are normal rotten doors," she replied, very matter-of-factly.

"Minker, keep watch behind while Englemare and I open the doors," directed Darkmere. Minker quickly flanked the rear.

Englemare and Darkmere pushed on the doors. They slid open with hardly any effort.

"Get ready. These doors have been used recently."

They made their way cautiously through the doorway. In the corridor, beyond, they heard the doors slam behind them. An amazing sight held their gaze:

White marble floors rose up into white marble walls covered with elaborate paintings. Pillars of white flanked each side of the grand entrance-way ahead of them. Before them, a carpet of red silk stretched across a gleaming, pure white floor, and along the sides of the carpet stood six gold chairs, each inlaid with diamonds.

They turned to each other in silence, and then turned back to see that everything was still there.

After looking up at the gold-embossed ceiling, Darkmere held up his hand, turned to the party, and began to silently speak. 'Do not be alarmed by this. This is an ability

I have, and few know of it — now you do. Just listen.'
Yasmin stared at him, dumbfounded.

'I do not trust what is going on here. Now if you
need to talk to me, just <u>think</u> about talking to me, and I will
hear you.'

'My, this is wild,' Englemare said to Darkmere.

'Now, Casiopiea — anything magical?'

She looked around and shook her head.

Darkmere told them all to be quiet, to disturb
nothing.

They began to move stealthily, almost in unison,
along the red carpet leading into the halls of Castle Bilac.

As they moved, they noticed doors that had not been
there before. These were all the same — the same height, the
same markings, and all had the same gold knobs with an "A"
carved in each.

In the silence, Darkmere began to wonder why this
seemed so unusual.

They moved on until they came to a corridor, which
rounded a corner. There they stopped.

'Casiopiea.'

'No magic, Darkmere — not yet, anyway.'

Darkmere motioned for them to follow, and they
discovered another set of double doors.

Casiopiea shook her head, as they opened the doors.

This hall was exactly the same as the last; the same
number of doors, the same spread of carpet — even the pillars
looked the same. They rounded a corner and came upon yet
another set of identical double doors.

"Someone is playing us for the fool; they know we're here. Casiopiea, try another spell," said Darkmere aloud.

"Understood."

She lifted her hands and began to chant the words of magic — then . . . nothing.

"Darkmere, nothing happened."

"I figured as much — none of your magic spells will work here. We also won't be able to get past this area until we go through these rooms. I'm sure our host has been expecting us."

"That's right!" Gowen exclaimed harshly, as he grabbed Englemare from behind and held a dagger up to his throat.

"What are you <u>doing?</u>" Yasmin screamed.

"Gowen — what you're doing is wrong. Leave him alone!"

"No, Darkmere, I will not follow your orders anymore! Englemare, I wouldn't move if I were you. There's poison on this dagger." Gowen turned quickly to ward off Minker, who was coming up from behind.

"I told you, Darkmere, we should have left him behind," chimed Casiopiea.

"And not face the music of your keeper?" Gowen said, looking at Darkmere and smiling. "Welcome home, Darkmere," said Gowen, still smiling as he sliced Englemare's neck. Hot blood slowly streamed down over Gowen's hands, as he laughed a demonic laugh. Darkmere's eyes widened. That laugh — he had heard it before. . .

"<u>See if you can find us,</u>" a snarled strange voice through Gowen's lips, just before he and Englemare disappeared.

The others looked at each other.

"There are only four of us left. What are we going to do?" Casiopiea asked.

"He won't die — will he?" Yasmin whimpered.

A laugh resounded throughout the room.

"Remember me, Darkmere?"

Darkmere's eyes widened. "Yes, Father!"

Chapter 18

Casiopiea, Yasmin, and Minker stared at Darkmere.

"Who are we going to meet next — your cousin?" Minker wondered aloud.

Darkmere stood, still as a statue.

"Welcome home, my son. Remember . . . I told you never to come back here? You broke your promise — but don't worry, for I welcome you back with open arms." The ground began to rumble . . .

"Duck!" Darkmere yelled. He quickly dropped to the floor, and the others followed him in rapid succession. Two giant arms sprung from the walls, flailing out at them, swinging wildly to and fro.

"Oh, I see you have become adept in your ways — or so it seems."

A buzzing began to ring in their heads. It quickly increased to an unbearable level, until only Darkmere could stand his ground. "No! You will not harm me!" he breathed out, pushing the noise from his head, while Casiopiea, Yasmin, and Minker rolled on the ground, clutching their heads: "Hear me!"

Suddenly, the sound subsided and the flailing arms retreated.

"So you are stronger than we thought. You have done well. Now, see if you can help this world of yours before I take complete control. I love you."

"And I never gave my word to you," Darkmere replied.

Silence descended, and with it, relief.

"Darkmere, what are we going to do?" Yasmin implored.

"Something is wrong: I know this place, yet everything is so different." Darkmere looked around, then nodded. "First we must play his game, but that won't last for long."

"What about Gowen and Englemare?" said Yasmin.

"He will torture them for sure — but we will find them. Let's move on."

They crossed the red carpet. Darkmere looked around and then stopped: he closed his eyes and tried to remember the years he'd made himself forget . . .

His memory came back to him: that voice, booming: "You will pay for your insolent behavior . . . now!" The sound of a whip cracking, resounded on the castle walls as he walked towards the voice, passing down the spotless hallway, down to the door: the solid gold door; pulling it open with his small hand . . . and peeking inside to see a vast, circular room made entirely of marble. And there, in the center of the room, the man in the black robe hurting someone. The man in black turning towards him. And then the rest, almost too brutal to remember: a hatchet, blood, and...

"Darkmere, Darkmere, are you alright?" asked Yasmin.

He shook his head to clear it: "Yes — let's go in that door" he suggested pointing to one in the middle on the left side.

They moved towards it.

"Minker, check it for traps."

Minker went to the door, then tinkered with it until it opened. "It's o.k."

"Look," Yasmin said, discovering a beautiful room inside with sculptures of horses standing around a crystal-clear fountain.

"Wait, let's go cautiously." Darkmere led them forward.

They approached the fountain. There was nothing to see but water.

"Wait . . . look," said Yasmin.

A second glance: still nothing.

"Yasmin," Minker said "I don't see anything except water."

"Don't you see? A beautiful fish." Yasmin pointed again.

"No. Where?"

"There." They saw a flicker in the water.

"A see-through fish," Casiopiea said.

"We don't have time for this," Darkmere said. "He expects us to sit around like this."

"But it has something to say."

"What?"

"Listen," said Yasmin.

A low hum broke the silence as the fish surfaced, beautiful gold highlights shimmering from its transparent body. It began to speak to them in a flowing melody: "I am trapped here — can you help me? Darkmere, he wants you. Once he has you, the people of the town will follow, and then he will triumph."

"We will try," exclaimed Yasmin, reaching out towards the fish.

"No!" Darkmere said, quickly grabbing her arm.

"We have to help it!"

"No!" He turned her towards him, just as a voice bellowed forth: "I will succeed! You and the whole world will fall at my feet!"

The fish disappeared, in its place a corroded corpse.

Yasmin stepped back. "You are heartless — we could have saved it!"

"It was never there, Yasmin," Casiopiea assured her. Darkmere looked Yasmin full in the face.

"He wants us divided — and then he will destroy us. Listen to me. He is weak. We can be strong, Yasmin!" He shook her, and she began to cry.

"Darkmere, I don't want to lose Englemare."

"We'll find him. We will find him," Darkmere said. He held Yasmin close and watched Casiopiea seethe.

'Do you have to be so friendly?'

'Only when it is necessary. Yes, Casiopiea.'

The black-robed figure paced up and down and back and forth. Then he stopped, a smile crossing his face.

"Gowen."

"Yes", replied the monotone voice.

"Go destroy them."

"No, Gowen!   Don't listen --"   The black robed figure covered Englemare's mouth.

"Go, Gowen." Smiling at Englemare, he said, "I will deal with you . . . soon," as Gowen walked away, sword in hand.

Chapter 19

The party left the first room only to find themselves in another, very different hallway: no red carpet here; no gold chairs either. Just empty, black space . . . or so it seemed. And then: "What the . . . !" cried Minker.

Suddenly, the hall began to spin, and bright light illuminated everything. Just as suddenly, the spinning stopped, and they came face to face with . . . a giant — but a giant what?

It stood twelve feet high, almost reaching the hallway's ceiling. Its legs were gigantic, its voice boomed through the room, emanating from a being so repulsive it was difficult for them to look at it. A claw the size of two human heads pointed directly at Darkmere.

The creature spoke: "You will listen and listen to me well — my desire is for you and only you. The others may leave, but I want you."

"I am not afraid of you!"

As the rest of the party began backing down the hallway, leaving only Darkmere and the enormous creature, it continued to speak: "Prepare to meet your maker!"

"Oh, and who would that be — my father? Please tell me."

"You will perish for your insolence! Give yourself to me — drop all your weapons and walk this way."

Darkmere felt his knees weaken. "No!"

"Come to me and no one will get hurt!"

Darkmere took a step towards the creature. "<u>No</u>," he said again, trying to move back . . . but he could not.

The rest of the party watched in horror. Yasmin's eyes brimmed with tears.

"Darkmere, I only want to talk with you. Come to me." The visage of the twelve foot monster changed into one of a beautiful woman, looking longingly at Darkmere, calling to him with lust and desire in her eyes and upon her face.

As Darkmere slipped closer, the voice now changed into a choir of chimes and symphonic beauty. "I will not hurt you. Please help me."

The rest of the party continued to watch, horrified and helpless. Darkmere was willingly approaching what had again changed into a huge, hideous creature, which now had slime dripping from its cavernous mouth, as it prepared to ravage its entranced victim.

"Come to me, my love," Darkmere came within her reach. The party watched the horrible creature encircle Darkmere, though he saw only a beautiful woman putting her arms around him to give him a hug.

And with these words, "You are for me. Come to me my love, my —" her beautiful arms closed like a vice around him. Struggling, he saw her teeth turn into fangs, then felt her wretched mouth clamp down on his neck. Unable to move, he stopped and looked up, and as his blood began to flow down the side of his neck, he finally screamed,

"You are an illusion — I will not obey your commands!"

And as he screamed, the truth was revealed to Darkmere and the party; the horrible creature changed again, this time to its original being — Gowen.

"Gowen," cried Darkmere, "STOP!"

Gowen still held a dagger which, having pierced his neck, now dripped with Darkmere's blood. Darkmere grappled with Gowen, shaking him free of the dagger, blood now flowing down both their arms. As they fell to the ground, Gowen screamed, "You will die. You will die. You will all die!"

They rolled on the ground. The party watched the struggle, unable to move, stilled by a spell. Darkmere's blood flowed freely, until soon they were rolling in a pool of blood.

Gowen reached for his dagger, seized it, and straddled Darkmere. Darkmere — weakened — could barely move.

Gowen put the dagger to Darkmere's neck and smiled: "So you thought you could outfight me — I think not. Rise!"

Darkmere slowly got up, with Gowen holding the dagger's point to his throat, placing pressure where it lay. Small drops dripped steadily . . .

"You must let me heal."

"Only enough so that you will not die." Then, "Yasmin, come."

Yasmin felt herself moving, but she knew she was being controlled by something else. Her arms rose, and she began to speak, but not of her own will.

Darkmere, though covered with his own blood, healed quickly. Gowen still pressed the dagger to his throat.

"Come, and everyone else follow," commanded Gowen.

He and Darkmere retreated, the party following in silence.

Chapter 20

They rounded a corner, and the hallway changed again. Along the walls hung a number of paintings of the same child in various settings. As they moved along the corridor, they saw the child grow up, becoming more and more familiar to them, until no one could mistake the face: It belonged to Darkmere.

"Don't dawdle — move!" Gowen commanded . . . while memories of the place flooded his captive.

They rounded another corner, this corridor the same as the first: red carpet down the center, six gold chairs, marble pillars and walls, the ceiling inlaid with gold.

Gowen took Darkmere to the first chair and sat him down. Darkmere remained motionless. Gowen instructed the rest of the party to take the remaining seats.

Then Gowen sat down, closed his eyes, and went limp.

Suddenly they were all transported to another room. With only five chairs — Englemare was no where to be seen. This was unnerving to them. They looked around and saw another hallway leading to a solid gold door. In the center of the door, a large "A" had been engraved.

Once again Darkmere remembered the voice: "You will pay for your insolent behavior."

He saw himself peering around the corner, as he had so many times before, then approaching the door, and opening it. Inside, he saw the massive circular room, and the man in the black robe...

And he remembered something else!

'Casiopiea, listen,' he began communicating to her. 'I know about a few things here . . . ' As Darkmere spoke to her instructing her of his plans, Gowen rose.

"Get up, Darkmere." He pressed the dagger once again to Darkmere's neck. "The rest of you form a line and follow me."

They silently did as they were told. They were following Gowen from the room when they heard crying and screaming.

"You will listen to me, you insolent fool!" shouted a harsh voice, followed by the sounds of a man crying out. Yasmin knew at once who it was; her throat constricted, and silent tears sprang to her eyes. The screaming continued and then abruptly stopped.

Gowen approached the golden door and knocked.

"Enter . . . enter."

They opened the door to see a magnificent sight — one Darkmere remembered only too well, except for the once black-robed figure, which now stood before him . . . completely revealed.

Something about his face was uncanny. He had Darkmere's features, yet he was older, grey hair streaking down the sides of a once-black mane. His expression was hard to fathom, yet he seemed pleased with himself.

"Hello, son . . . my darling little son!" came the well-remembered voice.

"I am far from little," Darkmere said in a low voice, standing his ground.

"Oh, so offended, son? And the rest of you may talk — but only talk."

Yasmin immediately burst out, glaring at the sinister figure, "Where's Englemare?"

"Time will tell, time will tell," he responded lightly.

Casiopiea spoke next. "I'm curious. Why does such a man as yourself — of your obvious stature — play a game such as this? It doesn't seem right. Oh, also I'm a little curious what your name is?"

"Oh, Casiopiea, I adore your tongue. Well, if you had such elaborate power, wouldn't you do this, too?"

"I don't think so."

"Well . . ." he turned away from her, dismissing her and addressing the others. " Anyone else have anything to say?"

"Can I have a drink and get out of here?" Minker remarked. "You know my fiancee died, and I'm kind of thirsty."

"That all depends on my son."

"Yes? What do you want from me?" Darkmere asked directly.

"I want your powers — to help me control everything."

"You mean that you don't have enough power, whoever you are?" Casiopiea inquired.

"Of course I have the power!   And my name is Alcamere."

Darkmere stood completely still, Gowen's dagger still at his neck.

"Release," Alcamere said.   Gowen stepped aside, lifeless and empty.

"Thank you," said Darkmere.

"You're welcome, son. Now will you join with me and my disciples, to rule the world?" His eyes fixed on Darkmere, as if piercing through his son's soul.

"No," Darkmere replied firmly, holding his gaze.

"Why not?" The menacing form loomed closer.

"Why not? Who do you think I am? I don't have to answer to you any longer."

"Well . . . then you will pay for it!" Alcamere raised his arms as he spoke, and a volent wind began to swirl round the room. "I gave you another chance, and again you turned me down. Now you will kneel before me. Do it now!"

Darkmere tried to resist, but found he could not hold out for long. Against his will he bowed to his father and knelt to the ground.

"Now I will show you how much you should not have been born! Your power should be mine!"

As the wind intensified, the party became more immobilized. Casiopiea started to lift her hands . . .

"CALIB ALCARUS MOOR!" Alcamere cried out. A whip materialized in his hand and he directed its stinging tip at Darkmere.

Casiopiea began to speak, but caught sight of something in the distance — a flicker.

She stopped her incantations and cautiously moved towards the glimmer.

Yasmin tried to move but could barely do so as Gowen began to yell, "Darkmere — you will not repress me any longer!" He reached in his pocket and drew out the small wooden box. He threw it across the floor at Darkmere, who saw it — and screamed.

"No, Gowen!" Darkmere cried out. The whip cracked down on him, forcing him to scream again in pain.

Alcamere continued to conjure, while Casiopiea, seeing his absorption with Darkmere, flew across the room towards the savior.

Darkmere's body began to scar, and Yasmin crept closer, attempting to heal him. Alcamere yelled at Darkmere, "You're a worthless piece of nothing! And I didn't like you killing my messenger!" followed by a loud crack of the whip, and another streak of blood across Darkmere's back. Yasmin noticed that Gowen had lost all his color, and he suddenly fell to the ground. She instantly rushed toward him.

Casiopiea, moving through all kinds of resistance, reached it! Aha!

It was then that Alcamere noticed and turned to her — "No!"

While the self-propelled whip continued beating Darkmere into a senseless pulp, Casiopiea turned and grinned at Alcamere.

"So, Alcamere, while you were occupied, I got something you didn't remember was here — yet your son knew it!"

She held up a small pouch.

"Casiopiea, come, give the bag to me." Alcamere spoke softly and persuasively, smiling at her, as the wind suddenly ceased. Yasmin, Minker, and Darkmere watched while blood ran down the length of Darkmere's body, as the whip continued.

Casiopiea approached Alcamere . . . very slowly.

"You are ravishing, Casiopiea." Alcamere's voice grew more seductive still. "Didn't you like me when I tried to strangle you back in Darkmere's house, but Darkmere interrupted us? I could give you more power than you could imagine."

"Thank you."

"You could come join me and help me, Casiopiea." He smiled.

"Yes, Alcamere, I'm here," Casiopiea declared, running to him, and opening the small bag. Alcamere screamed in terror.

At once, the wind began to swirl violently around Alcamere. He pleaded with her. "Help me, Casiopiea. Please!"

"Rot in your destruction!" Casiopiea exclaimed, watching him try to avert his inevitable demise.

Alcamere, and everything around him, was being pulled towards the bag. He fought, casting a spell: missiles shot from his hands, struck inside the bag, and disappeared.

He himself followed, until he too was sucked into the bag, while Casiopiea smiled.

"Darkmere?" she shouted.

Hoarsely, he responded "Yes! <u>Do</u> it!"

Casiopiea opened the bag wide. Alcamere came flying out, faster than a tornado, splattering against the far wall.

"Well, I guess he's dead," Casiopiea said.

"Yes, he is," Darkmere replied. Then he collapsed, as the whip disappeared from over his battered body.

Chapter 21

Yasmin rushed to Gowen, hoping to heal him . . . but nothing happened.

"Don't worry about him. Heal Darkmere," Casiopiea said to Yasmin, who spun around to sneer in Casiopiea's face.

"You are not the leader here, you good for nothing . . ."

"No need to fight now, ladies — I think we need Darkmere healed first," said Minker, nodding.

"O.k., Minker," Yasmin said, taking time to throw a nasty look at Casiopiea, before she knelt by Darkmere with Minker beside her. She placed her hands over his body to begin the process of healing, but nothing happened.

"Casiopiea, what's going on here?"

Casiopiea raised her hands and began to speak the language of magic.

"Yes, just as I imagined — there is still strong magic here. Let's get them out of this room."

Minker, Casiopiea, and Yasmin tried to move Darkmere's limp form into the hallway, but it proved difficult. Every few inches, they had to stop, until finally they got him out into the corridor.

Yasmin placed her hands on his barely moving chest and began to pray: "Help me — help me to help him!" She concentrated as they all watched, and waited.

"Nothing is happening!" Yasmin cried in dismay.

"Don't panic, Yasmin — just try again," said Minker.

"I will see if I can find anything to help," Casiopiea added.

While Yasmin began again to pray, Casiopiea returned to the circular room. She began searching for something, anything, that might help. And then she saw it: a small wooden box, open, lying in a pool of blood. Whose blood? Who knew? There was blood almost everywhere.

She picked up the wooden box and looked inside; it appeared to be just an ordinary wooden box. She held it up to her face . . . and then she noticed a small green glow that appeared to be fading. She quickly closed the box and ran out of the room.

"Anything happening yet, Yasmin?" asked Casiopiea.

"No, nothing. He's losing his pulse." Yasmin was close to tears.

"Let me take over."

"What? Casiopiea — you're no healer."

"But this is." She held up the small wooden box, which they all immediately recognized.

Casiopiea placed it in Darkmere's bloody hand and began to speak to him inside his head.

'Come on, you good for nothing bastard — live!' Then she started screaming out loud: "Darkmere, stay alive — we need you now!"

Darkmere's arm twitched.

"Aha," said Casiopiea, turning to Yasmin — "Heal him now!"

Dumbfounded, Yasmin again began the process of healing, and this time it worked. She smiled and looked into

Darkmere's beautiful blue eyes when they opened, then looked around and focussed on Casiopiea.

"You're welcome, Darkmere," Casiopiea said.

"Let's clean up!" Minker declared.

"Where is Gowen?" asked Darkmere.

"In there . . . he collapsed."

Darkmere reentered the circular room to tend to Gowen. He knelt and opened Gowen's hand, placing the wooden box in his palm.

The box began to glow, and the glow to intensify, until it radiated throughout the room, heating it up like a warm campfire in a cold winter night.

After a few minutes, the glow ebbed and Gowen awoke.

"Gowen?" said Darkmere, looking him straight in the eye.

"Yes?"

"Are you o.k.?"

Gowen looked around, dazed. "I feel very odd — as if I've slept for days."

"You were in a trance," Darkmere told him.

"Are you o.k.?" Gowen asked.

"Yes." Darkmere replied.

"Where are Englemare and Symra?"

"Symra is dead, Gowen. And we have to find Englemare."

"What happened?"

"It does not matter. Guam is protected now, and Alcamere is dead."

"Alcamere?" asked Gowen, completely bewildered.

"Yes, Alcamere . . . my deceased father," Darkmere replied.

"Oh, I'm sorry."

"Let's go find Englemare," said Darkmere.

"No need," said Casiopiea.

"What do you mean?"

"He's here . . . come slowly."

Cautiously, they followed Casiopiea through a small doorway. Inside they found a room made of gold: gold walls, ceilings, and floors, with ruins all around. In the middle of the room there stood a huge stone slab. On it lay a figure with a sheet draped over it. They all knew what it was.

"I don't know if you really want to see this," Casiopiea said.

"Uncover it, Casiopiea — this is something we all have to see," replied Darkmere.

Casiopiea uncovered the figure, revealing the hideous sight that lay there: Screaming in terror, Yasmin ran from the room, not able to look upon Englemare's face, which could not be distinguished any longer.

Chapter 22

They comforted Yasmin while Darkmere and Gowen covered Englemare's mangled body, readying it for burial. Then, before leaving, they decided to check the rest of the castle to ensure there were no hidden tricks Alcamere had left behind.

They all stayed close together, the five that were left — Yasmin, Minker, Gowen, Casiopiea, and Darkmere — and exited the circular room in silence.

"What about Englemare, Darkmere?" Gowen asked.

"We will come back for him later. Right now, we have to make sure we're safe."

They moved further into the hallway to see what might befall them.

The once perfect hallways were old and crumbling. They led to empty rooms with nothing in them — except perhaps the ghost of Alcamere.

'Darkmere, where did he keep his magic items?' Casiopiea asked.

'Wait,' Darkmere replied. "Everyone return to the circular room — there's no remaining danger. Casiopiea, follow me."

"Where are you going?" Yasmin asked.

"To find out where my father left his wares: Casiopiea is the only one who can help with the magic, and I need you the rest of you to stay here and keep watch."

As Darkmere left with Casiopiea in tow, Yasmin turned to Gowen. "You know, I don't like her."

"I know what you mean, Yasmin," he replied.

Casiopiea and Darkmere ascended the spiral staircase, up, up and up, until they reached the top, where they came to a small door engraved with etchings.

"Casiopiea."

"Yes, Darkmere," she said, raising her arms and chanting the words of magic. "It says only a family member may enter unharmed."

Darkmere approached the door and spoke.

"Calib, Alcar, Moor — open for me, I am of Alcar blood." Darkmere took a dagger and sliced open one of his fingers. He allowed the blood to drip over the door handle. When the handle was covered with his blood he grasped it and waited, while Casiopiea watched.

The blood on the handle began to sizzle, and so did Darkmere's hand, but he stayed and waited through the pain. Not until the sizzling ceased did Darkmere take his hand off the handle. An "A" was now plainly engraved in the door . . . and it opened.

What lay inside was a wonder to behold — even for a practitioner of magic. They saw a circular domed room with hundreds of bottles of liquids and mountains of rolled parchments strewn about. A wooden table stood in the middle of the room, and towards the far window there stood a large desk with intricate carving and writing upon it.

"I am impressed," Casiopiea said, peering inside the room, her green eyes widening more and more.

"Don't come in here, Casiopiea — not yet, anyway."

She stood and watched as Darkmere rounded the monstrous desk to sit in his father's chair.

As he looked around, Casiopiea watched him . . . and it was then, she knew: it seemed he belonged there, and that he was to be . . .

"Casiopiea — enter," he bellowed. She whirled about the wondrous room in delight.

"This is truly amazing — he was a wizard, a true wizard, with all the majesty it took to be a true —"

"Lunatic," Darkmere inserted, drily.

"What do you mean, a lunatic? Look at this! . . ." She took in every inch, until she caught sight of a black book covered with so much blood she could not read its cover. She went straight to it.

"Don't even think of touching it, Casiopiea. It would probably sever the flesh from your body . . . slowly."

"What did you mean when you said he was a lunatic?"

"You could tell; he had no one near him, no one around him, and he thought he could take over everything. But he left one lace untied — me. He was clever, I'll give him that much. I never really thought it was he who was trying to take Guam over — until recently. But he began to slip." Darkmere's eyes, now scanned the room. "Something is missing."

"Don't worry so much. Let's take some of the items here, and then let's go."

"We leave everything undisturbed — except for this." Darkmere sat and waited. .

Casiopiea wondered what he was waiting for.

Then something happened. The whole room began to glow green. Darkmere rose and escorted Casiopiea out of the room, closing the door behind them. Before their eyes, the engraved "A" turned into the initials "DA."

Casiopiea, flabbergasted, began to speak: "Darkmere, you do amaze me. Tell me about yourself."

"Not now," he said, turning and drawing her to him . . . slowly kissing her.

Her knees began to weaken. She steadied herself and stiffened her body, not wanting to show weakness. She looked up into his eyes. He held her gaze . . . and then released her. Now she felt as though her very being had permeated Darkmere's, and he felt the same way, as though his had permeated hers. Both were unconscious of the fact that they were not in control of the situation.

chapter 23

Darkmere and Casiopiea returned to the circular room to find the others telling jokes to one another. Darkmere interrupted, letting them know that the castle was clear and they could now begin the voyage back to Guam. He and Gowen took it upon themselves to carry Englemare's body from the castle, and found a place to bury him.

"So, Darkmere, will this castle be all yours?" Yasmin wondered aloud, trying to keep her mind on other things. Darkmere looked over the castle, seeing hundreds of ravens now flying above.

"Yes, I suppose so."

"What are you going to do with it?" asked Casiopiea, her mouth dripping with envy.

"Leave it the way it is . . . until there is a time for its use."

"Hey! Anyone want some?" said Minker, offering his special brew to any and all takers.

"No, Minker," said Darkmere, as the eulogy to Englemare commenced, Darkmere, Yasmin, and Minker each saying a few words, and Yasmin conducted the rest of the service. Then the party left the grounds, beginning their journey back to Guam while far in the distance a ruby and two crystals glittered in the far distance.

Days of travelling passed and night watches resumed, with Gowen and Yasmin alternating with Casiopiea, Minker, and Darkmere.

Casiopiea grinned inwardly realizing she still held the bag which destroyed Alcamere.

'Keep it safe.' Darkmere interjected.

'I wish you would stop reading my thoughts, Darkmere.'

'I allowed you to take that from the castle, Casiopiea remember that.'

Yasmin began to ask Gowen a million questions, keeping her mind off Englemare.

"Tell me about that box."

"It's just a box that was given to me."

"By whom?"

"A relative."

"Oh, so you and Darkmere are related through your mother?"

"Yes," answered Gowen. He looked longingly at Yasmin, and then added, "Tell me, Yasmin, are you o.k.?"

"Yes, a little shaken up, but all in all, o.k." Yasmin held back her grief for Englemare.

"That's good: I'm glad. How do you feel about Englemare?"

"Better," she lied.

"Good, I'm glad," Gowen repeated, running his hand through his hair, and letting out a long and labored sigh.

"Wait a minute, Gowen."

"What?"

"Oh . . . nothing." She hesitated.

"What?"

"I see you seem sad."

"No, I'm o.k."

"If you need to talk . . . I'm here."

"Thanks," Gowen said, turning away. After he had left her, Yasmin allowed herself one tear, which rolled down her face. For you Englemare, she thought.

Further down the path, their mood seemed to worsen.

"Hello," came a whiny voice from out of the woods.

The party quickly sprang to attack mode, ready for the next battle.

Again came an annoying voice from the shrubs: "Hello." The bushes began to quiver. Gowen and Darkmere stood alert, swords drawn, senses heightened.

The bushes parted. Darkmere, with a frown, put his sword away.

"Hi! How are you? I'm fine. You look o.k. — well, answer already." They were looking down at, a three-foot midget with one eye in the center of his head.

"Hello," piped Yasmin. "Who are you?"

"Copin," the short one replied in his whiny voice.

"And what are you?" asked Minker.

"I am a cyclops."

"A what?"

"A cyclops."

Darkmere rolled his eyes. Casiopiea looked at him. 'Are we going to stand here and talk to a three foot pain in the ass, or are we leaving?' she said in Darkmere's head.

'No, we are not leaving — and he will be joining us,' Darkmere replied.

'What?'

'That's right, sweetheart', said Copin in Casiopiea's head, simultaneously pinching her in the buttocks. And in that instant it became clear to all that Copin and Minker would be good buddies, as Minker scooted over to give Yasmin a pinch on her ass at the same time. Meanwhile, Casiopiea fumed. Darkmere asked Copin to come along with them.

'How did he talk to us?' Casiopiea demanded furiously.

'He can talk the way I can — and he can read our minds. But only on the surface,' Darkmere said.

'How come you asked him to join us?'

'He's a cyclops.'

'So.'

'They are rare. They also are an asset in certain altercations.'

Casiopiea rolled her eyes skyward. As they continued the journey towards Guam, Copin continued pinching Yasmin's butt. And when she asked why, all Copin would say was, "That's the way we greet people."

"Oh," said Yasmin, without enthusiasm.

Chapter 24

Their anticipation rose as they made their way closer to Guam. Though only a few of them lived there, it had become home to all.

Copin, talking up a storm to Minker, was beginning to annoy the others.

"Can you do me a favor and keep your voice down?" Yasmin asked politely.

"Sure, honey", replied Copin, pinching Yasmin's behind for the fifteenth time in fifteen minutes.

Casiopiea asked Darkmere, "Can you please ask him to be quiet?"

"Copin, keep it down."

"Aye aye, captain" said Copin. Then Minker offered Copin an introduction to Big Bill's special brew. Copin accepted too readily, brought the concoction to his lips and drank, until his one eye began to spin up into his head, and he collapsed.

Almost everyone began clapping, while Minker bowed.

Then they continued home . . . carrying Copin with them.

They settled down for the night and, as the watches commenced, Darkmere and Casiopiea began to speak.

He had been sitting by the campfire, watching its glowing embers beginning to dim, when Casiopiea moved herself closer to him.

"Tell me what's on your mind," she whispered in his ear.

"Just thinking about what happened here. It still does not fit. I know there is something missing . . . maybe —"

"Maybe nothing," she said, ducking beneath his perfect chin and running her wet tongue along the length of Darkmere's neck.

He closed his eyes and sighed, pulling her closer. "Casiopiea, you are beautiful."

"How beautiful?" she whispered, her hot breath cascading along his neck, sending spiders up his spine.

"As beautiful as the moon and the stars," he said, covering her mouth with his.

At first she began to tear at his shirt, then to take it off, feeling her way over his splendid, perfect form. Then she backed away, breathless, gasping, drawing him to her.

"Tell me I am the most beautiful woman you have ever seen."

"Casiopiea, you <u>are</u> the most beautiful woman — more beautiful than the cosmos itself." His eyes glistened, mocking her in the embers of the fire.

Her breasts heaving, she smiled seductively at him. They looked at each other, yearning to unite in the moonlight.

"Kneel," said Casiopiea.

Slowly, ever so slowly, Casiopiea stepped up to Darkmere and circled him, scrutinizing every inch of him as he knelt before her. Then she bent down towards him, breathing heavily, coming closer and closer. She let her lips touch his, quickly, darting away, not letting him complete the kiss — then beginning again.

"Can you stay?" Casiopiea said, feeling a stirring in her breasts beginning — as she moved before his bare-chested body.

"What's going on?" chirped Copin in his whiny voice, awaking from sleep and grinning at Darkmere, who was becoming quite disgusted with him . . . the moment now broken, the sun came up over the trees.

Chapter 25

As Copin busied himself with waking everybody up, Casiopiea composed herself and Darkmere quickly donned a black, short-sleeved shirt.

Copin passed Casiopiea, pinching her ass and speaking to her in her head.

'I know you all too well.'

She glared at him, her breathing growing more rapid. Then Darkmere passed. "Good morning, Casiopiea."

"Good morning." She cringed.

Yasmin said to Copin, "You know, you're kind of cute."

"Oh, thank you," he replied as he pinched her ass yet again.

At last the path grew wider and well-traveled. Darkmere and Yasmin were the first to see the outskirts of Guam.

"Look," she yelped Yasmin, running ahead. Suddenly, she stopped dead in her tracks.

"What is going on?" Darkmere sighed, surveying the new scene while the rest of the party caught up to them. The once gnarled and twisted road of Guam now lay straight as an arrow. The once dark and horrid Guam now lay clear, sunny and filled with life. There were people yelling and children playing. The once empty street now bustled with merchants. 'Today and Tomorrow Only' the sign read, 'Come One, Come

All.' But where had they all come from? The small main street was alive again.

Darkmere and the others looked around, amazed at the changes. Then he felt eyes glaring at his black cloak. And one thing, at least, was missing: the shack from which Alcamere had ruled.

They entered Darkmere's small, dark house, placing all their goods on the wooden floor, and sat down — satisfied they were home at last.

"So, Darkmere, what is next?" Minker asked.

"Interesting. Next, we feel the town out and make sure nothing remains that could surprise us. After we secure the town . . . we shall see. Gowen, take Yasmin and Copin with you. Minker can go back to the halfling village. And Casiopiea stays here."

Yasmin eyed Casiopiea.

"We should be allowed to practice our swordsmanship again," Gowen declared.

"Not yet," replied Darkmere. "We have to make sure that this town is safe."

They split up, securing the town. Only Darkmere found something odd.

PART II

Chapter 1

Casiopiea

She sends chills through my body
She captures my soul
I ache for her touch
but once she touches me
she poisons my soul — Casiopiea
She shows me something that
no one else makes me feel
She burns her brand deep
below where I reel
I can't stand living with her
yet she's buried beneath my soul

> *Show me a way to rid*
> *myself of her — show me a*
> *way to move on. I don't*
> *know why but I want*
> *her deep within my soul —*
> *Casiopiea*

It was evening; the sun had drifted off beyond the horizon.

"It's a little bit chilly," she said. "Would you start up the fire?"

He went outside to fetch wood while she shifted in front of the empty fireplace.

After a little time had passed, he came back, his arms full of wood. He lay the wood in a pile in front of the hearth.

She sat watching while he placed some of the wood in the fire.

"Darkmere?"

"Yes?"

"I have decided that it's time for me to get a companion — a familiar."

"Now?"

"Yes, now."

"I will help you, follow me," Darkmere said, placing the rest of the wood on the far side of the fireplace.

They left the house, passed the end of the main road, and turned down a small path . . . disappearing into the night.

"Gowen?" said Yasmin.

"Yes?"

"This is a nice town."

"Yeah, I know," piped Copin. "Where's Big Bill's, Gowen?"

"Oh, Big Bill's is straight down the street, on the left. And why do you want to go there, Copin?"

"Well, I'm meeting Minker there later on tonight. He's going to show me the ropes." Copin winked his eye at Yasmin as he smiled. He then brushed his light brown hair off to one side.

Yasmin grinned. "You two should go to the Lionheart."

"The Lionheart!" Gowen mused.

"Yes, the Lionheart — what's wrong with that? Englemare worked there. That's where I met him."

"Oh." Gowen looked down.

Then Copin added, "Hey, guys, I'm going to go now and meet you later for dinner. I want to find out what's inn in this town: Get it — inn?"

"Oh, Copin, you're so cute," Yasmin declared, pinching his cheek, sending Gowen's eyes rolling skyward.

"Thank you, my lady Yasmin," said Copin. When he had left, Gowen asked her, "Do you want to go back to my house, or are you going to the Lionheart?"

"I'll come with you," answered Yasmin. "I have some questions for you."

They found themselves standing before a colossal tower, that seemed to cascade down from the clouds.

"Follow me," said Darkmere, taking Casiopiea's cool hand.

They walked up towards the tower's big gray door and knocked.

"Enter, Darkmere," a voice replied.

They entered the tower and saw stairs leading upwards. They followed them.

They came to the top of these stairs, where another gray door stood.

"Enter, Darkmere," the voice repeated.

A small room with two wooden chairs: Darkmere sat in one, and instructed Casiopiea to do the same.

The door opened again, and an old man with a white cane and spectacles appeared.

"Darkmere."

"Yes."

"You will come with me. Casiopiea will remain here."

Darkmere followed the old man out of the room and down a corridor, to yet another gray door. It opened; inside, before a hexagonal table, sat a man cloaked in dark gray robes.

"Darkmere."

"Yes."

"Why have you come here?"

"First Casiopiea desires a familiar. She is ready to learn more from you. And second, I found this." Darkmere reached inside his robe to retrieve a small scroll, which he placed in the magician's hand.

"And you seem to be visibly disturbed by its contents."

"I am."

The magician opened the scroll and began chanting words of magic.

When he was finished, Darkmere walked over to him, removed his hood, and looked directly into the magician's eyes.

"You lie!" exclaimed Darkmere, moving swiftly around the desk, grabbing the magician by his throat, and throttling him.

"You may kill me if you wish — but that will not stop it!"

Darkmere backed off, and the magician quickly caught his breath.

"This cannot be true!" Darkmere shouted.

"Oh, but it is. It is, and you will rot in hell for it!"

Darkmere held himself still, glaring at the trickster. "You will before I," he said unsheathing his sword.

"Oh, must I help you play out yet another of your pretty scenarios? How tedious --" Darkmere shoved his sword into the magicians bowels and wrenched it out again. The man's eyes went wide. "I never thought you could do it — congratulations! I will see you in hell!"

Darkmere tore the scroll from the dead magician's hand and wiped the blade of his sword on the conjurer's clothes. Sheathing his sword, he scanned the room. He took some papers and a quill from atop the desk and penned a note:

<u>You are now the keeper of this place - live well, Krantos</u>

<u>Forever yours, Darkmere</u>

He rolled the note up and, without as much as a second glance, left the room, handling the note to the old man with the white cane. "Congratulations — you get to teach Casiopiea.   See you in a week," he said returning to Casiopiea. He told her what she was to do.

"What do you mean, stay here and I will see you in a week? What happened, Darkmere?" She asked, knowing <u>something</u> had just occurred.

"Nothing happened. Are you going to disobey what I have suggested?"

Watching Darkmere's eyes change to cold hatred made Casiopiea quickly back down. "Anything else?" She asked resenting his control over her.

"Yes — here," he said, giving her an emerald ring. "Wear it . . . if there are any problems, I'll know."

Chapter 2

Entering Gowen's home, Yasmin found a chair facing a window and sat down. Gowen sat next to her, sighing loudly.

"Let me see you," she said

"What?!" Gowen exclaimed. Yasmin giggled like a thirteen-year-old.

"I want you to tell me about <u>that</u>."

"What?"

She pointed to the familiar wooden box which lay in front of him.

"That is a gift. I told you."

"Then you wouldn't mind if I —" Yasmin picked up the box and began tossing it up in the air.

"Yasmin, please, put it down."

"Why? . . . I won't. You tell me why."

"Please . . . put it down, Yasmin, please."

"Not unless you tell me."

"Tell you what. . .alright, I will tell you if you put it down."

Instead, she threw the box up once more. This time she missed catching it; it landed and broke.

Sweating, Gowen scrambled for the box.

"I'm sorry," Yasmin cried, watching Gowen turn paler than a ghost. She became frightened. She ran over and knelt by him, wanting to cradle his head in her arms. "Gowen I'm really sorry — can I help you?"

"No. <u>Wait</u>." said Gowen, clutching the box to his chest while he gasped for breath.

"Tell me. I will keep your secret," she insisted. In amazement, she watched as the box slowly became whole again. Simultaneously, the color returned to Gowen's face, and his breathing returned to normal.

"Gowen . . . <u>tell</u> me," she said, running her hands through Gowen's hair and looking down at him.

"Gowen?" she whispered.

"What?"

"Your ears."

"I know."

"<u>You're</u> a half-elf, too?" Amazed, Yasmin pulled his hair back to reveal his pointed ears that signified that he was not fully human.

"Yes," he said unenthusiastically.

"But you look so human!" she exclaimed, almost on the verge of tears.

"I know."

"Who is human, your mother or father?"

"Boy, you <u>are</u> nosey, Yasmin. My mother is human and my father was an elf. I hope I didn't hurt your feelings." Gowen grinned.

"Tell me about your father. I am intrigued by elves. My family, the DeLovines, were of elven descent. It's my mother who came alone and messed with my changes of becoming a full elven princess."

"I see." Gowen grinned at the idea of Yasmin as a princess, all dressed up and no place to go.

"Well, now that I know more about you, tell me your secret . . . the box."

Gowen began to talk.

Meanwhile Copin strolled down the open roads of Guam, taking in the sights. He watched people being thrown from the open windows of the Lionheart, and the rich and elegant strolling out of the Crystalbird Inn.

He made his way to Big Bill's, a tavern which appealed to his sense of adventure. He sat himself down at the bar.

"Hey, what you want?"

Copin turned to see Minker standing there holding two glasses, one pink, the other green.

Copin jumped from the bar stool and grabbed the green drink. The rest of the night was a little blurry.

Darkmere sat in front of a freshly lit fire and opened the scroll again. . .

Quickly rereading it, he tossed it into the fire and decided it was time to get some rest. This night had become too long.

chapter 3

He emerged from the river, dripping in the morning sunlight. As the trees began to sway, he slowly made his way back to the dark house swallowed by the forest.

As he opened the wooden door, he stepped into the depths of the past . . .

"Yes, you will go to help him."

"No, I do not feel it is necessary."

"You have put this upon him, and you alone will fix it."

"No, I will never allow him to be free."

"You will be bound by him if you do not heed my words."

"Get out . . . ."

He sat down heavily in the rocking chair and began to feel that holding Gowen under his wing was not the right thing to do. It was time . . . now.

He closed his eyes. Swirling lights blinded his vision as he gave up his inner fight.

Meanwhile, as Gowen lay in bed, gasping for life, he held the box to his face.

"Hear me, Darkmere, hear me. I am your flesh and blood. I do not deserve your hatred . . ." He sighed, regaining ground, "I never meant to hurt you. Believe me or not, I am not - -"

A whirlwind of colors spinning to no end, lights bouncing off other lights; the ground below began to shake as the rooms merged — dark and light — a horrible creation. A loud blast, and all was broken. The two brothers lay devoid of feeling.

A knock broke the silence that had seized the house. Awakening with a sudden jolt, Darkmere became aware of the things that surrounded him. He heard another knock and opened the door.

Yasmin was standing there. He was not in the mood.

"Darkmere, I know about the box, and I insist you let Gowen free — he's dying."

"The deed is done. Now leave me."

She looked upon his weary face and continued, "Darkmere, pray tell, are you suggesting that you let him go?" She fluttered her eyelashes at him.

"Yes — leave me be."

"Oh, thank you, Darkmere — you're wonderful," she snapped, the sarcasm dripping from her mouth.

"Good night, Yasmin."

"Good night? But it's day! Let me come and help you lie down - you look woozy." As Darkmere began to wobble, Yasmin put her arms around him and lowered him onto the chair.

"It looks like you need to be healed." He nodded.

"I will heal you, but only if you," she smirked, "kiss me three times, and not just any kiss."

There was not much he could do except nod, and so she healed him. When he looked better she said, "How about it?"

"How about what?"

"You gave your word."

His eyes widened as he realized what he had done.

"I thought you cared for Englemare, Yasmin."

"I did, but he's dead now." She looked away.

"Yes, Yasmin, but it was only a short time ago," he said, realizing her thoughts were of him now, and that he had given his word. Break it! he told himself, but resisted the thought.

"You promised," she said.

"Come here," he whispered.

She came to him like an animal in heat and straddled him.

He kissed her and sparks began to fly in front of her eyes. He seemed bored.

They parted. She fluttered, "Oh, Darkmere, I knew you had such — we still have two more. Your word — remember.

He looked at her, struggling to control his anger. Don't kill her now was the thought that kept running through his head. He ran his hand through her short hair, then he kissed her as much as he could stand before becoming disgusted.

She almost melted to the floor when he took his hands away from her.

"Oh, Darkmere," she gasped.

His rage was barely contained by then.

She blinked into consciousness, and smiled. "Darkmere, kiss me again, and make it good this time."

He grabbed the back of her hair and pressed his lips hard against hers, and he thought:

"<u>You like her — don't hurt her</u>."

"<u>Be gentle</u>."

"<u>You are doing this wrong</u>."

His gentleness began to emerge, with her moving on top of him —

<u>No</u>!

He broke away, breathing more heavily than usual, and she gazed at his glistening chest, not a flaw marring his beauty. She could not help staring, and he could not move — time stood still, until there was a knock at the door.

Darkmere composed himself. "Who is it?"

"Casiopiea."

He arose and pulled his shirt on, "Yasmin, it's time to go — <u>now</u>!"

"Oh, okay — see you later, Darkmere." She almost swaggered out of the house, passing Casiopiea in her wake.

Casiopiea watched Yasmin nearly floating off as she left, and then stormed into the house.

"What is going <u>on</u>? I want to know right now!"

He explained that Yasmin had refused to heal him unless he kissed her.

"I want to <u>kill</u> her," Casiopiea shouted, "and I will!"

"No, you won't — not now. We need her."

"For what? She will die."

Darkmere grabbed her. "No — I told you no, and I mean no."

He held her while she kicked and screamed, until she calmed down.

With bated breath, she began, "I will kill her, and you will help me. I have your word on this?"

"Yes — not now. The time will come."

She followed him to the basement and closed the door.

Chapter 4

They sat across from each other.

"Darkmere," she said, "now that I've calmed down, will you please tell me what's going on?"

"You know that wooden box that Gowen has?"

"Yes."

"Well, I was the one who gave it to him."

"Tell me more."

"One night he visited me. I was trying to help him — and when I was sleeping, he tried to kill me. So I punished him . . . by creating the box."

"Go on."

"The box controlled his lifeline. I had complete control over when he suffered — it was his payback."

Casiopiea's eyes were wide. "He tried to <u>kill</u> you?"

"Yes, his father was sinister, he tried to enslave most of this town, and died trying. Gowen was controlled by his father . . . and was told to destroy me."

"Gowen went along with this?"

"He is weak. I didn't like what he had done, coming at me in the middle of the night, with a dagger in his hand, while I lie helpless in bed."

"Darkmere, I'm sure you are far from helpless. So do you still have control of him?"

"No. I let him go."

"Why?"

"It was time."

"What do you mean, it was time? You could have kept him under your control and we could have had him for ourselves, bending to our will." She waited for a reply.

"I do not have to explain myself, Casiopiea."

"I think you are bluffing, Darkmere." He quickly changed the subject.

"Gowen, are you alright?"

"Yes, Yasmin. Thank you for asking."

"You're welcome, I'm really sorry about last night with the box."

"It's fine now."

"I want to make it up to you."

Yasmin came closer to Gowen and hugged him.

"I don't know what I'd do if you died," she added.

"Probably go on."

"I guess", she said, feeling a little guilty.

"Casiopiea, why did you come back?" Darkmere asked.

"I have something to show you."

"What?"

"Darkmere, meet Crystalmere — my familiar."

Casiopiea waved her hand, and out of the emptiness a small crystalline dragon with beautiful green eyes materialized.

Darkmere placed his hand under Casiopiea's chin and lifted it up to look into her eyes. "He has your eyes, my dear."

- 116 -

"My beautiful eyes?"

"Yes, your most beautiful eyes." He kissed Casiopiea, drawing and lingering on her lower lip.

'It is a pleasure to meet you, Darkmere. I like your name,' Crystalmere conveyed to Darkmere in his head.

'The same to you,' replied Darkmere. "So tell me, Casiopiea, did you name your familiar after me or Alcamere?"

"You, of course," she said, kissing him again. "Darkmere?"

"Yes?"

"Would you like to go into the bedroom?"

"Yes — I would."

Chapter 5

Time passed: days into nights and nights into days, with Gowen and Yasmin beginning to get closer and Darkmere and Casiopiea's intimacy deepening. Minker and Copin's intimacy — at every bar and tavern in Guam — also deepened.

Gowen woke one morning and went to make tea and breakfast for Yasmin and himself. She was already in the kitchen.

"I thought," she said, "since you've been so kind to me, I could make some breakfast for you."

He gave her a kiss on the cheek, sending tingles down the sides of her body.

He turned, smiling at her. "I'll be back soon. I'm going to get a few things in town."

She admired Gowen's powerful physique as he departed, the door leaving her to cook and clean for him. Excited, Yasmin said aloud, "This will be the first time ever!" She began to cook — throwing eggshells into the pan right after breaking the eggs and tossing them in.

Meanwhile, Casiopiea untied Darkmere from the post in the basement where she had left him the night before.

"Casiopiea, why did you leave?"

"Because I felt you deserved a little punishment for treating me the way you did."

"How?"

"You didn't pay any attention to me when I asked you how you felt about me."

"Isn't it obvious? I've never —"

"You've never what — felt this way about another?"

"Yes — and you as well?"

"Yes."

"Then help me heal my wounded shoulders — I should never have trusted you, my piece of work."

"Piece of work? I hope that is a compliment, Darkmere." She narrowed her eyes.

"Of course it is," he smirked.

"I know you could have gotten loose, with your strength . . . and how do I know you did not, and then put yourself back in the simple knots I tied around you?"

"Because, Casiopiea, you have my word," he said, looking her full in the face, shifting from playfulness to complete seriousness. In that moment, Casiopiea saw his true weakness.

Gowen was strolling back from town with the few items he'd gotten from the country store. He listened to the birds chirping and watched the flowers blooming. And then he noticed an odd smell — smoke coming from every nook and cranny of his house!

He bashed in the front door, screaming for Yasmin. He went further into the smoke: still no sign. Then, through a little clearing, he could see her, smoke billowing all around her, from the pot of tea.

"Yasmin! Turn off the stove!"

Coughing, he ran out the back door and fetched some water. He tossed it over the oven, making it worse as smoke billowed throughout the house.

"Yasmin — come with me." He took her by the hand and sat down outside, to wait for the smoke to clear.

"What did you have in mind?" he asked.

"Well, oh . . . I figured, from watching you, that it was easy to cook. But, I . . ." She put her head in her hands and muttered, "I burned the tea."

"The tea?"

"Sorry."

"Just let me do the cooking from now on. It'll be better that way."

"I'm sorry — so sorry," Yasmin said, tears beginning to drop from her eyes. "Gowen, I really thought I could do it — but I failed."

"It's o.k." said Gowen, embracing her, holding her, and rocking her back and forth. In his arms, Yasmin felt safe. "Yasmin, I don't know what I'd do if you died."

"Probably get over it," she sniffled.

"No, never," he said, hugging her closer, the last of the smoke fading away. Which gave Gowen an idea . . .

As Casiopiea and Darkmere started to get on with their day, she instructed Crystalmere to check up on brother Gowen. 'Things in this town need livening up', she thought while Darkmere made a mental note of her thoughts as he watched her closely.

Chapter 6

A knock on Gowen's door interrupted his concentration: he was cooking.

"Yasmin, can you get that?"

She opened the door. "Gowen, nobody's here."

"That's odd," He appeared behind her.

"Maybe one of the children was having fun," Yasmin suggested.

"Probably", said Gowen, turning back to resume his cooking, while Casiopiea smiled to herself, enjoying his befuddlement. Crystalmere reported he was inside Gowen's house.

"Darkmere?"

"Yes, Casiopiea."

"I think it's time for me to go and continue my lessons in magic while —"

"While Crystalmere watches Gowen and Yasmin?"

Surprised, Casiopiea looked at Darkmere, then grinned. "You wouldn't tell on me, would you?"

"No."

"Well, I'll be back in a couple of days and nights."

"O.k."

"Who do you think is the most beautiful woman on the face of the earth?"

"Naturally, the woman next door," said Darkmere. Casiopiea whacked him as hard as she could.

"That <u>hurts</u>!" he said easily withstanding the barrage of blows to his chest. "Casiopiea?"

"Yes, ugly one."

"I think it's time for you to go."

"Are you going to tell me who is really the most - -"

"See you soon, Casiopiea", said Darkmere, shoving her out of the house, then closing the door in her face.

"You inconsiderate bastard!"

'I love you - now go on and make me proud,' Darkmere said in her head.

She sighed. It occurred to her that there might be a way to 'make him really proud'. With a devious smile on her lips, she took a room for the night at the Crystalbird Inn.

As the day wore on, another knock sounded on Gowen's door. Yasmin opened it and was surprised to find Copin and Minker standing there.

"How are you — anything doing?" said Minker, teeter-tottering his way in.

"He's just a little drunk," said Copin, whining.

The two crusaders entered, stayed awhile, joking and playing around, then took their leave.

At the same time, Darkmere set himself in his rocking chair to read from a book entitled <u>The Trials of the Government of Ancra</u>.

At once, a sharp pain seared through his body. The small man in dark clothes awoke to hear a voice: "Get him any way you can." He steadied himself and left the mountain:

it crumbled in his wake. The time had come . . . it had been a long time — much too long.

Casiopiea went to see the old man with the cane to study the scriptures of magic, learning as much as she could absorb. After a day, she understood as much as anyone else would have in a week. And so she returned to Guam, informing Darkmere she would again stay at Crystalbird Inn — where, unobserved, she watched Gowen and Yasmin declare their unbridled love for one another.

"Oh Gowen, I don't know what I would have done without you."

"Wait," said Gowen, and scrambled out to the dining room. He dashed back with a small intricate box in his hand, reached across the bed to take Yasmin's hand, and opened it. Then, holding her hand open, he knelt before her.

"Yasmin."

"Yes, Gowen."

"Will you marry me?"

"Oh yes — I <u>will</u>," she smiled, her eyes twinkling with delight as she opened the small box to reveal a beautiful diamond with pink gemstones set around it.

"You're sure you want no one else?"

"I'm sure now, Gowen."

He took the ring from her delicate hand, and slipped it on her ring finger. The two, beaming with delight, hugged each other. Gowen looked into Yasmin's big blue eyes, she looked back deeply into his . . . and they kissed.

"How disgusting! Crystalmere, keep me updated. I can't listen any more," Casiopiea said aloud, while she communicated the same to Crystalmere. The short man smiled in delight.

Chapter 7

Darkmere woke the next morning to find a note:

Darkmere —

Meet me at the place where Guam intersects with Krantos's tower.

— Casiopiea

Darkmere left immediately. He waited; there was no one in sight. He searched for Casiopiea through his brain, but could not find her. What was going on? It had to be a trap.

He sighed and slowly turned around, noticing, as he did, the sky growing darker and darker. Something was about to happen.

Casiopiea awoke from her sleep and peered out the window; it looked like rain.

She put on her grey robe and stepped outside; this time, she thought, to see Darkmere.

As she strolled down the street a small person bumped into her.

"Excuse me," a gravelly voice said.

"Of course," she replied.

"Excuse me," the voice repeated.

"Yes? May I help you?"

"I get a sense you could use some direction."

"What exactly do you mean?"

"I mean <u>power</u>," the man in the dark clothes whispered.

Casiopiea was immediately interested, yet wary. "Tell me more."

"Meet me in a little while at that house," the man said, pointing down the road, "and I will explain. Come alone — or I cannot tell you what you wish to know."

Casiopiea agreed, intrigued by the figure now walking away from her. A very interesting little man, Casiopiea thought.

The clouds broke. Torrents of rain drenched Darkmere as he waited for who knew what.

He had turned towards home — when lightning streaked across the sky, striking him full force in the chest, and knocking him unconscious. He lay still. The rain stopped, the sun peered through the clouds, and on his body, the only visible sign of the impact was the tear in his left shoulder. While it healed by itself, he awoke. Glancing at his left shoulder, he saw that the outline of a lightning bolt had been carved in it. He noticed that he felt different, stronger.

He rose, felt a little woozy, then returned home.

Meanwhile, Gowen and Yasmin had fun listing all the things they liked about each other.

Darkmere, arriving home, had forgotten about Casiopiea. He settled in his rocking chair and fell asleep.

Casiopiea approached the house where the little man had indicated he lived. She knocked, but there was no answer. 'Tomorrow', she thought, turning in the direction of Darkmere's house.

Knocking on his door, she found, much to her dismay, no answer there, either. 'Later', she told herself, and returned to the Crystalbird, where a stranger, a buxom woman with blond hair whom she had never seen before, caught her attention. When the woman suddenly turned and smiled, Casiopiea smiled back. As she did, a man called out, "Crendar." The woman turned away. Casiopiea entered her room and fell asleep, exhausted.

The small man smiled to himself, as he watched her through his crystal ball.

chapter 8

As morning emerged under the dew of the trees, Casiopiea awoke in her inn room. She scanned the room, and the dark wooden furniture; she looked out the window at the townspeople who bustled about, this way and that, then across the street, and somehow sensed — this day would be different.

She dressed and made her way down the winding roads until she came upon a little bent house right on the outskirts of town.

She approached the door, which was hanging from its hinges, and knocked.

"Oh, Casiopiea, come in," the small, gravelly voice responded, surrounding her.

She entered, dagger in hand.

"Put away your weapon, Casiopiea — I won't hurt you."

She turned a corner, finding herself standing before the small man with the determined look.

"Ah. How are you?"

"How did you know it was me? Are you like Darkmere?"

"No, not really — but, in a sense, yes."

"How do you mean?"

"I have some of the same abilities — given to me by him." He looked skyward.

"I want to know more about him and how I can become more powerful than Darkmere."

"You mean the Dark One?"

"Yes."

"Are you sure?"

"Yes."

"Sit down."

She did.   Suddenly she felt tremendous power run through her — a surge the likes of which she had never felt before.

"More?" he asked.

"Yes — I want more."

A second wave went through her.   She could not comprehend what was happening; a whirlwind of feelings — feelings of power, growth, and the sense she could destroy anything.   She smiled in her glory.

Soon the feeling vanished.

"What — why did it stop?"

"Do you think he gives this for nothing, Casiopiea?"

"Tell me more."

"Well, the Dark One is all around.   He can help you with your tasks.   He can help you become more powerful than Darkmere could ever be."

She nodded.

"Do you wish to become a messenger of the Dark One?"

"Yes," she said, unaware that the Dark One now had control of her.

"Come with me."

He stood up, bringing her into a room which had only four stone walls, with a stone slab in its center.

He said, "Kneel down, and I will give you your first task."

She knelt, and he began chanting words of a language so old and powerful, the trees began to hear and shudder.

After he stopped, a swift breeze swept through the room and around Casiopiea. She looked up, wide eyed; standing in front of her was an image of unnatural beauty.

"Casiopiea, welcome. You are now part of US. Worship the Dark One!"

She could not help but bow. Then the image was suddenly gone. She sighed.

"Now — here", he said, handing her a small pewter symbol of an arrow going through a heart. She took it.

"Hold it dear to you."

She shook her head, trying to make sure she was rid of the troubling image she had seen.

"Don't worry. It won't last long, Casiopiea."

"What did I just see?"

"A disciple of the Dark One."

She sighed.

"You have a first task for the Dark One — have Darkmere kill someone, to rid himself of the goodness which lies deep within him. Then bring him here."

"How?"

They spoke in hushed tones, and she left.

Chapter 9

Darkmere awoke the next morning feeling groggy. He sat down in the living room. Soon the room began to spin, and he put his head in his hands. No, I will fight this, he thought trying to focus on anything to keep him awake. Moments later, he collapsed.

Casiopiea opened the front door and bound Darkmere's hands and feet as the priest of the Dark One lifted him off the floor. The three entered the depths of the woods, where they came upon a stone slab protruding upwards on a slant. Strapped to it was a woman, revealed by her shape, but with her face covered.

As Darkmere awoke, the priest disappeared.

Darkmere peered at Casiopiea, sending a shiver up her spine.

"What is going on, Casiopiea?"

"You are becoming too amicable. I want to see you —" she grabbed the woman's hood and took it off — "kill your mother!"

"Never."

"You hate her!"

"Yes."

"Then kill her."

Darkmere gazed at the woman's wide, pleading eyes.

"No," Darkmere replied.

"Yes."

"No!" he said again, but, she persisted, and, after a brief but terrible struggle, he lifted his mother's head, kissed her, and then, with her eyes still pleading, severed her throat.

Then Darkmere fell to the ground.

The priest returned. "Very good, Casiopiea. Now we will take him to my house. Take her as well, what is left of her. Darkmere will understand." He smiled as they left. Behind them, the stone slab disappeared, along with all signs of what had just happened.

They took him and the woman's remains back to the shack, where they bound him head to foot. Then they woke him.

"Darkmere, you have been a disobedient boy."

He could not speak — before his face Casiopiea held his mother's decapitated head. His eyes widened and began to fill with disgust. Casiopiea screamed at him, "You are weak and helpless! You are repulsive. You are too kind! You detested her, hated her for having Gowen and staying by Gowen and not helping you! You despised her!"

She drew the bloody head along his squirming body.

"You weak, pathetic fool!"

She began to unbutton his pants, and slowly laid the head on top of him. He lost ground and collapsed.

She woke him again as the priest stood smiling in the shadows.

"Darkmere, you killed your mother! You, and only you! You did this and nobody else!"

He knew it was true and shrank from her, as she ran his mother's hand up and down his body. He became more and more rigid — and then it was done. When she screamed again, he did not flinch. He did not move, and did not feel. Then she untied him, and he did not lash out. He just looked at her. She was horrified as he got up and left.

Chapter 10

Casiopiea turned her worried eyes to the priest of the Dark One.

"Does he remember what happened?"

"No, Casiopiea - he does not remember that you made him do it. He only remembers that you found him, and that he did kill his mother."

"When I go back, he will read my mind and - -"

"And be unable to pick up what happened. The Dark One now protects you."

"I will see you later, then."

"Yes. Remember, any death that is caused by you will help you gain ground with the Dark One."

"Good afternoon."

As Casiopiea approached Darkmere's house, she felt a sense of dread. She opened the door to see everything on the floor: pieces of furniture, dishes, sculptures from the mantle — everything in disarray. Through one of the windows, she saw a lone figure standing in the distance. She hurried out the front door and around to the back of the house. There he was his back to her . . . standing there, not moving.

"Leave me be," he barely whispered across the wind.

"No. Darkmere, what you did - -" She felt tingles down her back as he turned towards her, glaring at her through the hood that covered him.

"Leave, Casiopiea — <u>now</u>!"

"No — Darkmere — I will . . . ." She began to feel worried as he slowly approached her.

"Casiopiea — if you do not leave now, I will not be held responsible for what I do to you. Leave!" he bellowed. She was frightened, for the first time. She was hastening away from the monster that grew within him when she heard a scream that ripped through her very being.

Chapter 11

For next few days they stayed away from each other - - Casiopiea at the Lionheart with Crendar, a woman she had met in the Crystalbird a few days before. On the fourth day, a loud banging on Crendar's door resounded off the walls of the inn.

"Who is it?"

"Darkmere. Is Casiopiea there?"

"Wait a minute."

He heard shuffling inside, then forced the door open — only to see the two women laying on the floor, opening their arms to him.

He entered and closed the door.

"Come here, Darkmere — I missed you."

"<u>We</u> missed you."

He stood there, as Casiopiea allowed Crendar to stroke her hair. Darkmere watched, and became nauseated. Casiopiea, he knew, had betrayed him.

"Darkmere, oh Darkmere, won't you . . . come here . . . please," Casiopiea stretched out her hand to him, and he held it like a boy holding his mother's hand. She drew him to her, and both women tried to remove his clothes — but he would not allow it.

Casiopiea began kissing his face and neck, and Crendar to feel her way all around his body.

He lay there, not reacting. Then Casiopiea said, "Crendar, leave him alone and come to me." The other followed Casiopiea's commands, while Darkmere's face began to turn as hard and white as stone.   Finally, he grabbed Casiopiea's arm and yanked her up.

"You are coming with me — now!" he seethed, speaking under his breath.   "Get dressed."

Casiopiea apologized to Crendar and left with him.

As Darkmere dragged her from the inn, she spoke. "Darkmere, that was rude — were you getting a little jealous?"

He picked her up and kept on walking.

He approached his house, walked in, and dropped her on the floor.   Then he proceeded to the bedroom.

"That hurt!   What are you —"

The bedroom door slammed.   She opened the door.

"What the hell!?"   She looked at him - blood marks ran down his back.

"You knew — you knew something was going on with me, and you stayed away — you knew."

"What happened?"

He turned on her, and threw her against the wall. "Casiopiea, I am losing.   I am going insane.   I don't want you and Crendar together."   He ripped his shirt open in front of her.

"What are the marks on your back?"

"Two nights ago I was asleep, and suddenly I was awakened by a voice — a deep dark voice, which sounded familiar — yet I don't know how.   I ignored it and returned to sleep.   Then the pain began, as though someone were tearing into my back like an animal.   I was not able to be healed. The healer I went to told me it was my destiny. You see, I did not believe it to be true."

"What are you talking about?" Casiopiea looked at him, confused.

"It was <u>told</u> to me that this would happen. A prophecy involving me that I was told in confidence, yet I did not believe it."

They looked at each other. She could see that something in his eyes was different, but she was not sure what. "What did this voice say?"

"That I will be destroyed. And ever since, I have had this feeling that I'm going mad."

"Let me help . . . maybe it's not true."

"How can you?" Darkmere looked Casiopiea up and down, and then his tone of voice changed. "Interesting, very interesting. Is that what you care for?" Darkmere asked, walking over to her and placing his hands on her neck. Her breath became short as he opened up the top of her robe to reveal the symbol of the Dark One.

"Darkmere, no — I don't only care for him," Casiopiea pleaded, looking skyward.

"You know, I never felt I could believe in the gods." Darkmere followed her gaze and continued, "Yes, they do exist, but they don't help in any way. So I see, then — you are not loyal to me. You have betrayed me Casiopiea. How do you think I can trust you, when your locality lies elsewhere?" He looked into her eyes and waited.

"Let me try, Darkmere," Casiopiea said, feeling that she might have made judgement on this god too quickly.

He searched her thoughts, and he saw she did not lie. "I will this time." He touched neck again, caressing it before and stepping away. He knew if she betrayed him he again, he would have no other choice but to kill her.

"Thank you Darkmere, you will be pleased." Casiopiea grinned, as did the short man, who watched through his them through a crystal ball.

Casiopiea was intrigued, and over the next few days she searched for the answers to the problems that were occurring. But each day left her more discouraged; there didn't seem to be anything to find. Each day, however, the words on paper, which Darkmere had burned in his home, seemed to become more real. He stopped eating and began to not want to see anyone. She knew she had to do something. She was afraid that he would perish — and she did not want that to happen . . . yet.

chapter 12

"Darkmere, get up."

He moaned but did not move from his bed when she approached him.

"Darkmere, I need to talk with you. Maybe I can help you."

He stirred a little, and then turned to her, his pale face showing his agony.

"What do you want?"

"I need to ask you a few questions," she continued. "Has this happened because of you killing your mother?"

He shook his head.

"Then why would it occur now — is there anything you know of that we can do?"

"Just keep looking," he said with halting breath.

"I will."

Without further thought, she began searching the town for the history of the family of Alcar.

Meanwhile, Gowen and Yasmin were planning their marriage. One day as they lay together, someone knocked on the door. Gowen lazily got up, Yasmin grimacing.

"Who is it?" he asked.

"I overheard Big Bill say that you were looking for some people to join you on an adventure — and so I came here."

"Wait a minute." Gowen unlocked the door and let in a woman who had long wavy blond hair, tailored clothing, and appeared to be in her mid-twenties. She strode in and smiled.

"My name is Abeline. What's yours?"

"Gowen."

"And I'm his fiancee, Yasmin." She came out in an outfit which barely fit, and extended her hand. Abeline took her hand and smiled.

"Come in and let's talk."

Abeline sashayed up to the kitchen table and sat down.

"Tell us what you do, Abeline."

"I wield a few weapons, and I practice the arcane arts."

"Something I know we would be interested in," exclaimed Yasmin. "Do you do anything else?"

"That's about it. I am very interested in travelling — and love people."

"A kind of all around person," Yasmin replied, then added, under her breath, "*bitch*!" Gowen gave her a kick.

"What did you say?"

"I said 'ouch.' My legs have been hurting me. Too much sex, I guess!"

Abeline went on, "So when do I get to meet everyone?"

"Later. I'll set up a meeting, and then we can all get to know each other."

"I'm staying at the Crystalbird, in town. Just leave a message there for me."

Gowen showed her out: when he had closed the door, Yasmin turned to him.

"I don't like her. There is something about her."

"I think she'll make a great addition to our group — and we'll let Darkmere decide."

The night came quickly, and Abeline paced her room.

"Where are they? I've been waiting - -"

She heard a knock at the door and straightened her dress.

"Who is it?"

"Front desk."

"Hold on."

She opened the door.

"This is for you."

It was a white envelope. She opened it:

Dear Abeline,

Meet me at my house, after the moon rises just above the stars.

Gowen Aries

She looked out the window, and saw it was almost time to go.

Meanwhile, Gowen had some to Darkmere's house to explain what had happened. Casiopiea had managed to get Darkmere out of bed and prop him up in the rocking chair.

"Darkmere, what's wrong?"

"A bad cold. What happened?"

Gowen told him about Abeline, and Darkmere agreed to see her; but Gowen would have to bring her to the house. Gowen agreed and left.

"I'm glad. We need help on our next mission."

"What mission?" asked Casiopiea, always intent to know more.

"I'll tell you later," Darkmere replied, sounding tired.

"O.k. I'll hold you to that."

"I know you will." Darkmere almost smiled.

The moon began to peek above the stars. As it did, Abeline put on her blue robe, walked to Gowen's house, and knocked on the front door.

They escorted Abeline to Darkmere's house, were they found a figure wrapped in a dark cloak, with Casiopiea standing next to him.

After they were all seated, Darkmere began to speak. "Tell us, Abeline, what has made you want to go out and perhaps kill yourself?"

"I am strong willed, and life in a small town bores me. Excitement is what I crave, and I am good at my skills."

He introduced himself. "This is Casiopiea, and you have already met Yasmin and Gowen."

"Yes. It is nice to meet you all." She extended her hand to Darkmere, studying the shadows in his face.

"Will you not be open and show me who you are?" she asked. Casiopiea closely scrutinized her.

"Yes, I will," he said.

Casiopiea's and Yasmin's eyes widened, as Darkmere unveiled his face.

Abeline watched intently, but did not break her gaze. She continued to speak. "I know I can help all of you."

"I believe you," said Gowen.

"You will come with us then on our next journey?"

"Yes, Darkmere." The name rolled off Abeline's tongue like candy. 'I've missed you,' she added in his head. Yasmin and Casiopiea looked dumbfounded.

"Meet us back here three days hence, and I shall tell you of our journey."

"Will Copin and Minker be coming?" asked Yasmin.

"Yes, they will . . . and Abeline will meet them later on."

Chapter 13

"I think she's very nice."

"What do you mean, 'nice'? She could take candy away from a baby and you would say 'she's nice.'"

"Now, Yasmin, Gowen is right — she's o.k.," interjected Darkmere.

Casiopiea's eyes widened. "Nice? She's a bitch."

"She is all right and she's coming along."

"Did you check her out?"

"Yes . . . and there is nothing adverse about her."

Casiopiea rolled her eyes. "Well, Gowen, Yasmin — I think it's time our leader got some sleep."

As they were leaving, Casiopiea ran out after them. "Gowen, I need to speak with you."

"Yes," he said, "what is it?"

Yasmin began stamping her feet. "I need to speak with you alone," Casiopiea insisted.

Impatiently, Yasmin agreed.

"Yes, what is it?" Gowen asked, wondering what Casiopiea could possibly want from him.

"I think you should know something," she said. "The other day I walked in on Darkmere and Yasmin, embracing." She waited, hoping for the worst possible reaction.

"What?" You must be joking!"

"No, I am quite serious. I asked Darkmere what happened and, quite frankly, he told me that Yasmin would not heal him unless — unless he kissed her." Casiopiea stepped back: She watched his face change color and his eyes boar themselves into her. "Are you telling me the truth?"

"I swear on Darkmere's grave."

Gowen looked at Yasmin, who had begun to tap her foot on the ground. He turned back to Casiopiea and swallowed hard. "Thank you, Casiopiea. Goodnight."

"You're welcome. I'm sorry."

Gowen returned back to Yasmin. Casiopiea watched in delight, then went back to the house.

"What was that all about, Gowen?" Yasmin wanted to know.

"Nothing, nothing at all. Let's go home."

Casiopiea supported Darkmere as he took his seat.

"I don't know about Abeline," she said. "Are you sure she's o.k.?"

"Yes."

"You seem better able to move."

"I am."

"That was a fast recovery."

"I'm not recovered yet."

"What do you mean?"

"I need you to find out some information for me — and to be discreet about it. Find out anything you can about a cult called Carum. . . Oh, I also see you like spreading gossip."

"Are you referring to Gowen?" Casiopiea leaned in close to Darkmere and kissed him on the forehead.

"Yes, my love."

"Well, I was telling the truth."

"I guess you were, but you know that this will cause some problems."

"Oh, well."

He reached for her face as she pulled away from him.

"Tell me about Carum."

"It is a cult and it has something to do with my condition and my Alcamere."

"He was an delightful person to meet."

"Whatever you say, Casiopiea." He studied her as she stretched.

"Darkmere, tell me what you would ever do without me."

"I would be much better off."

"Oh, really? Does Carum have anything to do with our next mission."

"Maybe."

"Maybe? Something is wrong here. You are not telling me everything. I too, know what you're thinking, in a sense."

"Show me."

"How do you know about Abeline? Tell me, Darkmere."

"Abeline and I were lovers once."

Casiopiea was stunned.

"Yes. A long time ago. She left me for Gowen. And then she left town with someone else."

"You mean you and he —!"

"Yes, Casiopiea. Now, I must go to bed."

"Wait a minute — you're not getting off that easily. Why did you two lie and act as if you didn't know her?"

"I thought I'd talk to you later, after I saw it was her. She's changed," Darkmere added.

"I won't allow her to come!" Casiopiea glared at Darkmere, jealousy pouring from her veins.

"We need her. Don't worry, I'm not going to marry her, my darling. Good night."

He left Casiopiea hanging. And then she knew what she had to do.

Chapter 14

Yasmin and Gowen walked back home.

"Gowen?" She sighed and nibbled on her lip.

"Yes?"

"Tell me what Casiopiea said."

"Oh, just that you and Darkmere kissed because you told him he would not be healed if he didn't. Is that true?" Gowen asked, stopping in his tracks and turning to Yasmin, who looked away.

"Gowen, listen to me. It was Darkmere. He has a sort of spell over me, and I don't know what to do around him."

"Don't give me any excuses. Tell me the truth!"

"If you really want to know, I did it just after Englemare died, and it was before I told you I would marry you."

Gowen watched every more she made.

"Gowen, I do love you. You kiss better than he does any day."

"Oh, really?" he asked, raising his eyebrows at her.

"Yes, please believe me. I am marring you, right?"

"Yes, but would you marry him if he asked?"

"No, I would not!" Yasmin retorted.

There was an achingly long pause. "All right, I believe you." He took her slender hand in his and resumed walking.

After a couple minutes of silence, Yasmin spoke. "I don't like her."

"Who?"

"Abeline."

"What do you mean?"

"There's something going on, Gowen — tell me."

"You won't like it."

"<u>Tell</u> me!"

"Abeline used to go out with Darkmere — until she dropped him for me. And then dropped me, and left town."

Yasmin stopped dead in the middle of the road.

"Yes, Yasmin. She used to go out with us both, she's harmless."

"Why did she leave?"

"She left because she wanted someone else," Gowen replied.

"And now you two are letting her come back into your lives?"

"Are you jealous? I love <u>you</u>, Yasmin — and only you. I'm <u>your</u> husband to be, not hers."

"But if she had stayed around, who's to say you would not have married her?"

"I would never have!" Gowen put his arm around Yasmin and they started back home.

"Why not?"

"Because I would never have met you."

"Oh," said Yasmin softly.

After making sure Darkmere was resting peacefully, Casiopiea left the house for the middle of town. "Crystalmere."

"I'm here."

"Do me a favor — go to the inn and find Abeline's room. Then watch her, and tell me what's going on."

"Yes, master."

'Casiopiea, come back here tonight.'

'Yes, Darkmere I will come back to you,' Casiopiea said. Darkmere could not keep his mind off her.

Chapter 15

Screams, screams in the night, skeletal hands reaching out, grabbing, groping, tearing — pieces of flesh, blood, bodies, rotting corpses, burning, burning, burning. . .

Startled, Casiopiea awoke midway through the night to the sounds of horrifying screams. They came from within, where Darkmere tossed and turned, sweat pouring from his brow.

What was happening? The screams stopped, and Darkmere began clawing at the bed. Quickly, Casiopiea began slapping her hands together. It didn't work — until suddenly he was propelled upright . . . and awoke.

"Darkmere, you're <u>drenched</u>. What happened?"

Slowly he lifted his gaze and looked at her.

"A nightmare."

"I know. What happened? I heard all these noises."

"What . . . kind of noises?" said Darkmere.

"Screams."

Darkmere rose from the bed and strode towards the door. Puzzled, Casiopiea watched. Just as Darkmere was about to leave the room, he had to clutch onto the door, fighting for his life.

"<u>Darkmere</u>!" yelled Casiopiea, running over.

"Just help me onto the rocking chair."

"But you're too heavy."

"Just try." The two of them wobbled into the living room, and Casiopiea helped Darkmere sit down. "It's happening again, isn't it?"

"Yes. I don't know how long I can withstand this. I feel as though I'm being pushed inward from all sides. You see the small scroll there in the fire — how it's not burning?"

"Yes."

"See if you can retrieve it. First, put out the fire. It's just about out anyway."

"She waved her hand and uttered some magical words, and they watched the fire fade.

Casiopiea reached her slender hand into the fire, retrieved the scroll, and snapped her fingers. The fire began to burn again.

"Here you are, Darkmere," she said.

"I am impressed."

"You should be."

Darkmere, forcing a pained smile, untied the red ribbon that kept the scroll from unravelling, and began to read aloud. began to read aloud. "The prophecy — the Alcar prophecy." He had to pause to catch his breath . . . and his hands began to shake.

"Let me," she said.

"No — I will continue." He sighed. "The fifth generation will become like the fourth — insane — and will perish."

"What does that mean, Darkmere?"

"I will perish and go mad in the process."

"Read more."

"The fifth generation will have a half-brother who is a half-elf."

"Gowen is half-elf, but he looks so human."

"He is — anyway, let me keep going. The fifth generation will be betrayed by a close friend and Darkmere Alcar will be the end of the . . ." The scroll fell from his trembling hand, which Casiopiea reached out and clasped.

"What does the last part say?"

"World," said Darkmere, strained.

"Darkmere, this isn't true."

"It is the truth. Remember you asked me about what happened at the wizard's tower?" Casiopiea nodded. "I tried to get rid of this curse, but I was told through magic it was truth. Plus the fact of the matter is I am following in my father's footsteps. When I received that scroll, I could swear I burned it, yet it reappeared. I am going insane." Darkmere looked away, disgusted.

"Listen, Darkmere," said Casiopiea, picking up the scroll, "a prophecy is made to be broken. The future is yours to mold, not something determined by a piece of magical paper."

'Bring the scroll to me . . . I can help,' said a gravelly voice inside Casiopiea's head.

"Darkmere, I will see if I can find out more to help you. Stay here . . . I will return."

"No! You will not go anywhere with that scroll." Darkmere grabbed a startled Casiopiea's hand. With amazing strength, he turned her around to face him.

He looked at her eyes and then down the length of her body, while Casiopiea, with all her might, tried, but could not budge. He took her by the neck.

"Casiopiea, this symbol has something to do with what is happening," he said of the amulet she wore. "I can feel it." He pulled it off and beheld it in the palm of his hand.

"No, Darkmere! You said you didn't believe in gods."

"No, I never said that, I just believe that I can't trust them."

"Why, maybe this one can help you."

"I highly doubt it, Casiopiea. Go ahead and see."

"Stop being a martyr! You disgust me when you talk like that. I will be back shortly. Anyway, have you got anything to lose? I think not."

'Bring him with you — bring him to us. He is losing the power of choice — and we can help him regain it,' urged the gravelly voice within.

"Will you come with me to find out?"

"Maybe."

"Maybe? Darkmere, look at you — you're half the man you were!" Casiopiea raised her hand to meet his hardened grip.

"No! Leave, Casiopiea . . . now!" He pointed to the door. A crazed, mad look had filled his face.

Looking at Darkmere, she felt her life was in jeopardy. She fled the house, hearing sounds of destruction behind her. She did not like what was happening to him.

'Casiopiea, I can help — I can always help,' the gravelly voice intoned.

'Crystalmere?'

'Yes.'

'Anything on Abeline?'

'Maybe.'

'If nothing is happening soon, go and watch Darkmere.'

'Yes, mistress.'

Casiopiea quickly made her way to the small house that belonged to the Dark One's priest.

Chapter 16

'Go now.'

'Yes.'

Abeline left her inn room, with Crystalmere following. They turned from the main road of the town down the winding path that led past Darkmere's house into the woods. Abeline sat down on a rock and waited, unaware that Crystalmere sat in the trees above, watching.

"Oh Gowen . . ." Yasmin hummed.

"Yes."

"I want to get married today."

"Today? But there's so much to do and so little —"

"Don't worry — I'll take care of that. Minker will get the halfling village to come. I'll make a dress of my own, and I'll pick a halfling to be my bridesmaid. And I'll get flowers, and —"

"And, calm down — my best man will be Minker."

"You mean you won't have Darkmere be your best man?"

"Only if you have Casiopiea." Gowen grimaced.

"I won't bother you. How about two days; we can do it in two days, can't we?"

"Two days . . . hmmm," said Gowen, drumming his fingers on the kitchen table. "O.k."

"Thank you. I love you so — so much," said Yasmin, kissing Gowen on his face and arms. Taking his hand, she led him to the bedroom.

Meanwhile, outside, Minker and Copin giggled as they watched through the bedroom window.

"You know, Copin, let's go have some fun. These two need to be left alone."

They left, whistling a funny tune and grinning.

Casiopiea, opening the door to the small house, saw her savior.

"Casiopiea — I am glad you came to see me. I feel you should help Darkmere. He is losing himself, feeling distraught. Together, we can help him. You must find him another kill."

"Who?"

"Anyone who means something to you."

"Nobody means anything to me . . . except Darkmere."

"No. You have a friend."

"Who, Crendar?"

"Yes, Crendar. Have Crystalmere go to watch her . . . and see."

"All right." She closed her eyes. 'Crystalmere.'

'Yes.'

'Go and watch Crendar. How's Darkmere?'

'I will watch him soon. I'm still watching Abeline.'

'Forget Abeline. Go and watch Darkmere, and then, if he is well, watch Crendar.'

'All I do is watch people.'

'Is there something wrong with that?'

'No, master.'

'Good.'

"Casiopiea, now we must pray." said the priest of the Dark One.

Crystalmere left to check on Darkmere, who was asleep. The familiar left to look in on Crendar. Abeline approached Darkmere's window. She made her way around to the front door and went inside. Walking slowly, she let pieces of her clothing fall to the floor as she approached the bedroom door. She opened it gingerly, then grinned at the magnificent sight of a helpless Darkmere. Gently, she laid herself next to him in the bed.

Chapter 17

A wind began to rise . . . blades of grass stood on end . . . while the people of Guam took a second glance at the sky.

They had been going about their daily chores and tasks when the sky started to turn gray, the gray was followed by a tinge of red that floated over the people, before the sky changed to black.

Too familiar a sight for comfort the townspeople scattered into their houses, closing their doors and locking them.

A downpour seemed imminent. A shiver ran through Casiopiea's body. The little house shook. A figure, surrounded by boundless light that seemed to flow everywhere, entered. As Casiopiea looked up into the glow, things began to shift, and then the walls of the small house crumbled into dust. He stood there in all his glory.

"Casiopiea. How are you?" The voice resonated everywhere around her.

"Who — are — you?" Casiopiea asked, trembling.

"I am your God. Bow before me."

The urge was overwhelming. Casiopiea bowed before deep, piercing gray eyes. His white-blond hair touched his broad shoulders, enshrouded in black ceremonial garb, which came to a point on each shoulder.

"I, I — am. . . overwhelmed," uttered Casiopiea, hardly able to look at him.

With a wave of his hands, the house walls returned to their original shape and size. He had made it possible for her to look upon him - and not lose her sanity.

"Is this better, Casiopiea?"

"Yes, it is."

"I'm glad. Now let's discuss things, while I reveal to you your future self."

Darkmere tossed and turned. Abeline laid her warm hands on his bare chest. Barely able to contain herself, she smiled in the knowledge of her growing accomplishments.

"Darkmere," she said, sly as a snake between the sheets. He rolled over and moaned.

"Darkmere," she repeated firmly, snapping her fingers. He opened his eyes.

"Casiopiea, what do you want?" he said, his eyes two empty pools of water.

"I want you."

"But I can't."

"Yes, you can," she whispered in his ear, running her hand down his chest.

He rolled over and smiled as Abeline began kissing him. Her face showing her triumph as she kissed him. When she was finished, she got up and slapped him in the face. As he fell into unconsciousness again, she rolled him onto the floor, left the house, and returned to her inn room.

'It is done, Etten.'

'Very good, Abeline. Very good.' He smiled in the night sky.

Visions began floating in front of Casiopiea's face - visions of people she'd met, places she'd been, and things she wished to possess. Then a vision of Darkmere loomed in front of her.

"You see . . . he will betray you, Casiopiea."

"What do you mean, Dark One?"

"Watch."

Casiopiea began to see herself with everything she ever wanted: Darkmere as her husband, power, wealth, slaves, and magic powers she had not even dreamed of. She was to be given the position of Queen of All Things, with Darkmere by her side . . . on his knees. A golden throne stood before her. She approached it, with Darkmere following. But, just as she was about to sit, the vision changed. She saw Darkmere taking everything away from her. And then the vision vanished.

"What — how, why?" Casiopiea begged.

"Don't worry. Just show him our way, and he won't be able to take anything away from you. He will be bound to you forever."

A twinkle came into Casiopiea's eyes. "When do I start?"

"Now. Go get him, and have him kill Crendar. Then bring him to me . . . after you have killed one as well."

"I will." Casiopiea smiled, her fiery green eyes twinkling with deviousness.

Chapter 18

The next morning dawned just as Darkmere awoke, his face nearly burned where he had been slapped by Abeline. He got up and realized he wasn't wearing anything. Slowly, he approached the mirror - to see his left cheek beet red. He could not remember the night before. Why? What was going on? He did not like it.

He got dressed and went into town, forgetting to close the door, mindlessly strolling. He went in and got a new black shirt and food supplies for home. Before he left, he bumped into Yasmin.

"Oh, hi, Darkmere — how are you?"

"A little tired."

"Well, the two of us were going to tell you together, but I'll say it now — Gowen and I are getting married."

"Congratulations," said Darkmere with little enthusiasm.

"Well, tomorrow, we would like it if you and Casiopiea would come to our wedding at Big Bill's tavern."

"I will be there. Invite Abeline, Copin, and Minker."

"Invitations have already been distributed to Copin and Minker. But Abeline?"

"Yes . . . invite Abeline."

"O.k., I guess. See you tomorrow, Darkmere." Yasmin smiled at him, swaying her hips slightly.

"It's at noon tomorrow. Don't be late. You're too cute to miss." Darkmere sighed as she met up with Gowen outside and the two of them kissed warmly. He turned and left the two alone.

"Gowen," Yasmin asked, after a while.

"What is it?"

"Darkmere and Casiopiea are coming tomorrow. What is it, Gowen, are you upset? You know Gowen, you're so adorable."

Gowen blushed. "Come on, you little imp." He forced himself not to tell Yasmin of the growing jealously that plagued him.

The two went on, making wedding plans, while Copin and Minker set up the decorations in Big Bill's.

"Hey, Copin, you want to be in on it when Bill and I create our next potent concoction?"

"Sure what are you going to call it?"

"Well, we can call it the Red Killer."

"But that's kind of ugly."

"You come up with a better one, then."

"How about the Cyclops Twist."

"Boring. I'm sure we'll come up with something. Let's get these decorations up and then create something special for the bride and groom."

Copin started laughing when Minker fell off the bar stool, cracking it in the process.

"I'm gonna tell Bill!"

"Go ahead — I've broken many before, and he never did anything to me."

As the decorations for the wedding went up, Casiopiea and Crystalmere lured Crendar into the forest with a note:

> Crendar, meet me at the North Woods.
> Love and kisses, Casiopiea.

Crendar left the Lionheart that afternoon and never returned.

Not again, thought Darkmere, as he unwillingly slew Crendar . . . taking out his aggravation on her.

"So, Casiopiea — you were the one who had me kill my mother. Am I right?"

"Yes, you are. Revel in the feeling that you felt — no remorse — and you can join me."

"In what? I don't believe in anything except . . . I don't trust anything else."

"Not even me?"

"I, yes I do." Darkmere stated unwillingly. Something was in control of the both of them and he could do nothing about it.

"And?"

"And, I love you, but I don't feel I can worship this deity, a deity who has people go opposing what they believe."

"And what is it that you believe in, Darkmere?"

"I can only believe in myself."

"I understand."

"Thank you that." They kissed beneath the blood that dripped from Crendar's dead body, and Etten began to smile.

Chapter 19

That morning, the festivities got underway. Big Bill's tavern filled to capacity while the townspeople busied themselves in anticipation, talking about Gowen finally getting married.

"I can't believe, after all these years, Gowen is getting hitched!" said Big Bill, presiding over his tavern.

"What do you mean?" inquired Copin, "He's never been before?"

"No. Have you?" wondered Minker, slugging another drink down his throat.

"Well, once there was this beautiful girl. She was sooo beautiful," said Copin, shaping circles with his hands.

"What was she, fat?" pressed Minker.

"No. She had such an amazing eye, purple and blue. It was the most —"

"Spare me, Copin. I like people to have two eyes, except maybe for you."

"Oh, you like him?" Big Bill offered.

"No, he's a good friend," said Minker, eyeing Bill, who stood with his hands planted on his sides.

"Lighten up, you!" said Big Bill, slamming Minker in the back and sending him flying into Copin.

Bill's laugh reverberated around the room. The wooden planks shook.

Right then, Gowen sauntered in.

Bill shouted a greeting, and the whole bar broke into applause for Gowen, who turned beet red.

"Hey, Bill," whispered Gowen, "I need to talk to you."

"The man needs room — move out of the way!" said Bill, escorting Gowen to the back room. Minker and Copin came tagging along.

"What's up, Gow?" said Big Bill.

"I'm a little bit shaky."

"Well, have a seat."

"I never thought this would happen, Bill," Gowen said remembering what Casiopiea had said once again.

"I know what you mean. I remember when that other woman dumped you just before . . ."

While Bill, Gowen and Minker reminisced and Copin listened, Abeline strolled into Big Bill's, smiling. People gasped. Furtively, a small bald man ran to the back room: "Bill, sorry to disturb you — but she's here, Gowen. The woman who dumped you — she's here!"

"Thanks, Willen," said Bill. Willen quickly departed.

Gowen looked up. "Abeline . . . I know . . ."

Bill looked into Gowen's eyes.

"Gow, does something still linger between you and her? I mean, she almost married you."

"No. Nothing, nothing at all," he sighed, getting up. "I'll be back at noon, waiting to be hitched to my bride-to-be," he declared, striding out smiling at Abeline as he passed her.

She followed him outside.

"Do you think he will keep his word — or could Abeline win him back?" A woman from one of the tables wondered aloud.

"I think he'll keep it!" answered another in a high, shrill voice.

"I think he'll do more than just look at Abeline — what a find!" said a brawny man. His wife jabbed him in the side.

While the townspeople busied themselves gossiping, Abeline ran up to Gowen.

He turned to face her.

"I wish you the best of luck," she said. "No hard feelings, right?"

"Right. Are you coming to my wedding?"

"Oh, yes — I wouldn't miss it for the world!" she said with a smile. She kissed Gowen on the cheek and gave him a hug.

"I'll miss you, Gowen," she whispered in his ear. "You'll make a wonderful husband to Yasmin . . . I'm sure!"

She pulled away to watch a little girl skittering back to Bill's to tell everyone what she'd seen.

"See you later, Gowen." Abeline left, looking over her shoulder once to see Yasmin staring at him.

"Gowen, it's bad luck for me to see you now . . . Maybe we should call the whole thing off. Do you love me or Abeline?"

"I love you, Yasmin." Gowen said and his jealousy flared as he added, "Who do you love, me or Darkmere?"

Yasmin gaped and began to cry. "No, I love <u>you</u>, Gowen. I <u>told</u> you what happened. What else do you want?"

"Nothing, nothing." Gowen suggested, "Let's pretend we haven't seen each other. I will forget the whole thing. Yasmin?"

She looked up, tears forming in her eyes. "Yes?"

"I do love you," Gowen said, clasping her head in his hand and bending down to gently kiss her.

Yasmin smiled and nodded as they parted. "Alright, Gowen, I will see you later.

He beamed, reassured, before she scurried off.

Chapter 20

As Gowen and Yasmin came down the aisle towards the homemade altar in Big Bill's, they walked past just about everyone in town. Casiopiea and Darkmere were dressed in black. Minker wore his usual browns, Copin was in green, and Abeline in radiant blue. Almost every halfling in the area was in attendance.

Gowen was dressed in black and white, and Yasmin sparkled in a white dress that looked as though it had been handed down many generations.

As the couple held hands and looked into each other's eyes, the ceremony began . . .

"And does anyone here feel that these two should not be joined?"

As a man in a brown robe made his way through the bar and up to the couple, a tense silence settled over Bill's. "Yes, I do," said the stranger.

"<u>What</u>?" said a perplexed Gowen, while Yasmin, and most everyone else, sneered at the intruder.

"Well, I can't have you marrying her without my permission."

"And why is that?" Yasmin wanted to know.

"Because you can't get married without having your brother at your side," said the newcomer, promptly removing the hood of his robe, revealing a man in his early twenties who looked to be Yasmin's opposite. She was light-haired; he was dark. But there was one feature so distinct, any observer could see they had to be related, their wide set eyes — big and blue. Yasmin stared in astonishment.

"Thaddius! What are you doing here? How did you find me? And why are you wearing holy robes?"

He put his arm around her and started to lead her away from Gowen.

"I need to know one thing, Thaddius."

"Yes?"

"Why are you wearing holy robes?"

"Because I became a priest."

"You — a priest?"

"Yes, me."

Casiopiea raised an eyebrow. "Can you believe this?"

"Yes, I can," said Darkmere.

"Are we going to have a wedding or a family reunion?" Big Bill wanted to know.

"Wedding first, then family reunion," said Thaddius.

Yasmin and Gowen turned back to the priest.

"Are we ready now?" he inquired.

"Yes."

"Now, who has the ring?"

"I do," Minker smiled, searching in his pockets. "Here it is."

The ceremony ended as quickly as it had begun. "I now pronounce you — Yasmin and Gowen — husband and wife. You may kiss the bride."

Gowen smiled and, quivering, bent down to kiss Yasmin, while rice was being thrown everywhere around them. Then the party really took off — everyone began dancing and singing, and — of course — drinking too.

Copin and Minker both came up to Gowen and Yasmin.

"So, here you are, married couple," whined Copin.

"Here it is, just for you two, the drink of all drinks — the Passionate Red," said Minker, offering a glass to the married couple.

"Drink up!" said Copin.

"I'm game," smiled Yasmin; Gowen frowned.

"Well, Gowen, what are you waiting for?"

"I can't drink."

"What do you mean?"

"I'm allergic. . . . Sorry."

"It's O.k. I'll drink one," Yasmin beamed.

"And I'll drink the other," said Minker.

At once the whole bar broke out into a chorus, yelling "Go, go, go!" and banging fists on the tables while Yasmin and Minker began to slug the drinks down and the bar cheered and clapped uproariously.

Meanwhile, Darkmere and Casiopiea slipped out the back door.

chapter 21

As the festivities mushroomed beyond the tavern to dancing in the streets, Casiopiea plotted and planned, until she saw the town begin to reflect the red skies left by the setting sun.

Abeline, after awhile, noticed that the two had left . . . and stayed patiently behind.

"Casiopiea."

"Yes, Darkmere."

"What do you have next in mind?"

"Oh, so you know already — you are too quick for me."

"Do you feel it wise?"

"Well, I can't kill her, so I might as well kill him."

"You're so pleasant."

"I know, I know," said Casiopiea, smiling slyly and running a finger over Darkmere's waiting lips.

"So you noticed they left, too," Abeline muttered to Gowen.

"Forget them . . . I can," said Gowen, as Copin began singing and Thaddius and Yasmin continued to reminisce.

"So Yasmin, how does it feel to be married to the king of cooking?" Minker smiled.

"I feel — let's see, not much different. Now I can fool around more often, without having to go out and find anyone," she giggled, beaming.

"You always were the same," said Thaddius, giving her a light push.

"Tell me why you became a priest," Yasmin said, more seriously.

"I felt it was time to grow up, and . . . this seemed to be the best way."

"I'm sure," smiled Yasmin as Gowen came over, and wrapped his arms around her.

"Yasmin, this feels very comfortable. I like this arm rest."

"Cut it out," Yasmin giggled.

"Should I leave?" Thaddius said aloud.

"No, no, I like you, Thaddius, but I think we should put an end to that cyclops's singing days!" chimed Gowen.

"I agree, let's go!"

Thaddius and Gowen got up, strolled over to Copin, and much to his chagrin, picked him up and turned him upside down.

"No, no, please leave me —" Copin began. But Gowen stuffed a handkerchief in his mouth. Then the two put Copin down and shook hands, while Big Bill's and the rest of the crowd's laughter echoed through the small town.

Chapter 22

"I am sick and tired of your superficiality. Do you know anything about this deity you're so busy worshipping?" Darkmere demanded.

"Yes, I know that, after tonight, I will get my rewards . . . aplenty. I have done all that he has asked, and by tonight my accomplishments will be great."

"Do you have an agreement?"

"You and your agreements! Do you always abide by the rules — or have you no sense of adventure? You are nothing, Darkmere — nothing!" Casiopiea screamed at him.

"Are you angry because I killed Crendar? Or is it that you are too in love with yourself? Do I not satisfy you? Or are you merely the most insensitive being living on this planet?"

A fight ensued. Bitter words flew back and forth between the two of them, until the ground began to shake and a voice exclaimed,

"Darkmere . . . Darkmere, you are torn — torn between the good that lies within you and the evil that presides. Do you not wish to extinguish the good . . . forever? As well as rid yourself of the horrible feelings that make you senseless?" The voice waited . . .

"I will extinguish these on my own, thank you. I will respect you, but that is all," said Darkmere, when a vision — all consuming — suddenly appeared before them.

"But I can help you, Darkmere," the vision appealed.

Darkmere, taken aback, as was Casiopiea, still stood his ground.

"I am sorry, but no — I reject you . . . I believe in —"

"<u>No</u>!" cried the vision. "Casiopiea, take your stand by my side and wait for us! Meanwhile, do what must be done."

Casiopiea nodded and set off on her mission, commanded from beyond.

"Now, Darkmere, we are alone. Do not try to impress me with your talk. Join me and you will triumph!" The Dark One waited.

"<u>You</u> will not bend my will. I am touched by no one but me — you do not scare me. Why does a God, such as yourself, beg a mere mortal such as I, to join him? Desperation must be growing in you — you cannot be."

"I will hear no more of this! You insult a <u>God</u> — I, who stand before you, and expect respect? I think not! I am your God!" The Dark One raised his hand and struck Darkmere across the face, sending him flying to the floor.

"Now you will listen — and listen well to me. I want you by my side, and if you do not obey, I will not understand. I will see you again. Do not forget me — or what I have said!" The vision disappeared, leaving Darkmere stunned . . . but able to comprehend the impact of the Dark One's words.

Casiopiea left Darkmere's fuming. She pulled a black robe over her clothes and went to the North Woods, where she waited until the moon peaked over the horizon.

The evening wore on towards dawn, until finally the crowd in Bill's dispersed.

Willen, the short bald man, who had returned for the festivities, walked up to Bill. "If you need me to help clean up, I will."

"Don't worry, Willen. I'll see you tomorrow, I'm sure."

"Then I'll go wish the couple well."

Gowen, Copin, Yasmin, Minker, Abeline and Thaddius were all sitting round the table when Willen came up to wish the newlyweds well.

"Thank you, Willen, and wish your wife, Alpea, well."

"Thank you, Gowen," said Willen, bidding everyone else good-night.

The rest of them stayed and told stories of the past, present, and future . . . until the wee hours.

"Well, I will bid my adieux first. Yasmin, my beloved sister, I will see you soon."

"Where are you going, Thaddius?"

"Oh, I will return . . . probably tomorrow," said Thaddius, holding up his holy symbol. Yasmin nodded.

"I hope to see you soon!" said Gowen warmly, getting up and extending his hand to Thaddius, his brother-in-law.

"I will see you soon, I am sure. Any friend of yours is a friend of mine, and that goes for the rest of you." Thaddius smiled as Copin and Minker came over to shake his hand. Then he left. After him, Abeline took her leave, followed by Copin and Minker. When they were gone, the couple were alone for the first time in many hours.

"You ready?" Gowen said.

"Last one there is a rotten egg-breath," said Yasmin, and she began running in her wedding gown towards the Crystalbird Inn . . . beating Gowen by several lengths.

"Well, I ask you — does that mean I get to say what goes tonight?" grinned Yasmin.

"No way," said Gowen, laughing as he picked her up and carried her over the threshold of Room thirteen.

Chapter 23

The dark and foreboding night lay still, as the black folds of a cloak meandered in and out of the woods.

Thaddius made his way down the deserted road that led out of Guam and into the North Woods . . .

'Darkmere, you will weaken,' came the voice.

'No, I won't,' Darkmere insisted.

'Yes, you will — you already have,' the voice in his head broke. Darkmere got up from the rocking chair and went outside, seeking solitude and peace at the cemetery where his father now lay — at least his father's remains.

As he approached the gravesite, the wind began to stir while Abeline watched him through a crystal ball and Etten laughed.

"Abeline, just watch . . . he will bend . .. he will be surprised . . . now . . ."

Abeline nodded, as they both looked in on Darkmere at the gravesite. As he stood in front of Alcamere's tombstone, a green glow encircled him. A beacon of light appeared on the horizon and then vanished . . . and Darkmere's glow suddenly disappeared, too.

Darkmere turned around. In front of him lay an empty grave, and at the head of the grave another tombstone. He approached it. As he did, pain began shooting through his arms and legs, forcing him to drop to the ground in front of the stone — which read <u>Darkmere Alcar Died This Day</u>.

"Never! You will not coerce me!" he bellowed into the night sky.

"Oh, yes! Yes! Look, Darkmere — now I command you!" The ground shook as the Dark One spoke.

As pain as sharp as knives shot throughout his body, Darkmere saw, standing before him, the ghosts of his ancestors: Bantamere, Crindmere, Zronmere, and, of course, Alcamere.

"You will never be yourself any more, Darkmere! You will live in torment for eternity!" At that, the visions of ghosts came together as one and then were sucked into Darkmere. He screamed into the night sky that enveloped him . . .

As Thaddius walked through the North Woods, his whistle echoed in and out of the trees. But small sounds that came from the woods began to make the hair on his back stand on end. He began to hurry. The feeling of being followed permeated his entire being.

He felt his feet betraying him. He could not move fast enough; all the while he was tripping over branches and stones. And then, a swift vision of darkness struck him, and he fell into nothingness.

The figure in black moved forward, bathed in sudden moonlight, dragging the body of Thaddius through the woods.

It stopped . . . and after a few moments had passed, an altar materialized where nothing had been before. For a time the dark figure stood a few yards away, and then began to approach to the body of Thaddius — now strapped to the altar.

"Waken," rasped a voice that surrounded and stirred Thaddius to consciousness.

"What is going on? Who are you?" he asked in terror.

The figure came up to Thaddius, and put a slender hand to his face, caressed it, and laughed.

"If you want anything, I will give it to you," cried Thaddius trembling with fear. "What do you want?"

"Your life!" the voice laughed, and the hand slapped Thaddius sharply across his face.

"Please don't kill me," he begged, desperately.

"And why not?"

"Because I didn't do anything to you," said Thaddius, gasping for breath as the figure took a dagger from the folds of blackness it wore and slowly dragged it down the length of Thaddius' chest, opening up his buttons as it went.

"Oh yes you did," the silky voice mocked.

"What? Who are you?" Thaddius scrambled inside to pray to his deity.

"I won't tell you until I'm ready, and for every time you speak, I will —"

Thaddius screamed as the figure sliced off the end of his left pinkie . . . and then his index finger, thumb, and ring finger. Thaddius, now sweating profusely, began to whimper.

"Very noble. You are getting good at this — and you haven't fainted yet!" the voice sneered.

Thaddius nodded, as he looked — wide-eyed — into a black void.

"Now I think a little pleasure is due," said the figure, taking the dagger and ripping open Thaddius' pants.

The figure began to caress Thaddius and, when he had become used to the pain shooting through his hand, began slicing up his body . . . laughing again.

"You may speak," the figure said.

"Why? . . . " cried Thaddius.

"You can thank your sister for this," said the figure, removing its hood.

"Casiopiea!" Thaddius gasped, quickly remembering her from the wedding.

"Yes, and as I said, you can thank your sister for this, Thaddius. It is unfortunate. You were so pleasurable." She smiled as she drove the dagger through his stomach.

"I like watching you die slowly . . . So, so sorry . . . Have you any last words?"

"What did she do?" Thaddius whimpered.

"She tried to take away something dear to me — Darkmere. And I'm getting bored by this. Farewell," said Casiopiea, ripping the dagger out and watching Thaddius's eyes go cold.

"His faith did not run too deep. I should have kept him around longer," Casiopiea said aloud, as the altar and Thaddius sank into the ground, disappearing forever.

Chapter 24

As the sun arose, Darkmere staggered into his house. Enraged, he sank into his favorite rocking chair. 'He will never control me.'

Casiopiea walked in.

"Good morning, my darling — how are you this morning?"

He glared at her, and images of Thaddius's death flooded his mind.

"Are you pleased?" she asked, her face flushed with excitement.

"So that's where you were?" he replied, in a tone that didn't please her.

"Darkmere, what is wrong with you?"

"Your deity — he is a fraud, mark my words. He will betray you and your attempts to gain power. That is no way to gain power."

"And you know about this?" Casiopiea sneered.

"Yes, I do."

"Darkmere, what happened to you?" she asked, surprised.

"Why do you ask?" he countered.

"Your eyes are glowing." Darkmere turned away.

"Tell me, Darkmere," she said, more softly.

"What — or else you will kill me? Or will I kill you first, my darling?" Darkmere seized Casiopiea's neck, lifting her off the ground.

"Please — let me go!" She rasped.

"Fine." He suddenly dropped her.

"Darkmere, I can help you get out your anger. You are holding it back."

"How? There is no cure." Beneath his brow, Darkmere glared at her.

"No. Come with me, my darling," Casiopiea said, holding her hand out.

He eyed her and, knowingly, grabbed her and carried her down to the basement. In the flash of a pirate's eye, screams of passion could be heard, while the sounds of a whip snapping resounded throughout the house.

Gowen woke up next to Yasmin, looked over at her, and smiled. He went downstairs, ordered breakfast and brought it back to the still sleeping Yasmin.

"Good morning, sleepyhead," he said softly, as Yasmin opened her eyes. She saw Gowen holding a breakfast tray full of food . . . and a rose lying across it.

"Oh, you didn't have to — but I'm glad you did! I'm starved." She sat upright as Gowen waited on her, then jumped in bed and alternately fed himself and her.

"This is going to be a great marriage. I've never been married before, and I'm glad I found you," Gowen said, kissing Yasmin on the forehead.

She smiled and nodded. "You are so amazing and interesting. I think this will be an original marriage, not like any other."

Gowen smiled, then leaned in closer and began to tickle Yasmin, while food began falling everywhere. In short order, a hilarious food fight between the loving couple broke out.

"Abeline, are you ready?"

"Yes," she said, as the Dark One hovered over her.

"I will triumph, and no one will stop me! What a fool Casiopiea is — she will help us destroy Darkmere's will. And when he is weak and helpless, he will beg us to help him, my darling. Do you wish to kill him?"

"Yes, I do," said Abeline, without emotion.

"Go. Begin to destroy his life first . . . and then the power that is supposed to be mine will return to me — and Darkmere will no longer be," said the Dark One, laughing. "Here, plant this," he added, handing Abeline a scroll with Alcar's name marked on it.

"I won't fail! He will come — or die!" said Abeline, slamming her fist on the table.

"Very good, you are obedient, Abeline. You put my other disciples to shame."

"Thank you, Etten."

"What is it, Darkmere?"

"I love your neck, Casiopiea," he replied running his hand up and down the length of it.

"Thank you. Well . . . do you like what I do?"

"Interesting . . . very interesting."

"Is that all you have to say?"

"I love all of you."

"You're not bad either."

"Thank you."

"You're —" Darkmere was cut short by his own scream; pain shot through his eyes, and his breathing became labored and intense.

"Darkmere! Can I help?"

Glaring at her, he shrieked, "I <u>hate</u> you! Leave or I will be forced to — no! — I will <u>not</u> be controlled by you!"

'You are very strong, but you will weaken.' Laughter echoed through Darkmere's head; he put his hands to his ears, trying to shut it out. Casiopiea watched him, wide-eyed.

"Can I help?" she repeated. When he did not respond, she rose and began to chant words of magic . . . but nothing happened. What is going <u>on</u>? she wondered, perplexed.

Then suddenly, Darkmere snapped out of it.

"Darkmere, are you — all right?" Casiopiea asked, still shaken.

"I am now — but we must leave very soon."

."What do you mean?"

"Come with me." He led her to a bookshelf and picked out a volume that looked a few centuries old.

"What is it?"

"My lineage."

"What is it for?" she asked, not following him.

"Casiopiea, did you find out anything else about the cult Carum?"

"No, I haven't had time."

"These episodes will come over me more frequently in the next days. I need information about this cult — by tomorrow, so we can get everyone together and leave."

"Why don't we just go?"

"Because I require everyone's help, and if I don't get it, we could lose everything." he answered gravely.

"What do you mean?" she asked, still baffled.

"I mean, I can save us — but you can't!" Darkmere said harshly, surprising himself.

"Darkmere, why would you want to save everyone? I thought you liked to <u>destroy</u>."

"Casiopiea, enormous tasks lie ahead. I'm telling you the truth," he replied deadly serious.

Casiopiea nodded and left quickly, knowing intuitively that Darkmere wasn't lying. It was then that she realized there was a lot more going on . . . and that Darkmere knew what it was.

Chapter 25

Abeline arrived at Darkmere's doorstep only moments after Casiopiea had left. She opened the door and entered. She didn't see him. She looked around, finding no one there. Where *is* he?, she wondered angrily. Exasperated, she left.

"You will not withstand this much longer . . . and trying to convince Casiopiea will do you no good. She is bound to me," said the Dark One, materializing again before Darkmere. Darkmere noticed the white hair touching the tops of his shoulders, something seemed familiar here. What was it?

"Etten — it's you! You two-faced —" Etten cut him off. "Yes, it is me, and this time I will see to it that your love is mine — and that your life is mine as well. I have achieved a lot more power since last we met."

"You are hiding something, and I will find it out. God? The <u>Dark</u> One? Who are you kidding?"

"I fooled Casiopiea and the rest of the world."

"Well, you don't fool me."

"Think again. Look around into every corner, Darkmere — because I will be in every one of them. Believe me when I say you will not remember this conversation . . . or me. I will push you to insanity," grinned Etten, vanishing, while Darkmere started screaming, falling to his knees, under siege from a new episode. He began to convulse violently and finally lapsed into unconsciousness.

Chapter 26

"Would you like to visit my mother?" Gowen asked.

"Of course. Why wasn't she at our wedding?"

"She doesn't like to come out of her house too often and, since Darkmere was born, rarely accepts visitors."

"Why?"

"She feels she failed the world, and because she never speaks with Darkmere, she feels worse. I could never help her . . . and she only lets me visit once a month."

"Let's go. I don't really understand why she feels she failed the world."

"I think it has to do with her getting involved with Alcamere, and the fact that she never helped Darkmere."

"What do you mean?"

"Well, Darkmere lived with Alcamere till he was ten, and then he was thrown out on his own. No one came to his assistance."

"Why?"

"Because we had other things on our minds . . . and we despised each other. I also think it has to do with the fact that things were different for him, that's all."

"That's horrible, Gowen. I feel sorry for him."

Gowen grabbed Yasmin and, looking her straight in the eye, said, "Don't ever feel sorry for him — he deserved it. He is —" he broke off.

"What?"

"He has no right to have anyone feel sorry for him, Yasmin. Don't let yourself . . . he is a grown man now."

In Guam's small library Casiopica began leafing through papers that might pertain to the cult Carum. With the help of the old librarian, she found a lot of information. Excited, she rushed back to Darkmere, only to find him lying comatose on the floor.

She knelt down and began praying, while Etten watched and laughed.

"So, Gowen, where does your mother live?"

"On the outskirts of Guam — not really that far from my house."

"Well, maybe we can get her to come into the town."

"Maybe," said Gowen as they walked hand in hand down the winding path. They came to a small blue-and-white house, deep in the woods, with nothing around it. The house had a border of beautiful flowers, and off to one side was a small garden.

Gowen knocked on the door. There was no answer.

"What?" said Gowen alarmed, noticing the door was unlocked. "Mom?" He opened the door, a lump swelling in his throat.

"Oh, she's probably just out back," said Yasmin, smiling to reassure him.

"She <u>never</u> leaves the door open." Gowen walked around the house, and found nothing.

He returned and cracked open the bedroom door, Yasmin close beside him, feeling a little strange. And then he saw her lying in bed. Gowen sighed in relief.

He went up to her and shook her sleeping body. No response.

"Mom, no!" Gowen knelt, bending over to listen for a heartbeat. There was nothing.

"Is she. . .?"

"Yes, she is," said Gowen, and a tear rolled down his cheek.

Yasmin hugged him tight and began rocking him back and forth.

"We have to have a funeral," he said, after awhile.

"Tomorrow?"

"Yes, tomorrow." They hugged each other for some time.

"Crystalmere, go find Yasmin and bring her here."

"Very well," said the little dragon, lifting off, turning invisible.

A voice wafted through the small house, "<u>Yasmin, Yasmin</u>!" Crystalmere landed and appeared, much to Gowen and Yasmin's surprise.

"Who are you?" exclaimed Gowen.

"Casiopiea's familiar. And Darkmere needs you, Yasmin . . . something has happened. He can't move."

"Let's go," said Yasmin, springing to her feet, much to Gowen's disappointment. "Gowen, are you coming?"

"No. I have to find a resting place for my mother . . . then I'll be there," said Gowen. "Tell Darkmere his mother is dead."

"I will, I promise," Yasmin said sympathetically, looking back at Gowen, who was now crying at his mother's side, before leaving to tend to Darkmere.

Yasmin followed Crystalmere out, while Gowen cursed Darkmere for taking Yasmin away from him and blaming him for ruining his whole life.

Meanwhile Abeline placed her scroll in a place where Casiopiea would be sure to find it when she went to meet Copin and Minker for lunch.

Chapter 27

Yasmin entered Darkmere's house . . . and gasped.

"What happened? You didn't do anything to him — did you?"

"No. Help him . . . I found him like this."

She knelt beside him.

"I hope he doesn't die . . . he's virtuous," said Crystalmere, and Casiopiea glared at him.

Yasmin placed her hands over Darkmere's chest and felt a stirring inside. She sighed and waited; nothing happened. She began to pray.

"Well?" said Casiopiea when Yasmin stopped.

"I can't help him . . . we have to leave him like this until he comes out of it."

"I don't accept that answer!" Casiopiea shrieked.

Yasmin had quickly resumed praying when Gowen, who had left shortly after Yasmin, stormed into the house.

"Casiopiea, stop ordering everyone around!"

"Why?"

"Just stop it!"

"Why? Because you hope he will die? Is that it? You pig!" she screamed, going for Gowen's throat. He side-stepped and grabbed her.

"Stop it now!" said Darkmere, rising shakily to his feet.

Casiopiea helped him to a chair.

"What happened to you?" asked Yasmin, concerned.

"Something is going on beyond our mortal control. We must leave here tomorrow — all of us."

"Why?" asked Gowen.

"If we don't go, and pay a visit to the leader of Carum — a cult whose leader knows more than I about this I will die — and so will you," he added pointing to Gowen.

"What?"

"You are related to me, you have the same blood, and what happens to me will eventually happen to you."

"How nice. Now you control my blood too?" said Gowen sarcastically. "By the way, our mother has died. The funeral is tomorrow morning, and I think she would want you there."

"I'll be there," Darkmere replied somberly.

"What do we do now?" asked Yasmin.

"We will meet here immediately after the funeral," he said, "and leave at once. Can you tell Copin, Minker, and Abeline?"

"Yes, I will." Yasmin assured him.

"I also need you to know that an episode like this might occur again — and until I pull out of it, Casiopiea will be in charge." He looked Gowen squarely in the eyes.

"What is causing this?" Gowen asked.

"I can't go into it now."

"Splendid. I must obey Casiopiea, be controlled by you, and have my mother dead — what's next? I'm leaving, and I'll see you in better company at the house, Yasmin! Good-bye!" Gowen stormed out, tripping over a black cat on the way home.

"He's really testy," said Casiopiea. Yasmin glared at her.

"Leave him alone . . . you witch," hissed Yasmin, before leaving them.

Casiopiea turned to Darkmere. "Those two have got something coming — do you agree?"

"Yes, I do, but not until this is over — we can't be rid of them yet."

"All right, torture is more fun." She smiled slyly at him.

"Yes. Now tell me what you found."

Chapter 28

Abeline entered Big Bill's and sat at a round table in the far corner to wait for Copin and Minker.

"Can I help you?" a small, red-haired waitress named Twyla asked her.

"A wine cocktail and an egg sandwich."

A little while later, Copin and Minker walked in, laughing, with beers in their hands.

"Good morning, Abeline, how are you?" Copin inquired.

"Very well. Have a seat. I've already ordered."

Minker pulled up a chair and plopped himself down on it.

The three began gossiping and laughing. Even the waitress joined in, commenting on Minker's 'sexy' expressions and the faces he made when he got drunk, which was almost all the time.

"Gowen?" called Yasmin, as she entered their house.

"I'm in here," said Gowen from the bedroom.

She saw Gowen sitting on the bed, plainly unhappy.

"Gowen, what's wrong?" Yasmin asked, sitting down next to him.

"Besides the fact that my mother's dead, that Darkmere is controlling my life, and that you find him attractive? . . . I think that should be enough."

"I told you — I love you. I don't think he's controlling your life, and I'm very sorry your mother's dead. What else?"

"I'm just sick and tired of seeing that repulsive face glaring down at me every second, breaking up our time together."

"Just <u>forget</u> him for now. And I will be back. I have to tell Minker, Copin, and Abeline that we're leaving."

"Where you gonna look?" Gowen grumbled.

"Big Bill's, of course. See you soon, my love, and don't be so angry," she said sweetly.

"Darkmere, will you be all right if I leave you here and go off to do some work?" Casiopiea asked.

"Yes. I will. If you come back and I am as I was before, just wait until I come out of it. Unless, of course, if it lasts long, find help."

"Who?" she wondered.

"You'll know if it happens. . . Wait! Tell me what you found on the cult Carum."

"They seem to be the anti-cult of another," she explained.

"Which one?"

"Nagas — the Devil's Cult."

Darkmere's jaw clenched while he thought about this.

"Did you find anything else? I need to know everything."

"You just have to promise one thing," she answered.

"What?"

"That I can toy with Gowen and Yasmin, as long as it doesn't affect you."

Darkmere consented. "Now tell me everything."

"I have your word."

"Yes."

"Here it is." She removed a scroll from the folds of her cloak and handed it to him. He opened it to find a map leading to the Temple of Carum.

"Amazing. I am impressed," he said, while Etten cackled, watching from above. "Anything else?"

"This description — here," Casiopiea handed Darkmere another scroll. While opening it, a sharp pain began to grow inside him. He hid it and began to read aloud:

"The Cult Carum, the counter cult to Nagas, derived their power from one crystal and two rubies." Darkmere stopped to glance at Casiopiea.

"Read on, there's much more," she said, watching the intrigue spread over his face.

"'A cult was performing a ceremony at the Time of the Lightning Bolts. They were evil, with a special set of powers derived from two crystals and one ruby. They wore black robes and worshipped Naga — the Evil One, the Devil. This was the cult of Nagas, the anti-cult of Carum, and was led by . . .' There is nothing more — what happened to the rest?"

"It was destroyed in a fire, many years ago. In fact, the date it seems to go back to, is this one." She opened a third scroll and leafed through it. "Here, look."

His eyes went wide.

"What is it?"

"You see, Casiopiea, it's —" the pain grew worse, Darkmere's eyes began to glow . . . and then he smiled strangely.

"Casiopiea . . . it's nothing . . . only that you should go and find solace — peace — within your own mind."

"What? You're losing it again, aren't you. Well, I kept my bargain. Now you will keep yours. I'll see you soon with more information." She left him dumbfounded.

'You will never try and speak to her about me again. I will have her for my bride . . . wait and see,' said Etten, laughing in Darkmere's head. Darkmere stood and took it, gritting his teeth until the laughter stopped.

You will never win, he replied, picking up the scrolls and taking them to his bed to read again.

Chapter 29

An old woman strolled down Guam's main street, bent over and clutching her cane.

"Excuse me," she said to Yasmin.

"Will you help me to the Crystalbird Inn? I would be so grateful."

"Certainly."

"Thank you," said the old woman, and the two set off, chatting as they walked.

'Yes! Darkmere, you are losing your sanity, just as I predicted. Soon you won't even remember your name.'

'Leave me be.'

'You're so, so weak — haven't broken your word to anyone today and haven't killed anyone . . . right?'

'By Etten's Skull! Leave me be.'

'Oh, I like that.' the voice chuckled. "Tell me how much you hate me," Etten said aloud, pacing around the bedroom.

"Listen — if I could get my hands on you — I would kill you without a second thought."

"Wouldn't it be easier to join forces . . . then you wouldn't have to do all that research?"

"No. Leave me be, before —" Darkmere stopped himself.

"Before what? What can you do to me?" Etten mocked.

Darkmere stared into Etten's eyes and began to concentrate.

"What do you think that will —"

Darkmere smiled deviously as the breath was taken out of Etten for a brief moment.

Taken aback, Etten began to tighten his grip on Darkmere. "You — a mere mortal — cannot do this to me, a God. I am disgusted by you — and I will not tolerate such obvious insubordination!"

A rumble ran the length of the ground underneath Darkmere, forcing him to fall to his knees. Through it all, he grinned.

"Etten, no matter what happens, you have already failed!"

At that Etten clenched his hand around Darkmere's neck and began to squeeze — yet nothing happened. Darkmere remained focused on Etten's eyes, not budging, not dying. Etten backed off, dumbfounded.

"I guess a little more power is in store, Etten?"

"Yes . . . and now you will pay for your insolence," said Etten, not understanding what had just happened. A mortal could never be stronger than the will of a GOD! Enraged at Darkmere he cast a spell that gave him the ability to change form. He changed into Alcamere, Darkmere's deceased father.

Smiling, he approached what had previously been Darkmere the man — now turned by Etten's power into Darkmere the little boy. With a whip he began to beat the child relentlessly, until he lay bleeding on the floor. Etten resumed his own shape while Darkmere lay twisted on the floor.   Etten laughed and laughed and laughed — yet something still disturbed him — something was wrong here. He took his leave.

The old woman stopped to turn to Yasmin.

"My dear, take this from me, for your kindness."   She gave her a bag.   As Yasmin took it, the woman waved her hands over Yasmin's head and smiled.

"Yasmin?" the old woman began, sweetly.

"Yes?"

The old woman's smile broadened.   "I think we have to talk about your husband and that Abeline."

"What do you mean?" Yasmin asked, trying not to show her growing alarm.

"Do you trust me?" asked the old woman.

"Yes, I do," Yasmin said without hesitation.

"Then just listen . . ."   The old woman began to talk about Gowen's adulterous ways, and about how appealing Darkmere was.

When she left, Yasmin was fuming — and in a hurry to find Darkmere.

Chapter 30

Gowen, a little bored, set his sights on Darkmere's house. Casiopiea did the same.

Yasmin rushed up to Darkmere's house and knocked impatiently: there was no answer. She pushed open the door and looked around. She began looking in each room. She finally headed for the bedroom.

"Darkmere? Oh, Darkmere . . ." Yasmin called out, softly pushing open the door. "I hope I'm not disturbing you." She heard no reply. "I guess I'm not disturbing anyone." She entered.

Scanning the room for anything of interest. Her eyes settled on . . . something. She walked slowly up to a heap, which looked like it might be a person, and horrified, knelt down.

"Darkmere?" she said, allowing herself gradually to look directly at the beaten face that had looked so magnificently beautiful before . . . and now was torn apart.

She tried to right his position, to see if he was still alive, but to no avail. She began to pray, desperately.

Yasmin, in the process of healing Darkmere, noticed his clothes had been shredded — by what? — and that he had huge welts everywhere. How could she do this without help? She renewed her concentration. "Give me what I need to heal this man," said Yasmin aloud, continuing to pray to her deity.

At that moment Casiopiea turned the corner into the narrow street that led to the house.

Yasmin placed her hands on Darkmere and waited. Suddenly, she felt a rush of power and smiled in gratitude. A burst of light, emanating from her hands, flooded the whole room and surrounded him — she saw his bruises disappear. She looked at the resting form of Darkmere and was amazed once again at her healing powers.

She sighed with the realization her deity had helped her heal Darkmere, knelt and hugged him.

At that very moment, Gowen opened the door to Darkmere's house, ready to confront his brother. He saw that the door to the bedroom was ajar. He took a fresh deep breath and opened the door.

"Yasmin? What are you <u>doing</u>?" Gowen stood frozen, his mouth agape, staring at the sight of Yasmin hugging Darkmere, who was dressed in nothing but his black underwear.

Yasmin jumped at the look of utter amazement on Gowen's face, betrayal and rage. Gowen turned around to see Casiopiea standing behind him . . . the same look on her face.

"I — I can explain," stammered Yasmin.

"I don't want to hear it, Yasmin," said Gowen, turning to Darkmere. "I want to talk to you!" Gowen screamed, shaking. Darkmere turned to Yasmin. "Thank you."

"You're welcome. Gowen, can I please have a word with you?"

"No.　Leave me be.　You disgust me!" Gowen, stormed out of the house, loosening his sword from his side and unsheathing it.

Casiopiea's nostrils flared.　"I can't believe you!　I don't want to see your face near mine again!　You unfaithful bastard!"　She marched out.

Darkmere stood up and looked at Yasmin.

"Let me get dressed, and then we will straighten this out."

"Are you sure you can stand?"

"Yes.　Wait for me outside."

Yasmin found Casiopiea and Gowen outside.　Feeling paralyzed with apprehension, she waited for Darkmere.

"Don't leave!　I will show him who should betray whom!" Gowen proclaimed.

"You will?" inquired Casiopiea.

"Yes, I surely will," said Gowen.

Chapter 31

When Darkmere emerged Yasmin was standing still as a statue, eyes glued to Casiopiea and Gowen.

"Yasmin, we will straighten the whole thing out," he said, startling her.

'Darkmere,' Casiopiea said in his head.

'Yes,' he returned.

'Show Gowen who is really boss,' said Casiopiea. As she spoke, he saw images of the old woman talking to Yasmin, and then the old woman changing back into Casiopiea, and he understood what had transpired.

'Casiopiea, you are a piece of work.'

'I will take that as a compliment, Darkmere.'

"Yasmin, come on," said Darkmere aloud, trying to calm her down while Gowen stood with his chest heaving, like a horse after a full run.

"Are you too much of a coward to fight me?" said Gowen, pointing his sword at Darkmere.

Darkmere immediately unsheathed his sword and the fight ensued — steel against steel, brother against brother, with Darkmere parrying almost every blow Gowen wielded, and Casiopiea and Yasmin watching like hawks.

When Gowen finally tired, Darkmere parried one of his blows, knocked him to the ground, and placed the tip of his sword to Gowen's chest.

"Why don't you just kill me and take my wife from me?" cried Gowen, forcing Casiopiea to muster all her strength to keep from laughing.

"Now listen to me, all of you. Yasmin just saved my life. That's all. Understood, Gowen? Casiopiea?"

"But why were you hugging him, Yasmin?" Casiopiea asked.

"He helped me get a message across to my deity — and I was hugging him for it," said Yasmin.

"But what happened, Darkmere?" asked Casiopiea. Darkmere removed the sword point at Gowen's chest and held a hand out to help him up. Gowen refused to take it . . . and Darkmere glared at him.

"While you were gone," he said to her, "I had an episode that almost ended my life."

"Yes. He had all these welts, wounds, and deep scratches . . . that would have killed anyone else. His clothes were restricting — so I took them off and healed him," said Yasmin.

"You took off his <u>clothes</u>?" spat Casiopiea.

"Just let's forget this whole thing. Go home, Gowen and Yasmin," said Darkmere.

Gowen took Yasmin's hand and left.

"So. Darkmere — did I do a satisfactory job?"

"Well, that all depends. If you go any further . . . and I go along, you will be with Gowen and I will be with Yasmin. And that doesn't bother you?"

"No, not if we can change them to wicked — and if you give me your word that I will be your only true love and that we will always be together."

"Yes, Casiopiea — I give you my word."

Casiopiea smiled. "Well, the old woman will be making very frequent visits now . . . and soon, very soon, Gowen and Yasmin will not be together. Are you all right?"

"Yes, I am . . . now. You and I have to stage a fight, so that when Gowen and Yasmin are no longer together you can comfort Gowen, while I comfort Yasmin."

"How repulsive a thought."

"Do you really want to go through with this?" Darkmere asked, knowing the only reason he was going along with this was to help himself.

"Yes. I'm sure you'll love caressing Yasmin's ugly body, instead of my lovely one."

"Come here, my piece of work. . ."

Casiopiea followed Darkmere into the bedroom, while Etten watched, angrier than ever.

Gowen barely knew what to say. "I'm sorry, Yasmin. I really thought . . ."

"What . . . that he and I? What a joke, Gowen Aries. I love you . . . and do you love me?"

"Yes. I will . . . always," said Gowen, hugging her, as doubt and distrust began to grow in the Aries household.

A small crystal dragon watched from above . . .

Chapter 32

'Darkmere, why are you doing what you're doing? You're becoming petty.'

'Leave me be, Etten . . . for once.'

'I will never leave you be.'

The next day was the day they had set to leave. It's about time, Darkmere thought to himself, knowing that his sanity was slipping away . . . quickly.

"Darkmere, I'll meet you at the funeral . . . I'll see if I can find anything more for you."

"Thank you," said Darkmere, getting out of bed and stretching as the sun was rising in the sky.

"Good morning, Gowen . . . do you want breakfast?"

"If you make it — no," said Gowen, smiling.

"No, I meant to go to Big Bill's. I forgot to go and tell Minker, Copin, and Abeline we're leaving today. I also was wondering if Thaddius came back — but knowing him, he probably didn't and won't."

"I'd like to see him again. He was a rather good fellow. Why do you feel he won't be back?"

"Because that is the way he has always been, unreliable." Yasmin yawned.

"Yasmin, I would be happy to go — with my wife — to breakfast."

"Then get up, sleepyhead," Yasmin said, grinning.

The two got dressed and headed to Bill's, where they found Copin, Minker, Abeline and about a dozen others, stretched out on the tables. What a night it had been at Bill's!

Gowen and Yasmin were amazed at the number of people lying around.

"What's going on?" asked Gowen, loudly enough to cause everyone in Bill's to sit bolt upright.

"Shush, Gowen — everyone here has a hangover," whispered Bill.

"What happened here?" asked Yasmin.

"Oh, our local benefactor — Sally Dragonas — made a hefty contribution, and we all celebrated last night. You should have been here."

"Sounds like a good time," said Gowen.

"Well, if you want to call last night a good time, I will give you permission. Just today is rough. I have to get everyone up and at 'em before the breakfast rush . . . can you help?"

"Sure!" exclaimed Yasmin, her voice loud enough to draw a few more glares from the people nearest them.

"I'll help too," said Gowen.

The three of them began escorting people to rooms, and helped to clean the place up, too . . . until they came to Minker, Copin, and Abeline.

"He started it, didn't he?" said Gowen.

"How'd you guess?"

"Instinct," smiled Gowen. He bent down to Minker and screamed, "<u>Wake up</u>!" causing Minker to jump higher than a bullfrog in summer. Copin and Abeline were affected as well.

"What'd ya do that fer?" mumbled Minker, all the while holding his head.

"Well, first I thought the great Minker never got hangovers . . . second, we are leaving on a mission today, and third wake up!" Big Bill just laughed, slapping his hand on his knee.

"What's going on?" whined Copin.

"Well, Copin, it's time for you to get serious and stop drinking so much . . . it's bad for you," said Gowen seriously.

"Yes, dad," said Copin, looking up and grimacing. Abeline also looked up, half-smiling.

"Good morning, honey," said Abeline to Gowen, causing Yasmin to lose her smile.

"Good morning, Abeline."

"Oh - good morning, Yasmin and Bill - nice day out for a day of sleeping."

"No - we are leaving today - with or without you. Darkmere needs our help," said Yasmin, glaring at Abeline.

"O.K. . . . I'm going," said Abeline, getting up. "Where can I meet you?"

"Meet us at Darkmere's at noon. First - we have to go to a funeral - and then we'll meet you."

"Who died?" asked Big Bill.

"My mother," said Gowen.

"What happened? She was so nice," said Abeline, her voice filled with sympathy and concern.

"I found her dead in her house, she had been sleeping. She died peacefully, at least," said Gowen, trying not to bring her too close to mind.

"When's the funeral?" Abeline asked.

"In about an hour, at the cemetery."

"Who are you burying her next to — your father, or Darkmere's?"

"I don't know," said Gowen solemnly.

"Well . . . I'm going," said Abeline.

"So am I," added Minker.

"I will, too," said Copin.

"And I will close the bar and come, too," said Bill a little glassy-eyed. "She was a nice lady . . . I'll miss her."

Meanwhile Casiopiea went to the old librarian. He had found nothing else but a description of each of Darkmere's relatives. She took that and thanked him.

Then she went to the priest of the Dark One. No one answered the door. How odd, she thought, pushing it open.

She looked in each small room . . . including the one where Darkmere had been strapped to the stone slab after his mother's death. This funeral will be amusing, she thought. I love the effect of magic, how —

"How we put Darkmere's mother back together — a nice <u>illusion</u> — so Gowen found her in a whole piece and it will be easy for her to be buried today," said the gravelly voice from just behind her.

Casiopiea turned to face him. "Why weren't you here when I came?"

"I had other things to attend to."

"More important than I?"

"Yes, there are other things a trifle more important than you."

"I wanted to know if you can find any information on —"

"Darkmere?" the man said, raising one eyebrow.

"Yes — how did you know?"

"He's written on your face."

"Oh, really?"

"Yes."

"Well, do you have any?"

"No, no more than you've found."

"But I'm sure you could find it for me."

"That all depends, Casiopiea."

"On what?"

The priest of the Dark One took a step closer and touched her face. "On how well you perform for me," he said, grabbing her robe and ripping it off her.

Casiopiea retreated, trying to maintain her dignity.

"If you think I would do this for you, you must be joking."

The priest's eyes burned with hatred. "Not only am I not joking, but I will force myself upon you if you do not cooperate."

"I will not take this any longer! When do I get my reward for making Darkmere kill those people, and for killing Thaddius for you?"

"In time . . . in time, Casiopiea my love!"

"What in time!' I demand satisfaction <u>now</u>!"

"I <u>will</u> satisfy you, now!"

A chase followed around the small house, strewing and knocking things about to the ground. Casiopiea, seeing an opening, ran for the door.   As she reached for the doorknob, the priest of the Dark One slammed his hand against the door, a moment before she could get to it.

Smiling, he said, "So, Casiopiea — I've got you cornered . . ."

chapter 33

As the funeral approached, Casiopiea was nowhere to be found.

Darkmere searched his thoughts for her but found nothing.

"Something's wrong," he said aloud.

Meanwhile, the priest of the Dark One smiled: "Casiopiea, I have been waiting for this moment since I first saw you. Make it easy on yourself . . . and come to me." The priest held out a hand.

"Never. And I want my payments! I have done what He asked of me — and I have received nothing."

"You still have not proven yourself. Go the easy way. Prove yourself with me, and you will get your rewards. Do the ultimate. Betray Darkmere, and all power will be yours."

"Is that it? Dark one — show yourself!" yelled Casiopiea.

An image appeared before Casiopiea. It was an image of Etten: the Dark One.

"Yes, Casiopiea."

"Do I get my rewards?"

"You worship me and I will reward you, when you have proven yourself."

"What is that?"

"Well . . . for what you have done, and to keep you going, here is your first reward: monetary wealth," said the Dark One, placing a box before her.

"How about magic?" Casiopiea insisted.

"In time, in time."

"In _time_! I risked everything for you, three times over, and now I am corrupting Gowen. What else do I have to do? You disgust me!" said Casiopiea, looking into the god's eyes . . . and seeing them waver.

"I will never betray Darkmere!" Laughing at him, she added, "You are impotent!"

"I have had enough of your talk! You betray a God! You will pay!" screamed the Dark One. "I will show Darkmere. _You_ will betray him — _and_ you will perish!" With that, the Dark One disappeared.

"I no longer believe in him," said Casiopiea, grabbing her holy symbol and ripping it from her neck. The priest screamed, then took hold of her, ripping her clothes off and throwing her to the ground.

"You will satisfy me," said the priest, straddling her.

'Darkmere, Darkmere, help me,' said Casiopiea in his head.

The signal came through. Darkmere left his home, bounding towards Casiopiea, bursting in on the priest.

He hauled the priest off her; then a fight began.

While he pummeled the priest, Darkmere roared, "You do not fool me! Etten!" Darkmere shook the priest . . . until he changed into the Dark One.

Casiopiea, stunned, looked at Darkmere. Immense power emanated from this mortal who held the Dark One, a god, in his grasp.

Then the tide turned, and the fight between mortals and Gods ended.

The Dark One, Etten, was now gone, leaving Darkmere on the floor, clawing for life.

Casiopiea ran to him.

"Get me out of this house!" Darkmere rasped. She helped him to his feet, and then outside.

Darkmere took his cloak off and gave it to Casiopiea.

"You saved my life, Darkmere, thank you."

"Let's get to the funeral, and then let's get out of here. A God is now angered, and there's no telling what will happen next."

"Who is Etten?"

"You will find out soon. I can't say any more."

Casiopiea now saw Darkmere in a new light. She resolved to have him for her own, to be controlled by her alone.

The funeral ceremony began; Big Bill, Minker, Copin, Gowen, Abeline, and Yasmin all sat in mourning.

"Where are Darkmere and Casiopiea?" asked Yasmin.

"Who cares?" said Gowen, coldly.

Yasmin recited the ceremonial script. Just as the last section of scripture was read, Darkmere and Casiopiea arrived.

"Thanks for arriving on time," said Gowen sarcastically.

"Darkmere just saved my life, Gowen. Consider that," said Casiopiea.

"Look — all of you — we are in grave danger. After this ceremony, we have to leave — at once."

Darkmere looked at his mother's body and then away . . . nauseated.

Darkmere said, "We have a mission, and we do not need <u>anyone's</u> sarcastic remarks. Are you coming, Gowen, or are you staying?"

Gowen swallowed hard. "I'm coming."

"Good. Yasmin . . . continue."

The funeral began again, and as Yasmin presided, Darkmere looked at Big Bill . . .

'Forget all you have just heard,' said Darkmere, looking into Bill's eyes, and then looking away.

Checking Bill's mind, Darkmere was amazed. Bill did not remember a thing that had just been said! Darkmere knew what this meant, that his power was growing. He smiled inside as the funeral service ended. His mother was buried and gone.

"Now get your gear . . . and meet at my house as the sun falls over this gravesite."

"You have an exciting life. You know, I envy you," said Bill to Gowen.

"Sure, but you did this once, too: adventures, swords." said Gowen.

"And sometimes I miss it."

"Well, I'll bring back some stories — and I'm sure Minker will bring back some new concoction for you two to work on."

"I'm sure. And come back in one piece!" said Bill, as the two embraced.

Chapter 34

They met at Darkmere's . . . to find that he had begun babbling uncontrollably.

"What are we going to do with him?" asked Gowen.

"We have to take him along. He saved my life, and he's saved all of us — we have to save his . . ." said Casiopiea.

"Then let's move fast," said Abeline, as they mounted their horses and rode. Gowen held Darkmere on his horse, trailing Darkmere's horse behind.

Casiopiea took a map that Darkmere had been reading and steered them on their way to the Cult of Carum.

They rode hard, with little or no rest. Darkmere lapsed in and out of sanity. When sane, he gave instructions, shortening their journey.

Three days later they arrived at their destination: a small village.

"The Village of <u>Darkmere</u>?" Minker exclaimed.

"What an odd thing," whined Copin.

Nobody seemed to be around — and Darkmere now had a fever to go along with his precarious mental state.

"Where is everyone?" asked Abeline.

"Don't look at me," said Minker.

They traversed the small place, listening to their own echoes. No one else was around . . . nothing.

They entered homes and businesses — not a soul to be found.

They wondered where the temple lay.

"What are we going to do now? Darkmere can't travel much longer, and we can't even find the temple," said Yasmin, applying a rag to Darkmere's forehead, mopping off the sweat.

"We must rest here . . . and then start searching for somebody who can help," said Casiopiea.

They settled down. Gowen and Abeline gently lay Darkmere on the ground.

"Casiopiea, you might want to do this. We need to remove his shirt. It's soaked through," said Abeline. Casiopiea removed Darkmere's shirt, with Gowen's help.

"How long do you think he will last? I can't cure him — I've tried," said Yasmin to Copin.

"I don't know. I really don't," Copin responded, looking down.

Chapter 35

'You are failing, Darkmere — soon, soon you will bend and be mine!' Etten laughed. 'Then . . . Casiopica's next.'

'Never . . . never,' said Darkmere, lapsing into unconsciousness again.

'Abeline.'

'Yes, Etten.'

'Go with my original plan — kill him when you know it's right.'

'Very well, my Etten.'

'Very good, my disciple.'

"I feel it's time to find someone to help us," said Casiopiea. She felt the strain of Darkmere's ordeal. He hadn't come out of the desperate state he'd entered for over two hours.

"Then let's go," said Copin.

They secured Darkmere to a litter, which they rigged up to a horse.

They made their way further into the village, checking every house and dwelling as they went, until they heard a noise.

"It's coming from over there," said Casiopiea, pointing to the deserted bar a little way ahead.

"Let's go!" said Minker, slugging down some special brew.

They cautiously entered the bar, swords drawn and spells ready.

They heard a clink coming from behind the bar.

Gowen went first, Abeline behind him.

They saw a man sitting slumped on the floor with a bottle in his hand. Gowen stood up and motioned to the others.

"Who are you?" he asked.

The man got up, revealing his unusually tall stature.

"I own this here bar — and I'm not leaving, you hear?"

"We're not asking you to leave. Just talk to us . . . we won't harm you," said Gowen.

The barkeep teetered out from behind the bar and sat at a table in the middle of the room.

"What happened to him? It's not the plague, is it?" asked the barkeep when he saw Darkmere.

"No, no . . . don't worry, it's not the plague. What happened in this village?"

"A man in black robes came here and put a curse on the people — and those who didn't die, fled."

"How it is that you are still alive?" Casiopiea wanted to know.

"Well, you see, little lady, I guess I'm just lucky."

"What happened to the Temple of Carum?" asked Gowen.

"It vanished. After the man cast his spell — oh my!"

"What?"

The man knelt before Darkmere. "Oh my — Naga
— stay away. Stay away!"

"No, no, he is not Naga — he is Darkmere."

The man backed up. "Get out — <u>get out</u>!" he said,
running for shelter behind the bar, his eyes void.

"He's mad," said Casiopiea, looking at Gowen.

"No . . . we will stay. This man needs one of your
rooms so he can heal - and he is <u>not</u> Naga. Here," said
Abeline, opening her pouch and retrieving six gold pieces
which she held out before the man. The man grabbed the
gold and was instantly taken with her.

"I will do what you need and help him," he said.

Chapter 36

They moved Darkmere upstairs, to a room above the bar.

"Is this o.k.?" the barkeep asked, showing them a big double bed and a nice, open window.

"No . . . we need a room that is dark, so he can get some sleep," said Casiopiea, bringing up the rear.

He showed them one of the corner rooms, secluded and dark.

"Perfect," said Casiopiea. They gently laid Darkmere in the bed.

"He's going to need constant attention. What are we going to do?" asked Yasmin, having just entered the room, noticing the strain on Darkmere's face as he began tossing and turning in the bed.

"I will stay here while you find the temple," offered Abeline. Casiopiea eyed her suspiciously.

"Casiopiea, she's right," said Gowen. "We need everyone else, and we can't leave him with just the barkeep; he might need help."

"Casiopiea, listen to me," Abeline replied, "I will not be needed. You are a user of the arcane arts and so am I. I am also a healer of sorts." Abeline emptied her pouches of healing potions and salves. "I can help him that way. You cannot. I am also a fighter. So you see, if he needs help, I can help him."

Casiopiea realized what Abeline had said was true and consented, resigning herself to what lay ahead.

They left Darkmere and Abeline with the barkeep.

"Where was the temple?"

"There," said the barkeep, pointing to where the mountains lay.

"On top?" Gowen asked.

"No, at the foot of the mountains."

"This is getting annoying," Minker said to Copin, who nodded as they got underway to look for an invisible temple.

Casiopiea knew she had to succeed, regardless of what lay ahead.

As the party left, Abeline smiled, then headed upstairs to where Darkmere lay.

Casiopiea took the lead behind Gowen, checking for magic along the way. As they approached the mountain, she sensed strong magic in their path.

'Crystalmere.'

'Yes?.'

'Watch over Darkmere.'

'I fear for you and wish to stay with you, Master.'

'If Darkmere dies, it will be more reason for you to fear for our destruction. Go.'

"I can stay by his side. Go back downstairs until I call for you," said Abeline.

"I will come when you call," the barkeep replied.

When he was gone, she went into the storage room at the end of the hall, where she gathered together all the rope she could find.

Returning to the room, she waited for Darkmere to settle down.

"There, that way . . . is as much magic as a god himself would have," said Casiopiea, pointing to the foot of the mountain.

"The temple must still be there — but hidden by what?" said Gowen.

"Probably someone having a good time and not wanting to be disturbed," said Minker. "I think the bar is the place to be."

"Why, are you afraid?" Copin whined.

"No, are you? You one-eyed —"

"Stop, you two — stop it!" Yasmin warned.

"Wait," said Casiopiea.

"For what?" Minker wanted to know.

"Concentrate . . . and look upon what we all have not seen."

Each looked again, and saw a white marble temple dwarfing the small village below.

What a place — it's beautiful."

They approached the stairs, which ascended to the magnificent domed temple.

Gowen took the first step . . . and a voice boomed out, "You may not enter."

"Why?"

"We must speak first."

"Wait! I know the name — Gualum," said Casiopiea, stepping forward.

"Yes! Tell me. I've not heard my name in so long."

"How long?"

"Decades."

"You mean this village has been like this that long?" asked Gowen.

"Probably . . . I can't be sure."

"We wish to enter. Our friend is sick . . . will you let us in?" asked Casiopiea.

"I will show myself, and then you may explain your plight."

The enormous golden doors of the temple opened, and out came an old man in white robes trimmed with gold. He slowly descended the steps.

"We wish to help Darkmere — he is dying." Casiopiea explained. When she had, they turned to Gualum.

"No. I will not help you," Gualum replied.

Chapter 37

Darkmere had ceased moving and now lay comatose. Abeline began fastening his arms and legs to the bed posts, making sure he could not move. She wrapped rope around the middle of the bed and over his chest, to ensure there would be no chance of his breaking out, and tightened it making it difficult for him to breathe. She smiled . . . and caught sight of something out of the corner of her eye.

She went to the window. Her vision unimpeded, she saw him.

Scrambling at her approach, Crystalmere backed away.

"You think you will get away with this, you little worm?" said Abeline, casting a spell directly at Crystalmere. In an instant missiles of fire shot from her fingers straight through the glass, right at Crystalmere, and sent him reeling to the ground with a thud. He collapsed. . . Abeline returned to Darkmere and, running a cool hand down his chest, laughed aloud.

Casiopiea sighed.

"What are we going to do now?" said Yasmin.

"I don't know," said Casiopiea, as a sharp pain knifed through her.

'Crystalmere,' Casiopiea thought to her familiar. . .

'Oh god — that witch is disturbing my fun! Do something, Etten! Make sure she thinks Crystalmere is all right.'

'Crystalmere, what happened? I felt a sharp pain.'
'Sorry, I just hit the wall, I missed a turn. Sorry.'
'Be careful, Please!'
'Yes, Master.'
'Is there anything going on over there. How is Darkmere?'
'Abeline and the barkeep are talking, while watching Darkmere. He has not changed.'
'Keep me updated.'
'Yes. I will.' Etten cackled as Casiopiea focused her attention back to the temple.

They reached the double doors to the temple and looked at each other.
"I'll go open it," said Minker.
After a few moments, Minker turned and smiled.
"It's open. You ready?" They went in, one by one, knowing they were entering a holy place, while Yasmin prayed for their safety.
"I see you came anyway," said Gualum, entering from another room. "Come with me. You must all care deeply for your friend, and for that I admire you."
They followed, not knowing what lay ahead of them.

"Casiopiea, it's difficult for me to breathe."

"That's the idea," said Abeline, kissing him again. Then her facade slipped away and she cackled viciously.

Thoughts flooded Darkmere as he realized who was lying before him and what had happened.

"Abeline!"

"Yes, it's me, my darling."

"Why am I like this?"

"Because, my darling servant, I want you this way — helpless, bending to my will — based on the reality of me . . . not a fantasy. And don't worry . . . any crying out you do won't be heard."

Darkmere glared at her.

"See what I mean . . . now you will be mine once again. And nothing and no one will stop me — not even you," she said, trailing her hand down Darkmere's face.

"What are you going to do with me now?"

"You will see . . . you will see," said Abeline, revelling in the idea that Darkmere would be hers — all hers.

Chapter 38

The adventurers followed Gualum into a very large room. White windows opened up into it. A white sofa sat on one side, and on the far side of the room sat a big white desk.

"What a room!" said Minker, looking around in awe.

"Thank you, thank you, my friend," said Gualum, patting Minker on the head.

Gualum made his way around the white desk and sat himself down. "Who is leader here?" he asked.

"I am," answered Casiopiea.

"Very well, then." A door on the right side of the room opened. "Go and find what you're looking for."

"Thank you, Gualum," offered Gowen.

"You're welcome, young man — and good luck."

"Well, Darkmere, how does it feel to be completely confined and not able to do anything?"

"Splendid, just splendid," Darkmere lied.

"You will be my slave," added Abeline waving her hands; out of thin air, an iron collar and chain materialized.

Abeline approached Darkmere and, pulling his head forward, placed the collar around his neck. With another wave of her hands, the collar closed.

"Now, if you do anything I do not like, that collar will constrict. You are bound to me for life, Darkmere . . . and I have bought you. You are my slave forever!" She laughed loud and hard, as she began to think about her first task. Darkmere remained motionless, looking at Abeline, knowing this could not be his fate . . . hoping it would not.

"Abeline, tell me — what have you bought me with, your life?" Darkmere asked, seeing it irritated Abeline and knowing what he had said had hit its mark.

"You will not speak to me in such a way!" Abeline commanded and waved her hand, forcing the collar to constrict around Darkmere's neck. Sweating, he waited until Abeline felt it was time to release her hold.

The party left the white room and entered a stone hallway quite different from the stark white walls they had just left. Rounding the corner, they came to a doorway.

"There's no way else but in," Yasmin said. Casiopiea gritted her teeth at the sound of Yasmin's voice.

"That's right, Yasmin — so Minker, check the door for traps," said Casiopiea.

He did so.

"Anything?" asked Copin.

"No, and it's wide open."

"So open the door," ordered Casiopiea.

It revealed a small room with tattered draperies covering the far wall.

They filed in, puzzled. There was nothing else there.

"Well, open them, Casiopiea," Minker mocked.

She nodded to Gowen, and he pulled draperies apart to unveil a series of paintings.

One was of a man dressed in a black cloak, wearing a head piece of lightning bolts. He looked over a man who lay on his back.

On a painting to the right, a group of people garbed in black stood around a fire and looked up into the sky.

On the left was a painting of the night sky with a huge lightning bolt streaking across the canvas.

"What do you think it means?" asked Gowen.

Darkmere, Casiopiea thought, remembering the lightning bolt etched in his left shoulder. She said, "I'm not sure. Maybe if we move on, we could learn more."

"But we'll have to search for another door that leads out, since back there it's just the same hallway," Minker advised.

They began searching for a secret door.

Yasmin had luck with her.

"Here! Come look," she said, showing them a recess in the wall beside the painting of the man in the black cloak. Giving it a push, they found a second room.

The collar released. "Darkmere, your first and only task — for now — is to satisfy me. I wish you to —" Abeline paused to take a shiny dagger out from her hip pocket. Bending over Darkmere, she ran the tip of the dagger down his bare chest . . . and then she smiled — "I want to have your baby."

"Why?"

"I don't like being talked to that way!" she screamed, and the collar around his neck tightened again, this time to the point that he could hardly breathe . . . and then released.

"Don't ask such foolish questions. I want to have your baby, and you will make sure I do. I will rape you if I have to, and each time I do, I will scar you for life. Am I understood?"

"Yes," said Darkmere.

"Yes what?"

"Yes, mistress."

"Thank you." Abeline smiled.

The second room was filled with all kinds of musty debris. More tattered draperies lined the walls. In the middle of the room stood a dais, and upon it rested a long staff.

"Look," said Yasmin, pointing to the floor; a faint pattern of a lightning bolt ran the length of it.

"Leave the staff alone until I can determine whether or not it's magical," warned Casiopiea.

"I will open the drapes," said Minker.

"Darkmere!" Yasmin and Casiopiea exclaimed in unison. What Minker had revealed was another set of paintings. One was a portrait of Darkmere that seemed to stare right out at the party. His outstretched hand held a crystal in it, and in his left eye there was a red colored gem.

"What does this mean?" asked Yasmin.

"I don't really know," said Casiopiea. "Maybe the staff will tell us."

Casiopiea turned to the staff and cast a series of spells.

"Well?" Copin wanted to know.

"It's magical . . . and I don't know what it is."

"Should we touch it?"

"Yasmin, is it of an evil quality?" Casiopiea asked.

Yasmin looked intently at the staff. "No. We can take it with us."

Casiopiea picked up the staff.

Chapter 39

Hours had passed when Crystalmere, barely able to move, struggled to his feet hobbled off to find Casiopiea.

Abeline had set about torturing Darkmere, inflicting dagger wounds in his body, and summoning Etten forth.

When she left the room to talk with him, Darkmere, dangling between life and death, struggled to free himself from the ropes of his prison bed.

"So, Abeline, you want to know if you're pregnant yet?" Etten spoke.

"Yes."

"Not yet."

"I will <u>kill</u> him! She returned to the room to find Darkmere gone. She looked out the window and saw him climbing down to freedom . . . until the collar constricted around his neck. Fighting for air, he lost his grip and fell to the ground.

"Etten, revive him and let me bring him back — and this time give me iron cuffs so he can't get out."

He disappeared, but not before leaving Abeline with the ability to levitate Darkmere back to where she knew he belonged.

The party found still more paintings of someone they thought was Darkmere.

"Look at this statue."

"It's Darkmere. What's going on?" said Casiopiea.

"Beware of the Devil — Naga. That's what it says on the statue," said Gowen.

"That's Naga?" Casiopiea responded.

"I'm confused," said Minker.

"So am I," added Copin. "All I see is Darkmere . . . Naga?"

"Look!" cried Yasmin, as the room began to change. Suddenly, the room they had been standing in became a background to five more now appearing before them.

They heard a voice:

"Good luck — the secret lies before each of you. Go where you are drawn."

"You mean this is where we find out what's going on?" asked Minker. There was no answer.

"We must each make a choice," said Casiopiea, approaching her door and opening it.

Casiopiea entered a long hallway at the end of which she saw Darkmere. "Darkmere?" Casiopiea called. Then she saw a man quickly approach Darkmere from behind, grabbing him and putting a dagger to his throat.

Said the man, "Casiopiea, I can show you all the power in the world — come with me and forget Darkmere. What you see is a facade — see how scared and helpless he really is. Come with me." The man held out his hand to her, and her, feeling as though she were in a dream, made a fast choice. She walked towards the man . . . and . . .

Pain shot through Darkmere's body as he lay helpless before Abeline. His limbs were now shackled, leaving him completely unable to move.

"So, you feel it now! Casiopiea will betray you at the drop of a hat. So much for your love and caring — and now you will feel it as each of your "friends" betray you, leaving you with nothing, Darkmere! Nothing!" Abeline cackled as Darkmere felt Casiopiea's true betrayal.

"Abeline, I can understand what you're doing — but how did you and Etten . . .?"

"How did you know?"

"I figured it out — I'm intelligent, remember."

"Etten has given me everything. And now I've had enough of your talk — be quiet and wait for your destruction."

"Thank you."

"Who?"

"Mistress."

Abeline smiled, secure in the knowledge she now controlled Darkmere . . .

Chapter 40

One by one, each member of the party betrayed Darkmere, sending him reeling with pain. And then it was Gowen's turn.

Gowen walked through his door and peered down a long hallway.

I will be strong, he thought, walking cautiously down the corridor.

"Gowen," a voice boomed out.

"Yes," responded Gowen.

"Come, follow my voice."

Gowen proceeded further down the hallway, until it suddenly opened up into a wondrous green field.

At once Gowen felt completely happy, seeing the trees surrounding the field, feeling the sun beating down on his shoulders.

"This feels so good! I wish —"

"You wish what?"

The feeling was broken as a dark cloud formed above him, shrouded in the shape of a black cloak.

"Darkmere, why do you not leave me be — I could have a happy life, but you keep on nagging at me!" Realizing Gowen had now shown his true feelings, Darkmere stepped back.

"So that's what you feel for me — annoyance, nothing, disgust," Darkmere approached Gowen, the anger now rising in his eyes. He unsheathed his sword, circling Gowen, and began taunting him.

"Come on, deformed half-elf — you took everything from me. I was given nothing, while you were given everything. I will take what is yours, and you will never again have what you want: happiness!"

It seemed to Gowen that what Darkmere said had truth in it. He looked up at Darkmere and saw the pain in his eyes. Darkmere swiftly brought the sword over Gowen, wounding his arm. "Come on. Are you that weak that you're unable to fight for yourself?"

"No!" shouted Gowen and began to parry Darkmere's blows.

Back and forth the fight continued, and with each exchange of blows Darkmere bested Gowen. Another blow caught Gowen off balance, knocking him to the ground.

"I will destroy you and all that is good, just because you live, you."

"Darkmere, I love you," said Gowen, moving away from his brother as he saw his rage grow.

"You don't love me! You did everything to destroy me! And now I will destroy you!" Darkmere loomed over him, blocking out the sun, his black cloak flowing in the wind.

"Die!"

"No!" cried Gowen, and he stood up and looked into Darkmere's eyes . . . and then he knew . . .

Gowen and Darkmere became young boys. Anger still permeated Darkmere as he watched Gowen standing next to his own father, an elf.

"Kill him, Gowen."

"Yes, I will, father," Gowen felt himself say.

Gowen saw himself approach a now-sleeping Darkmere with a dagger in his hand. Breathing heavily, he came closer, until he stood right over Darkmere. He lifted the dagger and plunged it down . . .

Breathing very heavily now, in slow motion, Gowen returned to the present.

"No! Not again — I will not betray you, Darkmere. No!"

He collapsed to the floor, the field he'd been in now gone. Awakening, he found himself still breathing heavily, and sweating. He looked up from the floor . . . into Casiopiea's face.

Darkmere was sweating profusely feeling Gowen had not betrayed him — hoping he would have — but clear that he did not. He felt something inside him disappear, and felt that Gowen had found out something he did not want anyone to know. Abeline laughed at his realization. "You weak, pathetic fool!"

Chapter 41

"Gowen?" Yasmin asked.

He slowly rose and looked around, knowing, knowing, yet not wanting to know.

"Yes. I just met Darkmere."

"So did we."

"Tell us about what happened to you. You are the only one who came out the way you did," said Casiopiea.

"I was asked to betray him."

"And did you?" asked Copin.

"No," said Gowen simply.

The others all looked at each other. Gowen suddenly understood.

"I guess I was the only one who stuck by our real leader, right?" he fumed.

"How were we to know?" Yasmin told him. "The situations we were given were probably different from yours, since you are his brother and all."

"Yasmin, how could you?" he exclaimed. "Do you know what everyone else went through?"

"No. I —" Yasmin looked down.

"We have to get out of here now!" said Gowen. "I fear for Darkmere's life."

"What do you mean? You fear for <u>your own</u> life! I am leader here, and we do what <u>I</u> say. We go <u>on</u>, and find the answer to —"

All at once, the doors and walls around them began closing in on them. Water poured in through the walls, quickly covering the floor. The only one who did not get wet was Gowen. . . .

The voice of Gualum boomed out: "You have all failed! Except for Gowen, you do not care for your friend. You have all lied to me and you will pay!"

Casiopiea, scrambling for higher ground, turned to Gowen. "If you really care you will help us out of this, Gowen. If you don't — you will betray us."

"So, Darkmere, do you wish to be helped, and live with me?" Abeline asked.

"I've had enough of this!" said Darkmere, the anger rising in him, the green glow emerging and encircling him. Abeline's eyes went wide, as she watched the iron cuffs begin to expand.

"Etten — now! Help!" Abeline screamed.

Darkmere left the bed and lunged at her. "I've had enough of you and your trying to control me, you witch!" He put his hands around Abeline's neck. "You are scared of me . . . a weakness in you, disciple of the Dark One! This is for Etten's skull!" Darkmere cried as he began squeezing the life out of her.

Gowen pulled Casiopiea from the rising water, slipped, and fell into it . . .

"I'll help you," said Casiopiea, knowing she still needed them to get out of this. But the solid ground she was standing on suddenly collapsed, and she was again plunged right into the water, struggling for her life.

They were all beginning to drown.

"No!" yelled Gowen, and he dove under to find a way of plugging up the water . . . nothing.

Diving again and again, he still found nothing that could stop the flood.

"Gowen, I don't think I can stay much longer!" Yasmin gulped.

"Hold on!" he called out, before going under once again. They waited anxiously for Gowen to surface, but he had disappeared . . .

"No! I will not allow you to destroy my life!" Darkmere shouted.

"I, I — listen!" Abeline gasped.

"To what?"

"I am with your child, Darkmere!"

Startled, Darkmere released her, knowing she spoke the truth.

"Now, Etten!" she screamed, and Etten appeared, larger than life, grabbing Darkmere and picking him up off the floor. Still, the collar did not constrict, and the green glow continued to emanate from Darkmere.

Etten began grinding his teeth, looking at Darkmere and smiling. Through sheer will, he made the glow around Darkmere disappear and the collar begin to shrink around Darkmere's throat. Etten left him a crumpled wreck, motionless on the ground.

"This time no more," Etten told her. "He will awaken as he was — crazy, losing his mind. We can't risk him getting any stronger. And you are carrying his baby, congratulations.

The water was just above their necks, and they were barely able to breathe. Their doom was nearly upon them, when Gowen resurfaced, just inches from the ceiling. In an instant, they were transported, still drenched, coughing and gasping for air.

They found themselves in a room: different, again, from any other they had seen or been in before. The ceiling peaked at a point just above a pyramid of eight-foot swords, in the middle of which a golden scroll rested on a pedestal.

"Do we go now or later?" whined Copin, dripping on the floor.

"We have to go on," Gowen said.

Chapter 42

Darkmere, again in a crazed state, looked wildly into Abeline's eyes.

Abeline smirked, "Too bad you won't be here for the birth of your first son, Darkmere. I think I'll name him Ettenger . . . of course, Etten, for short." She began pacing back and forth in front of Darkmere. "Of course he will be honored in knowing he worships Etten and does his bidding. He will feel fulfilled in his duty — don't you think?" Abeline smiled, stroking his face and kissing it once more.

"I have to go leave — but I'll be back soon. It's marvelous not having to worry about you," she said, strolling off, leaving Darkmere suspended in mid-air, bound head to foot.

Crystalmere crept up the steps of the temple, hoping he could make it to Casiopiea in time.

They approached the space where the scroll lay.

"Do not enter — the curse of the devil Naga will be upon you."

"Who is the devil Naga?" asked Copin.

"You know. You all know."

Casiopiea brought out the staff and searched for an inscription.

"Beware the word of Etten," she read aloud.

Suddenly, the walls began to shake and the swords to glow, and the party beheld a wondrous sight.

A man made entirely out of gold stood before them. "Beware Etten — beware the Dark One!" he spoke.

"<u>What</u>!" Casiopiea screamed, realizing she had been betrayed by her own deity . . . realizing Darkmere was now in danger, yet not knowing how or why.

The gold man held out his hand with the scroll in it.

"Hand him the staff, Casiopiea, now — before it's too late!" yelled Gowen. Casiopiea quickly did so.

The man vanished . . . and the temple began to crumble.

At that moment, Crystalmere pushed himself into the white room of the temple.

'Casiopiea, come quickly! Darkmere will be killed!' he cried, and collapsed.

Casiopiea's anger rose, and she began to run. Gowen ran next to her, somehow knowing they were all in grave danger.

Upon reaching the white room, Casiopiea found Crystalmere. Stopping to pick him up, they all continued towards the village. Meanwhile, Abeline, having killed the barkeep, also moved with a purpose.

The golden staff materialized in front of Abeline. She picked it and returned to where Darkmere lay.

"Thank you Gualum, you were so stupid and now you're gone, swallowed up by your own goodness, giving up your life too easily, as will Darkmere."

"I knew it — Abeline!" Casiopiea screamed, seeing her with the staff she had held in her hand moments before.

"You witch!" screamed Yasmin.

Casiopiea put Crystalmere down. As Abeline caught sight of her, hatred poured from Abeline's eyes. She hastily turned on her, not realizing that Casiopiea was opening the scroll she had found in the temple.

Abeline laughed. "You are all helpless, you fools!"

She threw the staff in the air. As Casiopiea began reading the scroll aloud, the street to the temple began to collapse.

"The staff is headed straight for Darkmere!" screamed Yasmin.

"Grasp this, Abeline!" said Casiopiea: "You of Etten will become the object of his mockery, and he will betray — end this life of yours!" Abeline's eyes went wide. Falling to the ground, she began writhing, gasping for breath. The party ran to her and held her down, while Casiopiea plunged a dagger into Abeline, killing her. The temple crumbled to dust. Abeline's body suddenly ignited and burned before their eyes. Suddenly a man's scream came shattering from above, causing them all to run, except for Casiopiea, who collapsed to the ground.

Chapter 43

As they scrambled up the stairs to where Darkmere lay, passing the mangled body of the barkeep . . . Gowen stopped them.

"Wait! Where's Casiopiea?"

"Who cares, Gowen? Let's go help Darkmere," said Yasmin, taking Gowen by surprise once again.

"Look, he might be dead already," said Minker. "Copin and I will go find Casiopiea."

They mounted the stairs two at a time and came to the door where they expected to find Darkmere.

"Open it," said Yasmin, breathing heavily, hoping only that Darkmere was not dead. The door creaked open. He swallowed, fearful of what they might find inside.

What they saw amazed them. Yasmin stepped up, wide-eyed, beside Gowen.

Lying on the bed, bound head to foot, was Darkmere, glowing green, while a beautiful jeweled dagger was suspended in mid-air just inches from his heart.

'Wait,' said Darkmere in their heads, as they noticed that, in the wall directly adjacent to him, there now was a hole the diameter of the staff that Abeline had thrown.

Meanwhile, downstairs, Copin and Minker had managed to pick up Casiopiea and bring her into the bar.

Then they went back to pick up Crystalmere, placing the familiar next to Casiopiea.

"What do we do now?" whined Copin.

"Go get Yasmin — look!" said Minker, taking a second glance at Crystalmere, noticing black char marks along the crystal dragon's side.

"He's dying fast . . . go get Yasmin," said Minker, trying to keep the familiar warm.

Copin ran up the stairs as fast as he could.

"Yasmin! We need —" Copin stopped in his tracks at the sight of the dagger in mid-air over Darkmere's chest.

'Tell Yasmin quickly and take her out of here,' Darkmere relayed to Copin.

'Yasmin, come with me,' Copin said, taking Yasmin's hand, leading her out of the room and down the stairs to where Crystalmere lay.

Yasmin asked Minker to move away, she placed her hands on the familiar, and began the task of healing him . . . hoping he wasn't too far gone. She waited and prayed.

In the meantime, Darkmere spoke to Gowen.

'Come slowly, very slowly,' Darkmere said in his head. Gowen took each step as though in the balance hung the difference between life and death. When he reached Darkmere's side he stopped.

'When you remove this dagger, you are to give it to Casiopiea. I will probably give out from the amount of effort this takes — don't worry about it. Let me rest for as long as I need to. Tell Casiopiea not to leave the dagger unattended — and never to leave it near me — is this understood?'

Gowen nodded, as Darkmere looked into his eyes.

'Now place your hands on the dagger and pull with all strength.'

Gowen followed Darkmere's instructions. The force he was pulling against was so powerful that he was barely able to move the dagger.

'Pull as hard as you can, and when you have it, run out of this room — understood?'

Sweating from exertion, Gowen nodded and began wrenching the dagger very slowly away from Darkmere's heart.

Yasmin pulled away as her healing proficiency once again saved another's life.

"Is he -?" Minker asked.

"He's fine, and so will she be, when she wakes up."

Darkmere spoke in Yasmin's head, 'Don't come — stay where you are, and make sure that everyone else does, too!'

Gowen had managed to wrench the dagger loose and tow it across the room. Feeling it pull back towards Darkmere, he got out as quickly as he could.

Making his way downstairs, Gowen saw Casiopiea rubbing her eyes and getting up. He grabbed her.

"Casiopiea! I need you to take this dagger and keep it with you in a safe place."

"How can I keep it, if you can barely hold it?"

'Because you're a magic user,' said Darkmere in her head . . . before drifting out of touch.

Casiopiea nodded, and Gowen placed the dagger in her hands.

Casiopiea took it, gingerly slipping it beneath her robes.

"What happened?"

"It was suspended over Darkmere's heart — it was the staff," said Yasmin, glaring at Casiopiea.

"I'll go see if he's recovering," said Casiopiea, leaving the rest of them standing in her wake.

She entered the room. "Darkmere. I like you like this, Darkmere."

"Casiopiea, he's sleeping. He said to let him sleep as long as it takes," said Gowen.

"Then we'll leave him alone."

"I think we should untie him first," added Yasmin, standing in the doorway.

Casiopiea nodded. As she set about unbinding Darkmere, she noticed the wounds across his chest, and the thick indentations about his body where the rope had been.

"Yasmin, heal him."

Afterward, They went downstairs and saw Crystalmere waking.

'I missed you,' said Casiopiea.

'I'm glad I'm back,' Crystalmere answered in Casiopiea's head, sighing as he snuggled next to her.

"How disgusting," said Yasmin, her hatred of Casiopiea festering.

"We'll have to wait till Darkmere wakens before we can leave here," said Gowen.

Chapter 44

As the days passed they became restless . . . except, of course, for Minker and Copin.

"Hey, Minker, I bet you can't guzzle this down," said Copin, picking up a bottle of vinegar, covered with dust, and handing it to him.

"I'll bet you five silver I can drink the whole thing."

"I wanna watch this," said Yasmin, as Minker picked up the bottle and dusted it off.

"Good year."

"What do you mean 'good year' — it's vinegar!"

"Exactly!" said Minker, opening the bottle and drinking it down . . . until there was nothing left.

"There!" Minker smiled triumphantly. Then his smile disappeared. "I think I'm going to —" he ran out of the bar.

"I'll only give you three silver — since you lost it as soon as you drank it," called out Copin, smiling towards the doorway.

"I guess," replied Minker returning. He held out his hand to Copin, who placed three silver pieces in his palm.

"Now, I dare you to —"

"Will you two stop it! We need you to stay awake — just in case something else happens," Gowen commanded. "Our lives might still be in danger. I'm just making sure we continue to live."

They waited another day and a half. "He still hasn't gotten up," said Casiopiea, coming down the stairs. "I'm worried about him; he hasn't had anything to drink or eat in days, and now he's sweating profusely again. He won't have enough water inside to last the rest of the day."

"Maybe we should wake him," said Yasmin.

"No!" said Gowen. "He told me specifically not to wake him. Just wait a little while longer."

"Only a little while," said Casiopiea, taking more water from the pump outside and then going upstairs to watch over Darkmere.

Night came . . . but nothing changed.

Casiopiea ran down the stairs. "We have to wake him. He's dehydrated and he's having nightmares."

Gowen conceded and he and the rest went upstairs. They were amazed at how pale Darkmere's face had become. Though his skin was usually on the pale side, it was now paler still.

"Yasmin."

"I know I should charge for this. I would make a fortune," said Yasmin, causing Gowen to wonder what was going on with her.

Yasmin healed Darkmere, and while she did, he awoke.

"Darkmere, I was so worried about you," said Casiopiea, looking at him.

Glaring into her eyes, he propped himself up. She knew that he knew that she had betrayed him.

"Are you — uh," asked Yasmin, "I mean are you sane?"

"Yes, now. Tomorrow we go back to Guam, and then we will have a week before we leave again."

"Leave again? Where?" Minker asked.

"We are not out of danger by any means. We must go to Ranker to destroy Etten."

"Who's Etten?" said Yasmin.

"Etten wants us all dead . . . Etten is the one who did this to me . . . and Etten controlled Abeline, and Alcamere, and Etten is the one who destroyed Gualum." Darkmere saw he would have to take command once again.

Chapter 45

The next day came all too soon.

"We leave now," said Darkmere. They mounted horses and left for Guam. They travelled day and night until they reached it.

"Boy, I'm glad I'm home," said Minker, longing for Big Bill's.

"Minker, you want to go to Bill's?" asked Copin.

"Sure."

"Wait," commanded Darkmere. "We all have a week to supply and train. We meet back here then. Do not venture anywhere away from Guam — I might need to gather you sooner."

"Casiopiea?" he added when they were alone.

"Yes, Darkmere?"

"Do your best to change Gowen's ways to evil."

"The old woman?" Casiopiea smiled.

"Yes, the old woman," said Darkmere, opening the door to his house and finding a note with a dagger dripping blood pinned to the inside of the door.

"What does it say?" asked Casiopiea.

"'Darkmere, you will bend — and then you will be my slave forever.'" Darkmere read. "It is signed 'The Great and Powerful Etten!'" Darkmere crumpled the note in his hand.

"Tell me about this dagger, Darkmere," said Casiopiea.

"Soon you will know. Right now, I need the scroll you read to Abeline."

Casiopiea reached into her cloak to remove the scroll. As she did so, she noticed that the dagger began vibrating, humming to get out . . . she quickly closed her cloak.

"I am curious to know why you didn't use the pouch you got in Alcamere's tower."

"There was not enough time." Casiopiea swallowed and looked towards him. "Darkmere?"

"Yes."

"I didn't mean to."

"Just get Gowen and Yasmin separated, and destroy Gowen."

"That will be easy."

"I don't know about that."

The morning dew coated the ground, and the rising sun signalled the beginning of another day.

Yasmin went into town to do some ordinary chores.

"Good morning, Yasmin," said the old woman, peeking out from a corner.

"Oh, good morning. I haven't seen you for a long time. How have you been?"

"Fine, I guess." The old woman began to talk to Yasmin, telling her how it wasn't such a bad thing if you wanted to experience other men, and how Gowen had been restricting her from having fun.

"Oh, no — I could never betray Gowen," said Yasmin.

"Oh no, never. Just go have some fun. You haven't been to the Lionheart in some time, have you?"

"How did you know?"

"I can see the sadness on your face and the fun slipping from your heart."

Yasmin agreed. By the time she took leave of the old woman, she was filled with a yearning to go to the Lionheart for a good time.

At the same time, a man checked into a room at the Bat's Eye bar.

After Casiopiea resumed her natural form, she strolled into the Bat's Eye. She sat down, alone, at a table near the back of the bar, and ordered a glass of black wine.

She would make her betrayal up to Darkmere, she thought to herself.

Gowen sat in silence, waiting for Yasmin. Something was beginning to bother him about her, but he couldn't put a finger on it.

Meanwhile, Yasmin strolled into the Lionheart, looked around the crowded bar, and smiled.

This is where I can just let loose, she thought. No Gowen — her thoughts were interrupted.

"Hello."

Yasmin turned to see a man in his mid-twenties with long blond hair. She smiled, brimming back: "Hi!"

"You want a drink?"

"Sure." Yasmin's smile grew into a grin as the two went off into the crowd.

After finishing her drink, Casiopiea got up to go back to Darkmere. Someone else watched her leave.

Casiopiea entered Darkmere's house and sat down.

"Darkmere!" she called. "I brought you some black wine."

"Thank you," he said, emerging from a dark recess, almost scaring Casiopiea.

"What have you been up to?" Casiopiea asked.

He sighed. "Not much."

"I've gotten Yasmin to go to the Lionheart without Gowen. I was able to conjure images in her head of the constraints that Gowen has placed on her."

"Perfect," said Darkmere.

"I need to ask you — after I killed Abeline, why did you scream? Or was that you?"

"Abeline wasn't the only one who died."

"What do you mean?" said Casiopiea, leaning closer to hear more.

"My son died."

"What son?"

"Abeline was pregnant with my son."

"<u>What</u>?" Casiopiea got up to leave. Darkmere put a hand up for her to listen.

"Casiopiea, she raped me and was with my child when you killed her," he explained with no emotion.

"Is that why you seem so low — because you couldn't hold her when she died — or did you like?" Casiopiea's voice constricted as it rose. "Did you like her more than me?"

"Casiopiea, I'm glad she's dead. She was part of the prophecy — Etten's prophecy. Don't get me wrong; I'm glad my son died. If he had lived, he would have been the slave of Etten. And no, she <u>wasn't</u> better than you!" he added, slapping Casiopiea across the face, sending her to the ground. "Casiopiea, you amaze me — <u>you're</u> the one who betrayed <u>me</u> — not I; you."

"Wait, Darkmere. I'm glad it was Abeline . . . I mean, I thought I might be the one who was sent to kill you, since I was worshipping Etten, too. I was fooled!"

"All right. Come here," Darkmere said, more gently. They headed for the basement.

Chapter 46

"What happened to her?" said Gowen aloud to himself, pacing the small house.

'Darkmere! Darkmere!' Gowen called in thought.

'Yes, what is it?'

'Yasmin has been missing for hours.'

'Wait a minute.'

Darkmere turned to Casiopiea.

"Casiopiea, Yasmin hasn't returned since this afternoon, when you left her."

"How nice," said Casiopiea, stretching and smiling.

"Well, I'll tell him where she is," said Darkmere, turning away from her.

'Gowen — she's at the Lionheart,' said Darkmere in Gowen's head.

Gowen quickly went to the Lionheart. By the time he got there, he was fuming.

He swung open the doors and began searching for Yasmin. He looked all over, and when he was ready to search upstairs, he heard something that disturbed him greatly.

"Oh Yasmin, you're so funny," came a young man's voice. "You want to go upstairs?"

Gowen's eyes burned.

"I don't know," said Yasmin.

"What do you mean <u>you don't know</u>? Go ahead, Yasmin. <u>Go</u>!" Gowen yelled out.

"Gowen, I —"

He turned abruptly and left the inn. Yasmin ran out after him.

"Gowen, wait! I can't catch up with you. All I was doing was having a good time — I'm sorry!" Yasmin screamed.

"Leave me be, and don't come home." He ran off, leaving her standing amidst a growing group of townspeople, who all frowned at her.

She started for Big Bill's. No — Darkmere could help her. She headed for Darkmere's, instead.

"Darkmere, I wish we could just go away together and never be bothered by —"

A frantic knock on the door resounded throughout the house. Darkmere, getting up and putting his cloak on, and positioned his hood once again to hide his face. He then sighed.

"Who is disturbing us?" said Casiopiea.

"Yasmin. Casiopiea, I think you should leave - till later, until I get her back to Gowen."

"It's working, at least."

Darkmere left the room, as Casiopiea quietly climbed out the window and returned to the Bat's Eye once again.

"Who is it?" called Darkmere.

"Yasmin. Can I come in?"

Darkmere opened the door, and in she rushed, crying loudly.

"I don't know what happened. I mean, I was just at the Lionheart, and Gowen told me not to come home. I don't know what to do." She leaned on Darkmere, sobbing. He patted her on the back, and began talking, just as Casiopiea entered the Bat's Eye, revelling in the seclusion of the place.

A man in black approached her.

"May I sit down?" he asked.

"Why not?," replied Casiopiea, puzzled by the black cloak that hooded him from sight. "Who are you?"

"My name is Tan."

They spent the rest of the evening talking together. Casiopiea was intrigued by this man, who reminded her of Darkmere.

Darkmere, she thought. "Oh my!" she said suddenly. "I have to leave. Will I see you tomorrow?"

"Certainly, Casiopiea. It's been my pleasure." He held out his hand. As she took it, a chill went through her body. Who is he? she wondered.

Darkmere told Yasmin it would be a wise idea to stay overnight, sleep on the couch, and go back to Gowen in the morning. Things would be better then.

In the meantime, Gowen had begun hurling their plates at the wall, watching them shatter.

'Casiopiea,' came Darkmere's voice to her. 'Stay at the Crystalbird tonight. Yasmin is staying here, on the couch. Your plan is working perfectly.' Darkmere said feeling disgusted at the pettiness of this deed, yet doing it for Casiopiea.

Chapter 47

The next day started off with a bang:

Knocking on Darkmere's door. Who could this be? he wondered. "Who is it?"

"Gowen."

"Gowen?" said Yasmin, rubbing the sleep from her eyes. Darkmere nodded, opening the door.

Yasmin scooted into the bedroom while Darkmere let Gowen in.

'Darkmere, don't tell him I'm here — he'll hate me —'

'Don't worry.' Darkmere then looked into his Gowen's eyes.

"Darkmere, I found Yasmin with another man," said Gowen, looking very downtrodden. "Should I take her back?" Gowen asked, not knowing who else to turn to.

"Don't worry, Gowen, it's probably not what you thought. You're overreacting." He wondered why everyone came to him. He wanted to be left alone.

Gowen left, and Yasmin came back into the room.

Yasmin, hugged him, making his blood pressure rise.

Casiopiea, who had already been awake for awhile, now went to meet Tan at the Bat's Eye. It wasn't long before she was asking him the question she wished answered. "Tell me — why do you hide yourself?"

"I look a little odd," he answered reluctantly.

Casiopiea smiled. "I'd like to see what you look like."

"You sure?"

"Yes." She followed Tan upstairs to his room, where he closed the door behind them.

"Are you sure you're ready?" he asked, hesitating.

"Yes," she assured him. He removed his hood, revealing himself to her. He had lavender skin, pointed ears, and lavender eyes.

"What, may I ask, are you?" she asked.

"An elf."

"But you seem so different."

"I am — I was born this way."

He touched her arm, sending chills up and down her spine.

"What about your touch?"

"I just have a chilling touch," he replied, moving still closer and looking into her eyes, intriguing her. "Casiopiea, do you think —"

"No," she stopped him. "But I have the right person for you."

"Yes? Who?" he asked eagerly, not having touched anyone in such a long time.

"You'll see later this afternoon."

"Alone at last," said Darkmere aloud. Taking a book off the shelf, he sat down in his rocking chair, and began to read.

Gowen sat at home, fidgeting, pacing the floor, hoping that Yasmin would forgive him.

Then came a knock at the door, and he ran to answer it.

"Yasmin," she called, not sure what kind of welcome she would receive.

He flung open the door, took Yasmin up in his arms, and lifted her off the ground.

"I hope everything's forgiven," he said

"I can explain, Gowen," she began.

"You don't have to. I love you. Promise you will never leave me, Yasmin."

Gowen hugged her again when she did and then, sweeping her up, carried her into the bedroom.

Casiopiea strolled down the street towards Darkmere's house, content with what she was about to do.

"Darkmere?" asked Casiopiea, opening the door to the house and sauntering in.

He looked up from his reading, disturbed once again. "Yes?"

"I have found the perfect treachery for Yasmin . . ." Casiopiea began relating her plan in hushed tones.

"Tan."

"Yes, my Lord."

"Is everything set?"

"Yes, it is," said Tan.

"Well, Gowen, do you think you can trust me to stroll into town?" teased Yasmin with a bright smile.

"Yes, I think everything will be fine. Go . . . and fetch me some dinner."

"Anything, my love." She kissed him on the cheek before setting out. She hoped he would truly forgive her. She vowed to herself that she would never, ever betray him.

Just as Casiopiea took her leave of Darkmere, he began to resent what lay ahead.

I'll go out and be alone, he thought, stealing away into the woods.

Chapter 48

The waiting was the hardest part. Tan left his room to take a stroll in the woods nearby. He gradually increased his pace, as he moved further into the woods.

Stepping out from behind a tree, seemingly out of nowhere, a man in black suddenly appeared before him, brandishing a sword. Shaking, Tan stood his ground.

"Who are you and what do you want here?" the stranger sternly asked him.

"I am Tan, and I am here to help."

The man stepped out of the shadows.

"I am Darkmere — and there is something you are not telling me. You spoke with Casiopiea, I know, and now you seek another?"

"Yes, I seek —"

"Yasmin," Darkmere declared. He watched as Tan moved uncertainly.

"Go back to your room, and you will get what you want. Gowen will find you and —"

"And nothing, Darkmere. Curiosity is all I have, and that is what I wish to have satisfied."

"I know now you worship the same, am I right? A test?"

Tan turned from Darkmere.

"No one thought I knew as much as I do, not even me, Tan . . . Go now, find what you seek."

Tan left Darkmere in the shadows and, when he was far enough away, knelt down and prayed. "He is much stronger than we had expected."

"Don't worry. Just do what you must."

Tan left the woods and returned to his inn room.

Once again, Casiopiea assumed the guise of the old woman. Maybe for the last time, she thought to herself, smiling.

She approached Yasmin, while Crystalmere watched.

"Good evening, Yasmin dear," said Casiopiea in a gravelly voice.

"Oh, good evening. I have much to talk to you about,' said Yasmin, glad to see her. The two began gossiping, talking endlessly, into the wee hours of the night.

Meanwhile, Gowen again paced through his house, wondering what had happened this time . . .

Finally, he sat himself down and sighed. "I have to trust her," he said aloud, resolving to wait and see what would happen.

After a few hours, Casiopiea brought Yasmin to the Bat's Eye . . . and began to get her drunk. When she thought Yasmin was good and ready, she began . . .

"Yasmin, I'll be right back," she said, "Stay and enjoy another — here."

While Yasmin drank, Casiopiea left her, changed back to herself and went quickly upstairs to find Tan. She called out his name, knocking on the door.

He opened it. "It's about time. I thought you would never come."

"She's downstairs — and she's a beauty. She will melt into your hands, Tan," Casiopiea said, grinning at him. "Good luck."

"Thank you, dear," said Tan, pulling Casiopiea close to him, sending chills up and down her body once again.

"Go, quickly," said Casiopiea, pushing him to the door. She watched as he headed downstairs to prey upon the gullible Yasmin.

Casiopiea slipped out the back door of the inn and back to Darkmere's. Disappointed at finding no one home, she sat to wait for word from Crystalmere.

"Good evening," said Tan, dressed all in black and towering over Yasmin.

"Hello! So nice to make your acquaintance," offered Yasmin, hiccuping again and smiling.

"Would you like to talk?"

"Sure," she said. He sat himself down next to her and began talking about everything under the sun.

In the meantime, Gowen had begun to pace in and out of his house, back and forth, up and down . . . then sat down and twiddled his thumbs.

"I can't wait any longer!" he exploded, jumping up and storming out of the house to look, once again, for his wife.

Darkmere returned home knowing that the plan that Casiopiea had concocted was probably in the works by now.

Gowen will be devastated, no doubt, Darkmere thought, and Casiopiea will be there to help him through it. He wondered how he was going to throw Casiopiea out so that it would satisfy her . . . so she wouldn't do anything too destructive. He also wondered if this was the only way to keep her occupied, or would he have to destroy her.

He opened the door to find her sprawled in his rocking chair.

"It's working?"

"Yes, it is — and I'm sick of you. You know I love you," said Casiopiea, grabbing Darkmere and pulling him to the bedroom.

"This will complete it, Darkmere. This will be the last time for us, for a little while."

"You are my piece of work," whispered Darkmere, and she grinned.

Gowen went to Bill's, no Yasmin. The Lionheart: no Yasmin. The Crystalbird: no Yasmin.

"Darkmere's, I bet," he said angrily, storming out of the Crystalbird, arriving there just in time to hear screams coming from the house.

"Darkmere! Darkmere!" Gowen yelled, opening the door at a run. He immediately had to duck, as a plate flew right by his head. More plates went flying, and he ducked to avoid them.

"You repulsive, grotesque, insensate!" shrieked Casiopiea.

"That's it, Casiopiea — get out!" returned Darkmere. The two turned to notice Gowen.

"I'm sorry if I am interrupting, but has anyone seen Yasmin?"

"No — now, please leave!" commanded Darkmere. "Both of you!" Darkmere glared at Casiopiea, while Gowen took his leave, resuming his search for Yasmin.

Where could she be? Let's see . . . I've looked everywhere but The Bat's Eye. Gowen thought, and headed straight there.

At that moment, Tan was leading Yasmin upstairs to his room.

"I'd like to see what you look like," Yasmin said to him, as he closed the door behind them. She began to remove his cloak.

Amazed, Yasmin exclaimed, "An elf — a purple elf! How wonderful!" She went up close to Tan and touched his chest, instantly feeling a chill go up her spine.

"Amazing. How do you do that?"

"This is my natural way."

"Oh," said Yasmin, smiling, as she tripped into his arms.

Chapter 49

Downstairs, Gowen approached the barkeep. "Have you seen a woman . . ." Gowen began to describe Yasmin.

"Yep. She went upstairs with some guy."

Burning, Gowen raced up the stairs to the room the barkeep had indicated. He charged headlong into the door, causing it to fly open, and found Tan holding Yasmin in his arms.

Mortified and amazed, he turned cold.

"Don't ever!" Gowen ran crying out into the street. "She said <u>never</u> — she <u>promised</u>!" he screamed, collapsing where he stood.

Casiopiea left Darkmere's as the last plate was thrown.

'Casiopiea — do I get a new set?' his thought called after her.

'Maybe,' she said, smiling, as she turned seductively, and walked away from Darkmere.

She walked down the main street, making herself cry . . . when she saw Gowen . . . poor Gowen.

"Gowen, are you all right?" Casiopiea asked, bending down next to him.

"She . . . ," said Gowen, pointing towards the Bat's Eye . . . and crumbled once again.

"Gowen, come on," said Casiopiea, lifting his face to hers. "I'm sorry. I know how it feels." Tears were running down her face.

"What do you mean? What happened?"

"Darkmere threw me out." Casiopiea began crying harder. Gowen leaned over to help her up.

"Maybe we can talk about it. Casiopiea?" he exclaimed grabbing her before she fell.

"I think I'll be fine. I will be in the morning, I hope. For now, I'll be at the Crystalbird. Thank you, Gowen. If you need anything, remember, I'm here for you. I'm sure things will be better in the morning." She hugged Gowen tight . . . and sniffled. Then she trudged off to the Crystalbird.

Gowen went home, took out a bottle of wine and began to drink heavily.

"I have to go after him!" said Yasmin.

"It will just make it worse, Yasmin. Don't go — come sit by me."

She realized he was right and sat down next to Tan. She began describing all her former lovers, before she married Gowen.

Tan sighed. "Would you love an elf tonight?"

She swallowed, the alcohol sloshing in her stomach.

"Sure . . . I'll show him," said Yasmin, removing her top.

He began to kiss her . . . until she passed out.

The next day almost everyone awoke with a massive headache.

'Darkmere.'

'Yes, Casiopiea.'

'The deed is almost done.'

'I'm glad. How are you feeling, having to look into the eyes of my pathetic brother?'

'That hasn't happened yet.'

'I thought you work fast, my dear.'

'Not that fast. Let's not spoil things,' said Casiopiea, stretching, readying herself to control another day.

Meanwhile Gowen, who had teetered down to The Bat's Eye, was now sitting at the bar and drinking heavily.

"Weren't you the guy who was here last night?" said the barkeep.

"So what," Gowen snarled.

"Just asking," the barkeep replied, backing away.

Gowen ordered another drink, just as Yasmin came down the stairs. Realizing all that had happened the night before, she was feeling mortified.

"Good morning, little lady," said the barkeep. Gowen looked up.

"Gowen — let me explain. It's not what you —"

"There is no need to explain," Gowen answered coldly.

"But I love you, and I am married to you," she cried.

"That can be changed."

"But why? I love you!" said Yasmin, tears running the length of her face.

"Here," said Gowen, prying off his wedding ring.

"No! Gowen!" Yasmin screamed, begging him not to.

"I don't think I need it any longer. You can now go and have fun without me," said Gowen, pushing her away, tears coming to his eyes.

"Gowen, you shouldn't be drinking, you're allergic. You're getting red blotches on your face. Now, come on, Gowen, you don't mean it," she cajoled him.

"Yes I do. <u>I want a divorce</u>. <u>Here</u>," shouted Gowen, throwing the ring at her and running out of the inn, totally distraught.

Chapter 50

Upon hearing what had happened to Gowen from the rumors flying about town, Casiopiea left the Crystalbird Inn. She walked over to Gowen's, and knocked softly on his door.

"If it's Yasmin — stay away," cried Gowen.

Casiopiea opened the door to find Gowen stretched out on the floor, sobbing.

She knelt beside him. "What's happened, Gowen?" she asked him, sweetly.

"Yasmin and I are through — we're getting divorced," Gowen managed to choke out.

"Why? I thought you two were happy."

"We were. And then something inside Yasmin changed, and she wasn't satisfied with me any more," he said pitifully. Then, remembering Casiopiea's predicament, he looked up into her green eyes. "Are you better?"

"I, well . . . Darkmere and I are through. This morning he told me we could never be together."

"Why?"

"Because he has this thing about being alone a lot of the time — and I was getting in the way."

"I'm sorry, Casiopiea."

"So am I, but I can't let it get me down, even if . . ." Casiopiea began to reminisce: walks in the woods, time spent — then the tears began to well up in her eyes. Gowen took her in his arms, and they wept together.

'Nice performance, Casiopiea.'

'Thank you, Darkmere.'

When Tan came downstairs, he found Yasmin crying, holding both her and Gowen's wedding bands in her hands.

"Maybe I can help," said Tan, sitting down next to her.

"No. Only Darkmere can help now," said Yasmin, getting up, leaving Tan to wonder if she deserved any better than she was going to get.

Hours passed, during which Gowen and Casiopiea bared their souls to each other.

"You know, I never thought we could have so much in common," said Gowen.

"Yes. It is quite amazing," said Casiopiea, raising an eyebrow.

"I feel much better. Will you come with me to get my papers signed?"

"Are you sure you want to do it so fast?"

"Yes."

They went to the courthouse that day.

'Yasmin has turned to Darkmere, not me.' Tan said.

'I know, and I am sorry.'

'What shall I do?'

'A decision will come to you, my son.'

Meanwhile, Yasmin reached Darkmere's. "Darkmere!" she screamed, banging her fists on the door.

He opened his door . . .

"Darkmere, you have to help me," Yasmin cried.

"What's wrong, Yasmin?"

"Gowen is getting a divorce — can you stop him?"

"I can try. But first, tell me everything."

He sat down to listen to Yasmin pour forth the story, beginning with her friend, the old woman, and then about getting drunk, and then not remembering much — up to the point where she saw Gowen in the Bat's Eye and the scene that had ensued. After much crying from Yasmin, the two left for Gowen's.

By the time they got there, however, it was too late:

"Gowen," called Darkmere, knocking repeatedly on the door. There was no answer. He opened the door, finding nothing.

"Yasmin, he's gone."

"We have to find him before it's too late, or he hurts himself," said Yasmin, pulling on Darkmere's sleeve.

"Please, Darkmere, I love him."

The two of them made their way into town; all the while Darkmere wondered if it was worth all the effort. He shook his head; he was not ready to rid himself of a magic-user yet.

As they hurried along, Yasmin was the first to spot them. Too stunned to speak, she froze in her tracks, her mouth agape.

"Hello Darkmere, Yasmin — how are you?" asked Casiopiea. She continued to hold Gowen's hand.

Darkmere nodded and looked at Gowen.

"Oh, Yasmin — here," said Gowen, shoving a scroll into her hand. "Open it!"

Yasmin opened the scroll, weeping as she read.

"Sign it here," said Gowen, forcing a quill into her other hand.

"No, Gowen, please!" Yasmin begged.

But he forced her to sign the papers.

"There. It is done. I want your things out of my house today Yasmin!" Gowen commanded, and turned to Darkmere. "I can't believe what a heartless piece of nothing you are! How you could do what you did to Casiopiea? Well, now she will be with someone who will appreciate her." Gowen threw a last icy glance at Yasmin and then led Casiopiea away.

Darkmere cursed Gowen for his goodwill.

"Yasmin — I can help you feel better."

"You can? Thank you, Darkmere," she mumbled, morosely following him back to his house.

Once inside, he slammed the door and turned to face her.

"Darkmere, what's going on?" she asked.

"Something you've always desired," he replied.

"Darkmere, you're scaring me," she declared, backing up against the wall behind her.

Darkmere finally cornered her. "This is what you've been anticipating since you first saw me. Now you can have it," he murmured, helping her to shred his clothes.

"No!" screamed Yasmin as Darkmere forced her to mount him and let her take all of him.

PART III

Chapter 1

Darkmere

*The darkness of the depths of my soul — it
soothes and comforts me in the way nothing
could.*

*My deep dark heart, it plagues me with deep
thoughts and sorrow, yet the feeling soothes
me.*

*Take me to the center of the darkness where
the hole grows deeper and deeper I fall and
where nothing will bother me -*

The darkness as I fall.

Tan paced his room, feeling the presence of a
unearthly being.
"She deserved it and will go through the test — she
has defied you too many times."
"You have found your answer, and I agree. Do what
must be done."

The birds began chirping as the sun rose on a new
day . . .

"Good morning, Casiopiea."

"Good morning, Gowen. Thanks for letting me stay here. Hmm...Yasmin never came to pick up her things."

"She will come . . . eventually. Let's forget about Yasmin and talk about us," said Gowen smiling. Casiopiea's insides turned.

"What do you mean?"

"You know — you and I . . ." said Gowen, brushing up against her trying to keep the pain of betrayal far away.

"What about us?" Casiopiea smiled innocently.

"Well, I had a wild thought."

"Yes, what is it?"

"How about you and me tying the knot?"

"Isn't it a little soon for you?"

"Not if you can handle it," Gowen grinned.

Casiopiea held herself back from hitting him; instead, she smiled sweetly.

"Fine, Gowen — whatever your heart desires."

"How about tomorrow?"

"Fine."

"Yasmin, are you awake?" said Darkmere.

Yasmin rubbed her eyes. Coming back to reality, she pulled away from Darkmere, wide-eyed:

"You raped me!"

"No, Yasmin — you took me and have been wanting to ever since you met me."

"But not like that." Yasmin blushed, knowing he was right.

"Come here, Yasmin. I don't want to have to chase you again."

"Why did you do that? You scared me."

"Don't worry. I won't do it again."

"Do you give your word?"

"Yes, I do. Come here," Darkmere repeated, holding out his hand to her.

She inched forward, taking his hand.

Darkmere drew her in and hugged her close. "See? I would never hurt you."

"I believe you," said Yasmin, smiling up at him.

"Don't worry . . . the time will be soon . . . soon," said Etten, watching Darkmere, as smoke rose from his fingers.

     'Darkmere'
     'What?'
     'I'm getting married.'
     <u>'What?'</u>
     'Yes.'
     'We never said marriage —'
     'Well, you want me to be thorough, don't you?'
     'When?'
     'Tomorrow.'
     'How nice.'
     'Thank you, Darkmere, my love.'
     Darkmere got up.

Cynthia Soroka

"Yasmin, if you will excuse me, I need to be alone. Gowen and Casiopiea are getting married tomorrow."

"What! <u>No</u>!" Yasmin wept on Darkmere's shoulder for what seemed to be hours, while his anger grew.

"Let's get ready."

"Sure, Gowen. I'd like to have it here, at your house — small and intimate."

"That sounds perfect!" said Gowen, sending word to Copin, Minker, and Big Bill.

Darkmere left his small house, holding back the feeling of wanting to destroy everything in sight.

He went into the forest and sat alone, trying to calm himself down. Soon, the green glow surfaced.

He reached inside his cloak pocket. Taking out a scroll, he began to read. He looked down and saw the image of the dagger above his heart . . . and he read some more.

After awhile, the glow faded and his blue eyes became fixed. He now knew that Casiopiea, Gowen, and Yasmin were trivial compared to what lay ahead. It would not be an adventure, but a nightmare.

The rest of the day vanished — the little time they had left.

Chapter 2

On the wedding day, Gowen and Casiopiea pledged their vows to each other before Darkmere, Copin, Minker, Big Bill, and Yasmin.

"Boy, this is strange - one day they are married, and the next day they get married," said Minker, looking a little confused.

"Maybe we'll get married next," whined Copin.

Upon noticing Darkmere holding Yasmin's hand, Casiopiea became annoyed.

'Darkmere how could you — remember your promise.'

'I keep my promises, Casiopiea — and I don't love Yasmin.'

'Oh,' said Casiopiea, all the while looking at Gowen.

"Darkmere," said Yasmin.

"Yes."

"Can we go?"

"Yes." Darkmere escorted Yasmin out of the house, while Casiopiea and Gowen sealed their union with a kiss.

"Well, I guess it's time to have a party, Copin." said Minker, opening up a bottle of Bill's special brew. Minker, Copin, and Big Bill set themselves to drinking.

After a few hours of sitting around and talking, Gowen and Casiopiea politely asked the three to leave so they could be alone.

"Casiopiea?"

"Yes, Gowen."

"Care to adjourn to the bedroom?"

She smiled in the knowledge that Darkmere was probably watching them, as Gowen picked her up and carried her into the bedroom.

But, Darkmere and Yasmin were at his house.

Said Yasmin, "Do you think they are together now?"

"Yes, I do."

"I hate him for what he's done. Darkmere, I'm glad you're here for me."

He nodded, sensing something was going awry.

After spending some time with Yasmin and cleaning up the house, Darkmere left for the woods to be alone and read some more. Frustrated, he walked through the woods.

"How far can I let this go?" he asked himself, almost regretting that he had allowed Casiopiea to marry Gowen. I will let this to play itself out. After all, it would help if Gowen changed. He concluded, remembering that this was not of any consequence in the scheme of things. He felt a breeze behind him and knew someone was watching him. He turned and spoke.

"So, Tan — how are you?"

Tan emerged from the shadows. "Fine, Darkmere. I see Casiopiea is otherwise occupied."

"Yes."

"You are angered — today you show it. It must pain you to be shackled to such a woman."

"I love her."

"Exactly."

"I will leave you."

"No, I will leave you be," said Tan. As Tan left the woods, Darkmere began to hear something all too familiar, a humming . . . a humming, but what?

He followed Tan's thoughts and waited. Darkmere watched as Tan went into his room and removed his robe.

Suddenly he withdrew a jeweled dagger.

'He has one of the daggers — that bastard!,' said Darkmere, momentarily getting up, then stopping himself. 'No, not yet. It is too soon.'

Darkmere drew a map and then sketched a pyramid in the middle — a pyramid of eight daggers.

The days wore on. Gowen and Casiopiea stayed together, and Yasmin grew more attached to Darkmere, not wanting him to leave her side.

Chapter 3

'Darkmere.'

'Yes, Casiopiea.'

'I feel strange.'

'Come meet me in the forest when the moon is full.'

At nightfall, Darkmere stole away to meet Casiopiea. Wild with desire, they made love to each other in the moonlight.

"I've been lost without you, Darkmere."

"I know."

"I don't know how long I can take this. I mean, I've tried to make him see how venting his anger could help him, but he just doesn't understand. He is really repulsive . . . not like you."

"Casiopiea — you're pregnant."

"You are joking, right?"

"No, I am not joking. You are only a few days along."

"No. That doesn't mean that he — no, it must be you — correct?"

"I can't say, for sure."

"Then I'll destroy it right now," said Casiopiea, turning to walk away. Darkmere grabbed hold of her roughly.

"No! You will go to term with it. If it's mine, I want nothing to happen to it."

"I can't believe this!"

"I will not allow anything to happen to it — understood?"

"And I suffer because of it!"

"You will be fine."

"No! I don't want it. I will kill it, Darkmere."

"No! If you touch it, you will regret it."

"What are you going to do — kill <u>me</u>?" Casiopiea sneered.

"Maybe," said Darkmere, knowing whose baby it really was. But he could not let her know . . . not now.

"Please, Darkmere — help me."

"I am. Tan has another one of the daggers."

"You mean like the one I have?"

"Yes."

"How many are there?"

"Eight."

"Tell me about them. Please, ease my pain."

"I cannot. Now go to your husband and tell him the news," Darkmere said not wanting Casiopiea, or anyone, knowing everything he knew.

"No."

"Then go. Leave me be," he sat, filled with worry and a sense of imminent disaster.

'Crystalmere.'

'Yes, Darkmere.'

'Watch over Casiopiea and make sure she does nothing to herself.'

'Very well, Darkmere.'

Casiopiea looked at Darkmere and said, "Who is Tan?"

"I have found out — he has come to test us all."

"How appropriate," she said, sarcastically.

"Go home, my dear, before Gowen misses you. Good night, my love."

"Why? Would you miss me?"

"Yes."

"Then I could not allow that, Darkmere," she said.

"Then go back to your spouse."

The next few days passed in anger and frustration.

Yasmin went for a walk, after berating Darkmere.

"What has happened to me?" she said aloud to herself.

"I've been wondering the same thing," said Tan, emerging from behind a bush.

"Why are you here? Who are you?"

"My name is Tan — and you have not been faithful."

"Faithful, what do you mean?" Yasmin looked at him, perplexed, as he removed his cloak for her to see him once again.

Annoyed and angered, she stared at his chest, where a holy symbol lay — her holy symbol.

"I _have_ been faithful — I pray a lot!" said Yasmin, realizing she had not prayed once in several days.

"You have one more chance, Yasmin."

"How do I know what you are saying is real?"

"Heed my words, Yasmin — you are getting too close to Darkmere."

"Well, what do you expect? I love him."

"But does he love you?"

"Yes, he does! I know!" said Yasmin, glaring at Tan. Who did he think he was, telling her who loved her?

"Good night, Yasmin," said Tan, disappearing into the night.

"I'll show him!" said Yasmin, kneeling down and praying. When she was finished she returned to Darkmere's.

Alone, feeling suffocated, Darkmere sat by the fire and watched the flames dance back and forth.

"How did you get into this situation?" a voice called out.

Darkmere looked around, seeing no one.

"Who?" he called out. "Who are you?"

"Oh, you know who. Don't be stupid."

"I thought you were gone, for now at least."

"I told you I would never leave you be, and I keep my promises, as do you. Your friend — or should I say lover — is coming back again."

"Thank you."

"The daggers will never reach you, Darkmere, never."

Darkmere shrugged off Etten's words, reminding himself that he — Darkmere — was too powerful. He turned to the mundane task at hand.

"Darkmere, Darkmere," Yasmin called, as she ran into the house.

"Yes?" he answered from the shadows.

"Tell me that you love me."

"I love you."

"I knew it," said Yasmin, throwing her arms around him, and hugging him.

Things were becoming complicated, with Yasmin asking for his love, which he really could not give for he had promised it to another, and Casiopiea constantly complaining about Gowen.

"Yasmin, tomorrow I will leave for a few days," said Darkmere. "I must find us a ship for our voyage."

"Can I come?"

"No, I must go alone."

He spent the night in horror, with Yasmin clinging to him to the point where he was ready to kill her. Holding himself back, he relayed his message to Casiopiea, and bade her goodbye.

'Don't kill anyone while I'm gone.'

'I'll try.'

Darkmere fell asleep . . . knowing tomorrow would be a long day for him.

Chapter 4

Candlespar, the place to be! The town had grown up around a series of long roads, all of which led to one place: the water, the Perched Ocean to be exact. It was a lively town, constantly filled with traders and merchants who came to want one kind of shipment or another. In the center of the town stood a long strip of stores and inns, leading out to the wharf.

The daily hustle and bustle of town momentarily subsided as a lone figure in black garb strolled down the main street. He made his way through town and down to the wharf, and a woman followed and watched, a glint of interest in her eyes.

She saw him turn a corner and playfully followed, slinking in and out of bushes, making sure he did not see her — but could.

She wore a seductive yet charming smile. She followed his movements, calculating her next move, until she heard a husky voice call out.

"Hey Eliza, get over here . . . I paid enough —"

"Shush!" she said, turning on him and glaring, putting a slender finger to her lips, then pointing: "I want to know what that is," she whispered.

He smiled, showing off all the black holes in his teeth.

"Eliza, I'll show you what <u>that</u> is," clutching his loins, his eyes went wide and his whole face grimaced from the kick she'd delivered flush in his crotch.

"Don't treat me like that, Prestoni . . . I will give you what you want after dinner." He fell to the ground squealing like a pig.

She hurried off, hips swaying, hoping to pick up the figure's trail. To her dismay, she had lost him.

Disappointed, even a little distraught, she headed back to her job at the Silver Spoon Tavern. She arrived just in time to see Prestoni stagger to the bar. It seemed to be a good time to hide herself, so she did.

chapter 5

"When that wench Eliza Young comes back, she will see who's boss!" she heard Prestoni snarling.

She was laughing from her hiding place in the corner of the bar when suddenly the tavern door opened . . . and in walked the mysterious figure.

Wheeling, Prestoni also saw him. He rose from his stool and without a second thought hurled himself at the figure, slamming his fist into the stranger's stomach.

Trying to catch his breath and unsheathe his sword at the same time — the stranger was thrown to the ground. Prestoni, along with one of his bar buddies, came at him again.

The figure rose and began swinging wildly, as howls of laughter burst from Prestoni.

"He can't even move!" he taunted. Eliza was transfixed by Prestoni's horror show. He was hurting a stranger . . . and for what? She could no longer contain herself. Coming out from the shadows, she spoke:

"Prestoni, leave him . . ."

She turned and looked into the stranger's face and was instantly star-struck; he was beautiful.

"This is for Eliza!"

She watched, horrified, as Prestoni, now joined by five of his friends, began pounding on the stranger.

Then screams were heard from the mass of fighting bodies. Suddenly, the stranger stood free, a dagger in hand.

Eliza noticed blood on the dagger. He now turned towards Prestoni. "No!" she gasped.

At the sound of her voice, the stranger quickly turned in her direction and it was all over. The stranger lay on the floor, dazed, with Prestoni standing triumphantly over him.

Eliza immediately went to the stranger and bent over him, revealing her ample self to the delighted onlookers. She saw blood running down the side of his head. Rising, she turned on Prestoni, who stood over them with a metal pan in his hand.

"You inconsiderate bastard! You had no right to do what you did! You don't deserve the right to live or to be running a ship!"

The figure moaned, and she knelt beside him and cradled his head in her lap. Prestoni groaned. When the stranger's ocean blue eyes met hers, Eliza felt herself melting away.

Prestoni, kicked her.   "Are you done being a nursemaid for today?" he sneered.

"Shut up, you insolent asshole!" Turning again to the stranger, she asked, in a candy-coated way, "Are you hurt?"

"Are you hurt?" mimicked Prestoni in a squeaky voice, fluttering his eyelashes and swinging his hips.

"Yes," the stranger said, as he slowly propped himself up against the bottom of the bar.

"What is your name?"

"What is your name?" Prestoni imitated, this time under his breath. Eliza turned to glare at him.

"Darkmere." Darkmere said disgusted with the fact he could not show his real strength in front of mere townspeople.

"That's such a nice name."

"Tha —" Prestoni started. Eliza stood up and punched him right in the nose. Then she smiled.

As Darkmere tried to stand up on his own, she turned to help him.

"Tell me, what are you doing here?"

"Looking for a ship to take me and a few others away."

"Oh, really? Prestoni is the captain of the finest ship on the ocean. It's so beautiful that everyone who sees him — er, I mean it — can't help but gasp."

When Darkmere looked at Eliza, she batted her eyelashes and made cute faces.

"Maybe he will show me the ship."

"That idiot?"

"Well, I'm looking for a ship, and a captain who will share the duties."

"But he just — and you're still bleeding. Let me help," she said, ripping off part of her barmaid outfit to dab his head with. In a flash, he crossed behind the seaman, grabbed Prestoni's arm and brought it behind his back. Without further ado, he twisted the dagger out of Prestoni's other hand, and held it to his throat.

"Are you going to stop this petty nonsense? I am not taking your girlfriend away! I'm looking for a captain and a ship."

Prestoni's five friends stood watching in shock, along with the rest of the tavern's patrons.

"Yes, I will yield — and she's not my girlfriend!"

Hearing that, Eliza got up and kneed him in the groin.

The bar erupted with laughter, and Darkmere helped Prestoni to a seat.

They began talking while Eliza watched. She wasn't finished paying Prestoni back. Considering Darkmere's fluid and graceful movements, she knew how she would do it.

When they finished talking, Darkmere shook Captain Prestoni's hand and left.

chapter 6

Darkmere proceeded down to the wharf, with Eliza following, keeping a good distance. Still, in short order, Darkmere turned around. "You don't have to keep hiding in the shadows."

She sighed and strolled up beside him.

"Are you going to see Prestoni's ship?"

"Yes. Do you want to come?"

"No, but I will."

She showed him the way.

"Eliza, tell me why you love Prestoni so."

She stopped, staring. "Are you insane?"

"It's written all over your face."

"Oh," she said, pursing her lips.

"Well? Must I read your mind?"

"I'll tell. You see, my name's Eliza Young. I was orphaned at birth. And if you ask any seafaring man around here, he will tell you about me. I'm known all over . . . Oh, there it is," said Eliza, pointing to a ship Darkmere could see was beautiful; finer than any ship he had ever seen. He seemed mesmerized. She watched him approaching the great sea vessel, standing before it.

"You were right. It is beautiful."

"Darkmere, <u>Darkmere</u>!"

He turned. "What?"

"Do you want to see the inside?"

"Yes," he said, and immediately stepped onto the plank stretching from the dock to the vessel.

She showed him every inch of the ship, from the fine captain's quarters to the exquisite wheel which navigated the big boat. She watched him and was amazed. He seemed to fit into this ship like a glove, the hard structure of his face melted away, like snow in a spring rain. His face became almost angelic. She could not help but stare as he looked off into the horizon.

"Eliza, Eliza," he mused.

"Yes?"

"How did Prestoni get this ship?"

"In a bet."

"Is he a good captain?"

"Yes, he is," she sighed.

"No. Is he a good <u>sea</u> captain?"

"Oh. Yes, he is." She was amazed, it was if he was reading her mind.

"Thank you for showing me the ship."

"You're welcome, Darkmere," she said, jumping up to kiss him. As he pushed her away, the stony facade returned to his face.

"Is there something wrong?"

"No . . . I just can't. I belong to another."

"So — so does Prestoni."

"I'm sorry . . . I can't."

The look on his face puzzled her . . . but she would try again.

He took her back to the Silver Spoon and asked to speak with Prestoni. They agreed upon a date to set sail, and Darkmere gave Prestoni a lump sum to seal their agreement.

As Prestoni gazed at the money in his hands, he noticed Eliza looking at Darkmere.

Darkmere got up and smiled. "Prestoni, we might need a barmaid on board . . . Think about it."

As he left, he saw Prestoni's face turn pale, almost white — while Eliza looked into Prestoni's face, smiling. Darkmere left the two of them to their own devices.

Chapter 7

The next day, Darkmere left Candlespar on horseback to return to Guam. He rode hard and fast, not stopping at all because he did not want to waste any time. He rode into town and immediately gathered everyone in the party together.

"So, did you find what we're looking for to get us to Ranker?" inquired Yasmin.

"Yes. A ship. The most beautiful ship you could imagine. And we leave three days hence, which means tomorrow we must head for Candlespar." Darkmere paused. "Casiopiea, what did you do to your hair?"

"I dyed it white — don't you like it?"

Yasmin put her arms around Darkmere and Gowen's insides turned.

"So tell us, Casiopiea, where are you and Gowen going with that baby of yours?" Yasmin said aloud, looking cross-eyed at Casiopiea's stomach.

'So you've told Gowen about the baby,' Darkmere said in Casiopiea's head.

'Yes.'

'Was he thrilled?'

'Yes.'

'Are you managing?'

'No.'

'Don't worry — I'm here now. And I hope your hair doesn't stay like that.'

'I'm disappointed, Darkmere.'

'Sorry.'

Casiopiea turned to Yasmin. "I will be keeping it far from you, Yasmin. I bet you and Darkmere have a lot of catching up to do," she hissed through clenched teeth.

"I want you two to cut out the bickering — now!" Darkmere commanded. "We only have one night to collect ourselves, and I don't need you two drawing everyone into a fight. Do you understand me?"

"Yes, Darkmere," replied Yasmin meekly, Casiopiea stood, glaring at him.

'I wonder, sometimes, Darkmere, if you don't really care for her,' she said, again, in his head. "Yes, Darkmere — our faithful leader," she said aloud, trying to kindle his anger.

"Now that's better. We will meet here at sunrise."

They all left, but not before Yasmin pulled Darkmere down to her, kissing him and exclaiming, "Oh, I missed you. When are we getting married?"

'Darkmere, you're breaking . . . have fun, my darling, and don't forget to give her my love. And beyond anything else — don't ever forget your word to me!' said Casiopiea inside.

Holding himself in, Darkmere kissed Yasmin and, smiling, added, "Soon, my love, soon."

He asked himself, why don't you just kill her and get it over with?

"How nice," murmured Yasmin. Darkmere led her home.

Chapter 8

"Darkmere, when are we getting married?" said Yasmin as she closed the door behind her.

"Not now, Yasmin. Just let me rest." Darkmere fell asleep on the bed.

Tan watched overhead, frowning.
"I think she's lost it."
"She has."

The next day they met at dawn, more or less ready to go.

"We have a new addition coming along," said Darkmere, "Meet Tan." Tan's presence took Yasmin by surprise.

"Nice to meet you," whined Copin, holding out his hand to Tan. As Tan took Copin's hand, a shiver went through him.

Minker smiled, introducing himself next, while Gowen glared, remembering that this was the man who had destroyed his marriage with Yasmin.

"Let's get going," said Darkmere, mounting his black horse and starting off at a trot down the path to Candlespar.

The journey took two days. As they rode into Candlespar, Eliza spotted them and ran into the Silver Spoon.

"Prestoni, they're here," she called out, excited.
"Who?"

"Your passengers for the Exodus."

"Thanks, Eliza. I'll be back in about two weeks."

"What do you mean two weeks? The last time you said two weeks, it turned out to be two months — and not one word from you!"

"Two weeks."

"Oh no you don't. This time I was invited. Do you think you're gonna stop me? You're —"

"Wait until later, and we will see. And do me a favor — tell Winfred to get off the bottle and onto the ship <u>with</u> the crew."

"Oh. So you think Winfred is going to deter me? I'll see you soon, my darling." She sashayed off as Prestoni got up and headed for his ship.

Darkmere dismounted, leading his horse up to the plank. Prestoni called out to him. "So nice to see you again."

"Yes, and you too," said Darkmere, extending his hand. Darkmere then introduced everyone to Prestoni. When he was done, Prestoni escorted them up the gang-plank.

As they were halfway up the plank, a woman screamed, "Wait, wait — I brought him!" It was Eliza, dragging a man with a beard and receding hairline behind her.

"Ah, Winfred. Meet our next set of passengers," smiled Prestoni as Winfred scrambled up the plank.

"Pick up your pants, they're falling down," Eliza called out to him.

"Thanks, Eliza," said Winfred, winking at her.

"This is Winfred, our ship's cook, blacksmith — and trader of worldly goods." Prestoni smiled with the pride that comes to a captain when he has a great first mate on board.

They all finished boarding the Exodus as the sun cleared the horizon.

Chapter 9

The crew began to loosen the mooring ropes. Suddenly a boy's voice yelled out: "Papa, papa!"

"Prestoni!" yelled Winfred.

"Yes."

"Come forward. Your son's screaming for you."

The task of setting sail was interrupted. Prestoni laid the gangplank down again, and disembarked. A few moments later he returned. "Darkmere, it is with my deepest regret that I must tell you we have to stay in port another night. My wife has taken ill.

"Understood," replied Darkmere. Eliza sighed. They stayed aboard, while the night grew long and fights ensued.

'Darkmere, I need to have a word with you,' came Casiopiea's voice.

'Meet me in the captain's quarters.'

While Casiopiea and Darkmere talked on deck, Gowen bumped into Yasmin.

"Oh, hello, Gowen Aries." she said.

"What is it, Yasmin?"

"I just want to touch you again."

"What! Get away from me . . . you are sick!"

"No, my former husband — I still love you."

"Leave me be!" said Gowen, storming off. Tan suddenly emerged from the shadows.

"Yasmin — come with me," he said half-dragging Yasmin off the ship.

He took her to a secluded area of town and sat her down.

"What are you going to do — rape me?" Yasmin shot out.

"No, Yasmin. All I want is your holy symbol," said Tan firmly.

"No! Don't do this, Tan, please. I worship him," she begged.

"Not any more, Yasmin. You no longer have a deity. I am truly sorry." He raised his hands, touching Yasmin, draining her of her once great and beautiful power, leaving her helpless and destroyed. Yasmin was no longer Yasmin, but merely a weak shadow of herself.

Back at the ship, Yasmin refused to let herself remember what had just happened. She wandered along the deck, dazed.

Meanwhile, Tan disappeared.

chapter 10

The next day greeted them with no sign of Prestoni.

"I wish to take a stroll," said Casiopiea. "I'll be back later."

"Just don't stay too long — I imagine we'll depart after lunch," Darkmere said.

"Where's Tan?" Gowen asked.

"He probably went to get his skin color changed," Copin offered.

"No, he probably just took a walk. Oh, and anyone else can leave — just be back in time."

Casiopiea departed the ship and went down the main street to the alchemist's store. She walked in cautiously, having some trouble steadying herself.

An old woman emerged from behind the door, holding a potion in a mangled hand.

"Thank you, I am well. I need a potion, a love potion."

"Ah yes — let me find one." The old woman began rummaging through a box with old flasks inside.

Casiopiea occupied herself looking around the store, while the old woman began humming.

"Ah, here it is, a potion — 'a la crevic,' as it is named in the terms of magic, a love potion. Here." Casiopiea extended her hand for the small flask filled with pink liquid.

"How much?"

"For you — five gold."

"Here," she said, laying five gold pieces down on the counter.

Turning to leave, Casiopiea saw the old woman grinning. She left quickly, feeling queazy.

Chapter 11

Casiopiea came to a fork in the road. Feeling very sick, she made her way back to the ship. As she took the road down the right path, a black bird hovered above.

Copin and Minker sat down with Winfred in the mess hall, and began playing poker to pass the time.

"So, Minker, Copin, why are you here?" Winfred asked.

"Well, money, adventure, and a good time. I also have to brush up on my skills." Minker smiled and took out a small pick and caressed it.

"I am here, because I want to further the ideas of cyclopis kind."

"And what's that?"

"Well, just live and help others to be free."

"That is a good idea." Winfred dealt the next hand.

"Darkmere," said Yasmin, smiling up at him. "It's such a nice day out, and I'm so glad I'm here with you."

"You know, we should be getting back to the ship."

"Yes, but let's just savor this moment. You thrill me," she smiled.

"You are the —" Darkmere stopped dead, staring at her.

"What's wrong, Darkmere?!" Yasmin was frightened of the way he was looking at her.

He turned abruptly. "Get back to the ship — now! There's been an emergency." He left Yasmin standing in her tracks.

Quickly rounding a corner, Darkmere found Casiopiea leaning against a tree.

chapter 12

"Casiopiea!" said Darkmere, moving swiftly to lay her down. Cradling her head in his hands, he asked, "What happened?" Then he knew. "The baby!" He looked at Casiopiea in horror.

"Ett . . ." she stammered, going limp in his arms.

Laughter rang through the heavens . . .

Darkmere gently picked Casiopiea up and carried her back to the ship.

Yasmin had meanwhile boarded with a smile on her face and sat down on one of the many crates. She turned around to see Gowen coming over to her.

Darkmere, running as quickly as he could, was stopped in his tracks by Tan.

"You know what has been done?" Tan said to him.

"Yes. Yasmin no longer heals." Darkmere said quickly, trying not to talk for too long, yet knowing this was very important.

"Yes, and I will not be coming with you. My deed here is done. Beware — for I hold two daggers, Darkmere. And whoever gets them first will have the power — and I will get them!" Tan vanished, leaving Darkmere to race towards the ship, hoping she would stay alive. Who knew what had really happened . . . save Etten?

"Where's Darkmere, Yasmin?"

"I don't know. He said something about an emergency," she replied, leaning back.

"An emergency? The only one, besides Tan, who is not back, is —"

"Casiopiea!" they said in unison. At that moment, they saw Darkmere coming aboard.

"What's <u>happened</u>?" Gowen let out.

"Quick, get me something to lay her down on."

Gowen took off, heading below for a blanket. When he came back, Darkmere told him where to lay it down.

Gowen had a bad feeling about what had happened. He looked up at Darkmere, and the tears began to well in his eyes.

"It's gone, Gowen," was all Darkmere could say. Gowen began weeping. And Darkmere mourned silently inside . . . knowing whose baby it really had been.

Yasmin, still smiling to herself, stood off in the corner.

Chapter 13

Darkmere got up, leaving Gowen to watch over Casiopiea. He could not handle it, unless he could understand why it had happened. He made his way down to the mess hall and sat with his head in his hands.

"Excuse me, but I couldn't help noticing — do you need anything?" offered Winfred.

Darkmere, looking up, saw Winfred's concerned expression.

"Maybe a cup of tea."

"No problem. I'll be back." Winfred went in the kitchen and found Eliza sitting by the door, watching Darkmere through the cracks.

"What you looking at? Haven't you got better things to do than to stare at him?" Winfred hissed, the jealousy pouring out of him like water through a sieve.

"Why do you care?"

"Well, I mean — forget it," said Winfred, turning away to make the tea. Eliza entered the mess hall.

She greeted Darkmere. She watched Darkmere turn and look up at her, attempting to control his anger.

"Yes, what is it?" he barely managed.

"Are you well?" said Eliza, sitting down next to him and putting her arm around him. She immediately felt him tighten, and he moved away, glaring at her.

"No . . . now just leave me alone."

"Maybe I can help."

"No, nobody can help . . . except me. Leave."

"I was just waiting for some tea."

The anger seemed to leave his face and returned to a stone mask.

Winfred entered. "Here's your tea."

"Thanks."

"Is there anything else I could get you? Some chocolate cake, maybe?"

"Fine."

Winfred left again.

"You know, he likes you," said Darkmere.

"And everyone else," she said unenthusiastically. But she was amazed at how rapidly Darkmere had been able to gain control over his emotions.

"Well, well — here it is — Wally's famous chocolate cake," said Winfred, coming back in and placing a slice in front of Darkmere.

Darkmere ate a piece, commenting, "Very good. But why is it called Wally's famous cake, not Winfred's?"

"Because my friend Wally made up the recipe."

"He made the recipe, but <u>you</u> made the cake," Darkmere noted.

"Do you need anything else?"

"See whether or not our captain's arrived."

Winfred took his leave.

Chapter 14

What's bothering you?" Eliza finally said.

"Nothing."

"What do you mean, 'nothing?' I heard the commotion on board."

"Casiopiea lost her baby."

"What happened?"

"I don't know."

"Where is she?"

"Unconscious."

"Unconscious?"

"Yes."

"How can you be so unemotional?"

"What do you mean?" he said, his voice flat and monotone.

"You started to get upset and then you covered it up . . . why? It's bad to hide your feelings, you know. And do you always wear black?"

"I'm quite well. And, yes I always wear black."

"What is going to happen when you snap and can't control yourself?"

"I can always control myself," he said, his voice rising.

"No you can't," she said. She bent to kiss him. He surrendered himself to her and returned the kiss with a passion she had never felt before. Then he backed away.

"See? I can control myself," he said. She stared at him, mesmerized.

Gowen stormed in.

"You inconsiderate bastard! Why in hell's name did you leave?" he yelled, cutting through Eliza's infatuation. She backed off, watching Darkmere, who did not flinch.

"Casiopiea will be well in a few days."

"Is there anything else we can do? I know the baby is gone, but . . ."

"Nothing yet, except to get this vessel under way. And without a captain, that's going to be a little difficult."

"I will see if I can find him," said Gowen, leaving the room.

Darkmere sighed while Eliza spoke. "Are you waiting for Prestoni?" she asked.

"Yes."

"Well, his return rate is about...whenever I'm around, he tells me he will be back the next day and he doesn't show up for weeks."

"Well, we'll wait until morning and then we sail — with or without him."

"Who will command the boat?"

With all the confidence of a former sea captain he replied, "I will."

"Oh," was all Eliza could say.

Chapter 15

Morning came, and so did a pelting rain.

"Any sign of him?" Darkmere asked.

"No," said Winfred.

"Then let's set sail."

Winfred was alarmed. "What? He'll be back — just wait."

"He has my money — and we will return his ship. I give you my word," Darkmere replied.

"What about Tan, Darkmere?" asked Minker.

"He can't come. He was called away," Darkmere answered, feeling restless.

"Oh," sighed Minker.

"I guess we can leave, then," said Winfred, looking downcast.

The long task of setting sail began — and as the ship moved further from the dock, a lone man with holes in his teeth ran the length of the pier, watching his ship sail into the horizon.

As the Exodus moved further offshore, four other vessels followed in its wake . . . with Prestoni at the helm of the fastest one.

"They stole my ship, and they will pay!" he swore.

Out to sea, Darkmere faced the crew and shouted, "Pirates in the distance!"

Chapter 16

As the four corvettes gained on the Exodus, their black crossbones furling and unfurling in the wind, the Exodus prepared for battle.

"Casiopiea," Darkmere yelled into her ear, propelling her out of her sleep.

"I will be behind you . . . we need you up there." He pointed to the deck, as she looked at him wide-eyed. He closed his eyes and placed his hands over her stomach. As he slowed his breathing, his hands began to glow green. Then they jolted off of her.

She sighed, "What's going on, Darkmere?"

"Darkmere, they're gaining on us!" a crew man yelled nervously from above.

"Come on!" Darkmere grabbed her arm, and nearly flew up to the deck with her.

The four ships were closing in on the Exodus . . .

"Ready for battle!" he yelled, turning to Casiopiea and smiling. Gowen and the rest of the crew watched with amazement as Casiopiea raised her arms and began chanting the old words of magic. They waited . . .

A tunnel of wind began to fly straight at one of the ships. In an instant, sails, wood and riggings began to collapse. Screams were heard, and then . . . the mighty ship toppled over.

"Destroy the Exodus!" cried a familiar voice from one of the other ships.

"Oh my God! It's Prestoni!" Eliza yelled.

"Go below, Eliza," shouted Darkmere.

"But Prestoni — No!"

"Leave," shot Darkmere, as fire-tipped arrows struck the waves within reach of the Exodus.

And at the first impact of a fire-arrow on the deck, an unearthly scream came from . . . Where?

Giving Casiopiea time to get ready for another spell, everyone on both ships turned around to see who was screaming.

As the fires spread, the screams became louder . . . and then overwhelming. A piercing cry shattered the sound barrier: "Darkmere — save me!"

"Who are you?" he yelled back.

"It is I — Phallon!"

Darkmere's eyes widened. He saw the other three ships readying another round of fire-arrows.

Chapter 17

"No — stop!" screamed Darkmere with all his might, as the wind once again began a crazy dance, spinning across and around and up and down — creating a cone of wind and water, water, and wind.

Grabbing the long bow and arrow, Darkmere quickly bounded up to the highest vantage point on the ship. As the wind shot through the sky, whipping towards the two oncoming ships, Darkmere strained the bow, the arrow lying precisely in its curve. And as the wind slammed into the second and third ships, extinguishing their fires and hurling them into a whirlwind, Darkmere let the arrow fly.

Eliza, seeing Prestoni standing on the bow of his ship, ran towards Darkmere screaming, "No!" But it was too late. The arrow hit Prestoni full in the chest, driving him to the ground.

And Prestoni — now a beacon to all — lay limp, a burning torch protruding from his chest, while the fires on Exodus subsided.

Eliza lay sobbing on deck, Darkmere, with satisfaction in his eyes, turned and walked past her, saying "He was going to kill us all."

chapter 18

Darkmere moved quickly to Casiopiea's side, supporting her and instructing her to sit down.

"I don't need to," she said.

"You will in a moment," said Darkmere. Gowen glared at him. Yasmin, in a corner, sat watching.

Darkmere turned to Gowen. "Get the crew and help the ship.!"

"What for? It's only a ship — and that's my wife!"

"I don't have any time for arguing with you. The ship is alive, and Casiopiea needs help.

Darkmere carried Casiopiea downstairs.

"Darkmere, what do you mean the ship's alive?"

"Phallon?"

"Yes, Darkmere" said Phallon. Casiopiea looked around but saw no one.

"Are you well?"

"Yes — and thank you."

"How did you came to be named Exodus? You know, I had a feeling about this ship," said Darkmere.

Phallon began describing how Prestoni had won her in a bet and then painted the name 'Exodus' over her own name. Casiopiea stared in amazement. Her amazement grew greater still, when, all of a sudden, a ghostlike figure began to materialize in front of her, — the embodiment of a woman, a beautiful ethereal woman.

Chapter 19

Phallon had flowing blond hair that cascaded down past the middle of her back. She wore a pure white gown from a long gone era.

"Darkmere, Darkmere," cried Casiopiea, seeing his eyes fixed upon this vision — it was as though they knew each other. She began shaking him, finally breaking his gaze.

He turned to Casiopiea, whose eyes were blazing. "Yes?"

"Who is that?" said Casiopiea pointing to the vision. The chimera had disappeared.

"That is Phallon — this boat we are upon."

"She is a <u>boat</u>?"

"Yes, who once was a woman."

Meanwhile, down below, Copin and Minker began singing songs and laughing, trying to make the ride an easier one.

Chapter 20

Darkmere sighed. "A long time ago — when I was just beginning my travels — I went on a journey. We set out on a mission across the seas, to find an item for a man. At least we thought he was a man. He had covered up his true identity. As we sailed, the seas grew turbulent. But we made it. We retrieved the item — though two of us died getting it."

"And?"

"We felt disgusted, realizing that chasing this item could cost us our lives. But I couldn't turn back — I had given my word. So we continued. We were attacked by sea monsters, and though we vanquished them, we lost two more of our companions. Then there were only four of us left. When the storm hit, we spent days fighting it. And finally, the ship broke apart. Only two of us remained: Phallon and I. We thought we'd lost everything — that it was the end. Yet after a few moments, we found a dinghy . . . and the item, floating next to it. It took us a week — with no food and hardly any water — to make it back. But we did. When we got close enough, we crawled ashore. Waiting for us was the man and his entourage. He picked up the item and said, 'You failed and you will pay!' And as I lay upon the ground, helpless, he turned my bride-to-be into a boat." He closed his eyes and sighed.

Casiopiea was nearly speechless. "Your wife-to-be?"

"Yes. Now go to sleep and all will be well."

"Wait — who was the man?"

"Etten, Casiopiea — the Dark One."

Chapter 21

The sun rose on the tall ship as it rocked slowly. The hammocks below swung from side to side, while Darkmere steered the boat that was now Phallon. The atmosphere was peaceful and calm, as was the sea; there was no one for miles around but the deep sleepers below and the ever playful sea-life that hardly ever broke the surface.

'It is peaceful, Darkmere, here upon the sea. Nothing bothers me here, with the constant movement from one place to another, till the day you came aboard. I was beginning to accept my fate, and then I felt you here, heard your voice, and knew your very breath. I don't feel, now, that I belong here anymore — and I would like a favor from you: If ever —'

'Yes, I will,' he said. 'You will not always be destined to this fate.'

The ship glided through the light breakers. The sun rose higher in the sky. It was quiet indeed . . . up here.

But below decks. . . things were not so quiet.

Eliza woke to see Winfred still asleep next to her. She shoved him and he rolled over. She grimaced as he snorted and woke with a start.

"Finally, you're awake!"

"What do you mean, 'finally'?"

"Aren't you upset by what happened yesterday?"

"No — he deserved what he got. No decent captain would ever try to kill his crew . . . he had no right. He knew we had to leave. It was as if he did it on purpose!"

"I don't know about you, but I don't think Darkmere had any right to kill him!"

"What about Prestoni — did he have a right to kill us?"

"Maybe he had a reason . . . maybe," Eliza sighed.

Winfred put his arm around her. "Maybe nothing," he said, as Eliza began to cry.

Chapter 22

"Gowen, Gowen, wake up," said Yasmin in a whisper.

"What is it?"

"Why we are staying with this? Why are we going on this boat, why do we follow Darkmere — why?"

"I am making sure that I do something constructive to help. We all want something better than we have. We would be just like everyone else, if we stopped and didn't do anything else. A life of sedentary nothingness."

"That's nice, but don't you think it's weird — about what's happened to Casiopiea?"

"It was my baby, too."

"If that's so, then why aren't you with her? She hasn't returned from Darkmere's cabin since last night . . . and I should know, since I'm going to be married to him."

"You and Darkmere!"

"Yes — isn't it nice?" said Yasmin.

"Do you know what you're doing?"

"Of course, Gowen." She gave him a sultry smile, looking into his eyes the way a vulture looks at a kill.

Gowen sensed something strange.

"I'm fine," she assured him. "I was just wondering if you are being pushed out of the picture."

"I'll go find her," Gowen said, getting up.

"Go do that — and good luck, Gowen."

"Yes," said Gowen tentatively, noting that Yasmin had begun to stare at the wall.

He came down the narrow hall leading to the captain's cabin. Was she right? What was going on here? What had happened to his baby, and why was Casiopiea staying away from him? Should he knock or just barge in? It was time to take charge.

He shoved his way in, only to find Crystalmere standing over a no longer sleeping Casiopiea.

He looked around, embarrassed.

"What's going on? Why are you disturbing me?" said Casiopiea, looking up at him.

"I'm sorry. I thought —"

"You thought what?"

"I'm sorry I disturbed you. It's just — Yasmin's been talking."

She glared at him, "What do you mean?"

"She said you and Darkmere —"

"What are you <u>talking</u> about! I just lost the baby, and you believe her stories! Get out now!" she screamed, pointing at the door.

He walked out like a lost puppy.

"Darkmere." He turned around to see Eliza standing in front of him.

"Yes?"

"I need to know why you killed him — you had no right!"

"<u>He had every right</u>!" Phallon's voice resounded. Eliza backed up.

"Who?" Eliza gasped, bewildered.

"That is Phallon — or Exodus to us. The ship that Prestoni hid from everyone, a ship that used to be a woman. Prestoni was going to destroy it — as well as all of us. Now leave, I have a lot to do," said Darkmere. Eliza dumbfounded, ran straight into Gowen.

Chapter 23

The following days seemed endless, and the tension continued to mount . . .

Casiopiea began her newest plan of destruction by asking Crystalmere to help her get to Yasmin.

She had Crystalmere — through her magic, of course — lure one of the shipmates down below, by implanting thoughts in his head. Once below, Casiopiea put a spell over the helpless crew member, and gave him the love potion she had bought on shore.

"Remember," Casiopiea said to the filthy seaman. "Once you see her, you will fall madly in love with her, and you will forget this conversation ever occurred."

She snapped her fingers twice, and the shipmate went back up on deck, not remembering a thing until . . .

"Yasmin — look! Land ho!" screamed Copin, from up in the sails, pointing.

"There's nothing there, Copin."

"Oh yes, there is," said the shipmate, approaching Yasmin. "Your beauty," he said, kneeling beside her. "I have never seen a beauty such as yours. You are radiating majesty even when you speak."

"Please leave me alone," said Yasmin, walking away. The man followed her, not leaving her alone for a moment, and attempting to kiss her all the while . . .

Chapter 24

Gowen and Casiopiea stopped speaking to each other. Gowen sulked around the ship, while Yasmin complained incessantly to Darkmere about the shipmate and anything else she could think of. Everyone else also began complaining to Darkmere as well. Only Copin, oddly enough, kept to himself, staying in the crow's nest, perched high up in the sails.

And as the fighting among them increased, the sea, too, became rougher.

When Gowen started to cry uncontrollably, for no apparent reason, Casiopiea's irritation grew.

And as she became more irritated, Darkmere became more remote.

And all the while, the seas began to rise and the skies began to darken. As the skies changed, Yasmin confronted Darkmere.

"What's wrong, Darkmere? I love you."

"It's over, Yasmin. Now leave me be."

She looked at him, clinging to the last strand of sanity left inside her . . . and then she lost it all.

And as she lost it, the waves swelled even higher . .

Then Darkmere slammed shut the door of his cabin and found blood stains soaked into his bed. This was the last straw.

He dashed out on deck to see an unearthly storm approaching. The waves shot higher and higher, and lightning tore through the skies — not ordinary lightning, but connecting everywhere, making arcs in the skies. Closer and closer it came. The thunder and darkness gave way to blood-red skies, as a blood-curdling scream came from Darkmere.

He fled below, while a face pierced through the skies — a face no one could bear to behold. He ran into Gowen's room, screaming, his eyes shining red, ablaze:

"It was never your baby — it was mine!!"

And Gowen, hearing this, bellowed his agony. "But remember, Darkmere — I didn't betray you!" screamed Gowen, as Casiopiea burst into the room. Seeing Darkmere's fury, she shrieked, "Darkmere! It's Etten!" Eliza and Winfred watched in horror from around the corner.

Darkmere wheeled around, staring at her, as the turbulence pounding the ship continued to increase. Then he raced up on deck, with the others following him.

Above them, Phallon's figure appeared, struggling to control herself on the waters . . . watching in horror, as the face above grew larger. And then, Phallon screamed. Everyone stared in disbelief at what loomed just ahead of them:

A whirlpool!

They all looked skyward, as the hideous face began laughing uncontrollably; they were being pulled, helplessly, into the whirlpool.

Chapter 25

And as the ship began spinning on the edges of the vortex, a figure dressed in blood-red robes looked into a glass door. As he gazed, the door began to open and the clouds began to clear. Soon, an image became visible. He saw the ship drawn into the whirlpool . . . and continued to watch as it disappeared into the center of the vortex. Then turning his back, his long blond hair flowing out over his crimson robes, he spoke:

"So that's them."

As another figure, covered in black robes, nodded . . . the portal closed.

About the author

Cynthia Anne Soroka is an entrepreneurial success! She owns and operates three businesses, had seven poems and one short story published. Her voice has graced many radio stations in the New York area and she has done numerous voice-overs for various businesses. Cynthia has always had a love for anything medieval, from sword to sorcery. This is her first full length novel.

Photography by Expressions Photography, Inc. Closter, NJ

Flash Blasters, Inc.
253 Closter Dock Road Suite 6
Closter, NJ 07624
1-800-FLASH-09
Other Products from Flash Blasters, Inc.:
EXAMBUSTERS Flash Cards series:
Biology part 1 ISBN#1-881374-23-8 part 2 # 1-881374-24-6
Chemistry part 1 ISBN#1-881374-25-4 part 2 # 1-881374-26-2
Physics part 1 ISBN#1-881374-27-0 part 2 # 1-881374-28-9
Earth Science/Geology Pt.1 ISBN#1-881374-21-1 pt.2# 1-881374-22-X
Essential English Vocabulary ISBN#1-881374-43-2
More Essential English Vocabulary ISBN# 1-881374-44-0
Into to French part 1 ISBN#1-881374-37-8 part 2 #1-881374-38-6
Intro to Spanish part 1 ISBN#1-881374-39-4 part 2 #1-881374-40-8
Beginning Japanese ISBN#1-881374-41-6
More Beginning Japanese ISBN#1-881374-42-4
Beginning Sign Language words ISBN#1-881374-49-1
Sign Language Alphabet & Numbers ISBN#1-881374-50-5
World History pt. 1 ISBN#1-881374-47-5 pt.2 #1-881374-48-3
American History pt.1 ISBN#1-881374-45-9 pt.2 #1-881374-46-7
Algebra I Pt. 1 ISBN#1-881374-31-9 pt.2 #1-881374-32-7
Algebra II/Trig pt. 1 ISBN#1-881374-35-1 pt.2 ISBN# 1-881374-36-X
Arithmetic pt.1 ISBN#1-881374-29-7 pt.2 #1-881374-30-0
Geometry pt. 1 ISBN#1-881374-33-5 pt.2 #1-881374-34-3
SELF HELP BOOKS
Biofeedback Without Machines
ISBN#1-881374-20-3
MINUS STRESS audio tape
ISBN#1-881374-52-1

If you are unable to find the books locally
you can order The Dark Chronicles Series
by sending the cover price plus $1.50
for the first book and $.50 for each
additional book to cover postage and
handling to:

Publishers Book and Audio Mailing Service
P.O. Box 070059, Staten Island, NY 10307

Specifiy title:

The Dark Chronicles-Volume I - The Beginning ISBN#1-
881374-70-X
The Dark Chronicles-Volume II - Red Blood
ISBN#1-881374-71-8
The Dark Chronicles-Volume III - Triumph
ISBN#1-881374-72-6

When ordering with a credit card call
1-800-288-2131, there is a $10 minimum
order. Visa, Mastercard, American Express
and Discover cards are accepted.